I0545211

THE LORDS OF THE DEEP

PATRICK LACEY & TIM MEYER

SEVERED PRESS
HOBART TASMANIA

THE LORDS OF THE DEEP

Copyright © 2019 Patrick Lacey & Tim Meyer
Copyright © 2019 by Severed Press

WWW.SEVEREDPRESS.COM

All rights reserved. No part of this book may be
reproduced or transmitted in any form or by any
electronic or mechanical means, including
photocopying, recording or by any information and
retrieval system, without the written permission of
the publisher and author, except where permitted by law.
This novel is a work of fiction. Names,
characters, places and incidents are the product of
the author's imagination, or are used fictitiously.
Any resemblance to actual events, locales or persons,
living or dead, is purely coincidental.

ISBN: 978-1-925840-62-9

All rights reserved.

"Welcome, welcome
The Lords of the Deep
Bring us new fortunes
and all ye seek

For there be no tomorrow
no light and no shine
the beasts of yesterday
hath eaten the hands of time

So welcome, welcome
The Lords of the Deep
Bring us new pleasures
from lands of foul sleep"

– excerpt from the poem "The Lords of the Deep"
Author Unknown

"Dead men don't bite."
— **Robert Louis Stevenson, Treasure Island**

"Let's jump on board, and cut them to pieces."
— **Edward "Blackbeard" Teach**

CHAPTER ONE

Donny Jordan spun around, rotating toward the Conquest Boston Whaler, and watched as the expensive boat shook atop a series of gentle waves. None of the other nearby yachts in Wilson Rhode's Marina bounced quite as much as *The Kerplunk*, which inspired paranoid thoughts in Donny's edgy, drug-addled mind. Moonlight glimmered on the oily-black surface of the cove. The eerie silence, coupled with the dead of night, furthered his dread.

It was *a wave, right?*

Of course it was. What else could it have been? A small hand of water patting the boat on the back, an innocent gesture from Mother Nature.

Donny turned and peered down the wharf, scoping out other boats, trying to decide which one to burglarize. Which one looked the most expensive and potentially had the most valuables inside? It was too hard to tell from their exteriors, so he had chosen to break into them all, or as many as he could until he got what he'd come for—enough pricey junk to pawn and secure his next fix. The cost of heroin had increased and Donny wasn't happy about it. Inflation had made the time between using longer, harder. His legs had been tingling all night and now his fingers were trembling too, no signs of either symptom letting up.

Nab as much as you can, Donny told himself, *and get the hell out. You only need enough to get through the end of the week. Payday.*

The big payday.

Wilson Rhodes, the proprietor of the Captain's Cove Marina, was on vacation somewhere in the Carolinas and wasn't expected back until next week. He was too cheap to hire overnight security, not even the occasional drive-by to make sure the boats were good and protected, to ensure there was no one like Donny Jordan sneaking about the shadows, breaking into his clients' treasured possessions. Rhodes was cheap, all right. Donny knew this because he'd worked under the stingy bastard for the last decade.

Don't want to give me a raise? Donny put his foot on the bow railing and jumped down onto the small deck. He made his way over to the cabin and found the entrance locked. *Fine. Don't. I'm going to get what I'm worth one way or the other.* It took three attempts to break the sliding barrier free from its track, obliterating the metal slide lock that had been good enough to deter your average looter but not Donny.

Once inside, he rummaged around the cabin. Stacks of nudie

magazines and a wastebasket full of spent tissues, a few newspaper clippings, results of local fishing tournaments, and a couple of goofy gag gifts intended for outdoorsy folks. A plastic, singing animatronic bass, the kind that wears itself thin after a few turns, stared with mute eyes. Disappointed, Donny backed out of the cabin.

One Whaler down, thirty to go.

The world shifted beneath him, more aggressively than *The Kerplunk* had less than five minutes ago. The sudden jerk forced Donny across the deck, and he desperately grabbed for the railing.

But the movement didn't feel like an ordinary wave. It felt like...

...something...

...underneath me...

Donny's brain projected the most ludicrous ideas, everything from giant three-headed sharks to tentacled sea beasts. It was the withdrawals fucking with him, he rationalized with the smarter half of his brain, the part of him that was still *him*. Still Donny. Not the drug-addicted scumbag he'd become.

The desperate need for arm candy stirred his paranoia. He pushed the images away, closing his eyes and shaking his head.

Then he stood frozen, listening to the soft sounds of the cove. The lapping waves. Crickets chirping in the sand grass. The thought-numbing white noise ducking behind it all.

Nothing.

No monsters.

As he stepped for the bow, toward the dock, something crashed into the boat, throwing Donny off his feet. He fell sideways and cracked his head on the railing. The impact stole more light from his vision, and for a brief second he thought he'd been taken underneath the surface, dragged into the depths of the cove. He continued to lie on the deck when the black fireworks faded from his sight. Thick wetness covered the right half of his face. He was scared to put his hand there, feel what he knew was there. He went through with it anyway. Not knowing wouldn't change matters. Sure enough, he came away with a palm full of blood, dark as motor oil in the absence of sufficient light. He gently patted around the side of his face, trying to trace the wound, trying to figure out the damage, estimating how many stitches this little misstep would cost him. He pegged the gash at about three inches, a sizable wound. But it wasn't the length that frightened him—the width and depth of the opening had caused his heart to beat irregularly. Split wide and furrowed deep. If he didn't get himself to a hospital soon, Donny Jordan might find himself slipping into a state of unconsciousness. The loss of blood might not kill him, but he didn't want to pass out here, on a customer's deck, only to be discovered the following morning a few feet from where he had kicked in the cabin door.

Donny rose to his feet feeling almost weightless, woozy, his vision beginning to blur near the edges.

He needed to scram.

Fuck the stashes, I'll get my fix money somewhere else.

There were some Section Eight housing apartments down the road from his current living situation *(clusterfuck it was)* and they were broken into at least once a week. Better yet, no one seemed to care about *those* places getting knocked over. He might not find a fortune in them, but it didn't matter. He only needed until the end of the week.

Payday, the phantom voice of his buddy, Rick, spoke in his ear. *Next week, we sell off the goods to our contact, and we're fucking golden, boys. We'll ride off into the sunset like the Magnificent Seven or some shit.*

Donny hadn't had the stones to tell him that not every protagonist survived that movie, that not every cowboy rode off into the sunset. Instead he had kept quiet, told his co-conspirator that he'd lie low until the deal went through, and not step foot outside his daily routines. Bring zero attention to himself. Rick had slapped him on the back, told him, "Good boy," and they had gone their separate ways with the plan to meet up next week after the goods were traded for cash.

The goods.

Whatever that meant.

It wasn't drugs, Donny was certain. It wasn't jewelry. It was *something else.* Something locked inside an old wooden chest. Something that made Donny uneasy whenever he'd been near it. Something...

...Evil?

The notion was absurd but Donny's mind often took him to dark places. Too many movies, too many nights drowned in alcohol, too many days spent shooting his arms up with smack.

He glanced around the boat, his eyes searching the water for the source of the disturbance. Something lurked below him, gliding through the waters, waiting to make another move, wanting to dunk him in the cove's black waters. Before the unknown thing could strike again, Donny jumped off the deck and landed on the dock. Crouching down, he tried to control his breathing, which had quickly gotten away from him. His heart stammered. Lungs seized, unable to draw complete breaths. Despite feeling like his bodily components were failing him, he craved a cigarette, that rush of nicotine. He fought the urge to pull the pack from his pocket and light three sticks at once.

Something splashed to his left.

He snapped his head in the direction of the dull noise. Nothing moving on the surface. Below it, a different story. Donny watched the displaced water bubble and swirl as if something had dipped under just before his eyes got there.

His knees grew weak.

Something prowled the cove's dark waters, weaving between the bulkheads.

Something big.

Donny sprinted down the dock, toward Rhodes's facility. Toward safety. Away from whatever roamed the cove.

Another splash sounded off to his right, maybe a fin knifing through the agitated surface. He didn't slow down, kept stamping his feet against the deck boards, making more than enough noise to wake nearby sleepers. He couldn't breathe but that didn't matter. Plenty of air waited for him where it was safe, away from the sea monster.

Monster.

Donny peered to his right. Something emerged from the water, a large arrow-shaped *something* with a tail that seemed to get thicker with its length. Donny's legs went numb and he almost tripped over his own feet. He didn't feel his bladder let go, soak his jeans.

The shadowy creature kept pace with him. After five more steps, Donny lost feeling from the waist down, and fell, tumbling across the dock. He landed on his back, his vision facing the star-lined night, a million bright freckles looking down at him from the cosmos.

A dark outline glided over him, twisting through the air, creating a maze of shadows above him. The triangle-shaped entity hovered over the wharf like a U.F.O from a faraway galaxy.

A head, he realized—it was the thing's head. And the thick tail? It wasn't a tail at all. It was the creature's body. The head swayed in the air, moving fluently as if in rhythm to some unheard song. It hissed, not words, but a long drawn-out sound, a slashed tire and the rush of lost air.

Before he understood what the thing was, before his brain pieced together the clues, the creature that shouldn't exist struck again.

Instinctively, Donny rolled over, off the deck and into the water.

An all-encompassing cold surrounded his body, filling him. He floated in the darkness, waiting for the monster to descend upon him and swallow him whole. Eating him in one bite wouldn't have been difficult. The thing's mouth was massive, big enough to comfortably fit him inside.

But the attack didn't happen.

He opened his eyes. Impenetrable darkness greeted him. He kicked his legs, swung his arms. He was moving. Moving away from the dock and the lengthy creature that had been born from his darkest thoughts. Gliding through the inky, frigid void, Donny felt a warm sense of relief. The shore wasn't too far away. Soon he'd find himself near the beach. He almost felt the sand underneath his feet, his toes sinking in, the welcoming stretch of the embankment. Pushing himself, he felt the safety wash over him, supplying his soul with comfort. He was almost there.

Almost.

Two oblong shapes glowed in the void ahead. They hovered there, blocking his path to the shore. He propelled himself forward, kicking his arms and legs in a fury. The shapes, like pennies tilted at an odd angle, grew brighter. The closer he got, the more they shimmered. Sparkled. Called to him. He thought maybe they were floating tokens, treasures stolen from the chest currently in his best friend Rick's possession. But when he drew closer, he realized it wasn't treasure. Not pennies. Something else. A shape formed behind them.

An *arrow* shape.

A head.

A mouth containing two long teeth and several shorter, sharper ones.

Before Donny could think of his wife and son, the family he had ruined with endless poor decisions, the need to further his drug habit, the shape in the water darted toward him, the coil of its massive body spiraling in its wake.

Then he knew pain.

And perpetual darkness.

CHAPTER TWO

3 DAYS LATER

The police officer led Daphne Jordan down a hall void of any charm. Sterile white walls every which way she looked with the occasional generic painting of vibrant flowers and sandy beaches. Not that she paid any attention to her surroundings. Her mind was elsewhere, had been since she received the call in the middle of the night.

"Mrs. Jordan?" the voice had said.

She'd nodded, foolishly forgetting there was no one in the room with her, least of all Donny, who she hadn't seen for a week or more.

"Yes," she'd said, her voice something above a whisper.

"I'm afraid I have some bad news."

And moments later, she'd known.

Now she was here, at the police station, waiting to identify the corpse of her on-again-off-again husband.

I'll do better.

That was what Donny had told her countless times before, each promise to his wife vanishing like the thinning hair along his head. From stress, he'd insisted. He was right of course. There was plenty of stress. He had a wife and child to support, and did so by working at the marina by day and by doing odd jobs at night. That was what he'd called them at least. Did he really think Daphne wasn't onto him?

He was using and stealing again. That much was evident by the cold sweats and the loss of appetite. His cheeks were sunken the last time they'd been together. Now, she supposed, they looked even worse.

She'd given him endless ultimatums. Get clean or get out. And for a while, he *was* clean. Things were looking up. They weren't exactly a gleaming example of a nuclear family but Jake had a dad who wasn't escaping in the middle of the night to shoot up. She'd almost fooled herself into thinking things would stay like that.

I'll do better.

Like hell you will.

"It's just up here," the officer said. She shook her head and was back in the lifeless hall, turning first to the right, then to the left. It felt as though she'd been walking for days. Her legs seemed to belong to someone else entirely. This morning, her mother had convinced her to take a Xanax to calm her nerves. Daphne didn't like the idea of being under the influence, not when she'd seen what Donny had gone through, but she needed something to stop the constant barrage of anxiety. The pill only offered a temporary escape. Now she felt groggy, zombie-like, and for a fearful moment, she wondered if this wasn't all some horrible dream.

The officer stopped in front of a door. "Here we are." His face was young and free of wrinkles, and though he couldn't have been more than five years her junior, she grew envious of him. Wondered how it would feel to be younger and without Donny. Free from this terrible burden. But she'd also be without Jake and no matter how bad things got, no matter what she saw in this next room, she couldn't imagine a life without her son.

"Are you ready?" the officer asked.

"Not even a little."

He nodded. "If you need a moment..."

"No. Let's just get this over with."

Another sweet, sad smile as he opened the door and led her inside.

The room was cold despite the heat wave outside. She shivered as the hairs along her body stood upright. There were drawers in the wall, just like on TV, and a half-dozen hospital beds, all of them covered with white sheets and for that she was thankful. She wondered which one was Donny.

A man in a lab coat sat at a desk, typing something on his computer. There were medical supplies scattered across his workstation: gauze, scalpels, even a microscope. She could've almost believed this was a science lab working on something miraculous, something important. A cure for cancer or Parkinson's. But the bodies reminded her that lives were not saved here. *Here* was a waiting room for whatever came next.

The officer cleared his throat and the man turned around. "Are you Mrs. Jordan?"

"Yes."

"I'm sorry for your loss." This spoken as though stated a thousand times before. Nothing like the youthful officer who had guided her here.

"Thank you. Where is he?"

The man locked his computer screen, stood, and led her to the farthest bed. He walked with a limp and she noticed a cane near his station. He couldn't have been younger than eighty. Liver spots covered his hands, which were gnarled with arthritis. "I'm doctor Harold Tripps and I'm the county coroner." His voice was raspy and he spoke with a whistle. From missing teeth, she assumed. "Your husband is right over here." He stopped at the last bed.

The officer stayed near the entrance, looking at his feet and sighing every so often. Daphne wished he'd accompany her for this next part. It felt safer that way. Instead, she felt alone. Abandoned. Gutter trash.

Better get used to it.

But she already had. Donny had been in and out of her life this past year, and since then she'd grown more independent. In a way, she'd been leading up to this day. All that was left were formalities.

"Are you ready?" Tripps asked, holding onto the white sheet. It was stained with something—not quite blood—but something oily that reminded her of pizza grease.

She exhaled, closed her eyes, steadied her hands. "Yes."

She heard the sound of the fabric being tossed aside and when she opened her eyes, she saw a dark blue mannequin.

That's not Donny, was her first reaction, but in the following moments her eyes adjusted to reality, and she realized that it *was* him. His eyes were closed, mercifully, but they looked ready to open at any moment. He'd come to life—she was sure of it—shivering and shaking like the last time he'd overdosed. But the bruises along his face and neck said otherwise.

She covered her mouth, surprised at the flowing tears. "How... I mean, the officers on the phone said he drowned."

Tripps's face showed no sign of emotion. "Before we go into details, young lady, could you first confirm if this is, in fact, your husband?"

She nodded. "Yes, that's Donny."

From behind her, near the doorway, the officer let out a sigh of relief.

"Very well. Now, it was initially thought that your husband died from asphyxiation underwater—drowning if you will—but now that we've had time for a brief examination, it looks as though he died before that was possible."

"How do you mean?"

He pointed to the bruises. "Blunt force trauma." He moved his hand toward Donny's head, which had caved in near the back. "Something heavy struck him. It's possible he tripped on the ship and struck his head on the way down, though unlikely."

"I'm not sure what you're saying."

"I'm saying, Mrs. Jordan, that there's a police investigation going on. Your husband was on that boat *illegally*. And it's entirely probable that someone else found him there. Someone who took action."

Fighting back the urge to cry, she nodded toward Donny's ruined head. "But what could've done that? A pipe or a bat or something?"

"The object would have had to be much larger."

"Like what?"

Tripps offered no other explanation, for no reason she could pinpoint other than the obvious—her husband was bruised and bloated and—well, he was dead. Did it really matter what had ended his life? When it came down to it, would *knowing* make a difference?

Daphne shivered.

"What about these marks on his flesh?" she asked, noticing little pockets of missing skin, deep puncture wounds that looked almost bite-like.

Tripps defogged his glasses against the fabric of his coat. "Yes, oddities, those." A weak shrug was all he had on the topic. "We'll do a comprehensive autopsy later. I intend to find answers to all our questions then. Best guess—maybe some crabs got to him before we did."

She shuddered.

"That'll be all, Mrs. Jordan. We'll be in touch with any further developments. I'm sure the officers in charge of the investigation will be in contact as well."

She found that hard to believe. She'd already been questioned by several investigators, all of them asking the same things in different ways, all of them speaking as if she'd had something to do with Donny's death.

A hand on her shoulder.

She forced back a scream.

It was just the young, naïve officer, whose name she still hadn't learned, offering to bring her back upstairs.

Back through the maze-like hall and up the stairs and out in the scorching heat. He told her things would get better.

"I've heard that one before."

She wiped away the last of her tears, thanked him for the help, and walked down the front steps of the police station. Across the way, countless tourists flocked by, families that were whole and happy. Children holding balloons and eating half-melted ice cream cones. It was hard to believe she'd just seen something so heinous, so vile.

At the bottom of the steps, she turned right and headed for the parking garage. Once she stepped past the ticket booth, darkness enveloped her. The sun did not penetrate the concrete walls. Her skin grew cold once more as she walked for her car.

Ten feet away, she suddenly stopped.

There was a man leaning against her vehicle, smoking a cigarette, exhaling plumes of rotten fog.

Watching her.

The man stepped forward and for a moment she was certain he was here to mug her.

But when she made out his face and recognized the scar along his chin, she calmed some.

Only some.

"Hey, Daph," Rick said. He tossed his cigarette to the ground and stepped on it. The ash remained lit, stubborn like Donny's partner in crime.

"Whatever you have to say," Daphne told him, "I don't want to hear it."

Another step closer and she saw his eyes dart right and left. He looked scared—*terrified*—which wasn't like Rick. Something was wrong. "Trust me," he said. "You'll want to hear it."

She made to speak but he silenced her.

"It's about Donny."

CHAPTER THREE

"What do you mean *killed?*"

Rick whipped his head around, scoping out the neighboring cars. *"Would you be quiet?"* he asked in a harsh whisper.

Daphne studied the empty parking garage. There was no one, not a single soul, visible down there. Rotating back toward her dead husband's best friend, she returned a cold stare. "I'm going to ask you one more time. What do you mean he was killed?"

Rick, who looked like he'd recently dug himself out from under a mound of garbage, gulped a mouthful of stale air. "I mean—I think he was murdered. What else do you think?"

"Who would want to murder Donny?" Her stern gaze caused him to take a step back. "Who would want to kill my husband? Drug dealers? Is that what you're telling me?"

"Daph, calm the hell down."

"No, I'm not going to calm down. Right now I have a seven-year-old waiting at home. I have to explain to him that he'll never see his father again." Tears began to plummet down her face. "Do you know how hard that's gonna be?"

Rick remained quiet, and cupped his hand over his mouth. His eyes darted back and forth, unable to stay fixed on hers.

She moved away from him, making for the door handle. "You have no idea."

He reached his arm across the door, blocking her. "Hear me out."

"Why the hell should I?"

"Because..." Rick worked his mouth, but no words came out.

"Move."

He didn't.

"Move."

He didn't. "I can't tell you everything."

Daphne rolled her eyes. "I don't know what you and Donny were up to, but whatever it was, I don't give a shit. That chapter of my life is over. Do you understand? No more posted bails, no more county jail visits, no more picking you two idiots up outside derelict buildings in Camden. No more of it. Get me?"

"I get you, Daph, I do. But I have something..."

"What is it?"

"It's..." He looked around once more as if the walls had eyes and ears and were interested in whatever came next. "It's a *treasure.*"

"A treasure?" she asked incredulously. "A fucking *treasure*?" Slowly, she shook her head. "What the hell are you talking about?"

"Come here." He strolled over to his car, parked three vehicles away, walking with a slight limp she hadn't noticed before. It must have happened recently.

"What did you do to your leg?"

He looked down, rubbed his knee, and returned his focus to the trunk of his car. "Nothing. Banged it."

"Nothing or you banged it?"

"Does it matter?"

She folded her arms across her chest. "You're acting sketchier than usual. Which is saying a lot."

"Just trust me."

"Oh, yeah, because you're such an outstanding citizen with no criminal background whatsoever. Yeah, I'll trust you. No problem."

"Sarcasm isn't necessary."

"Do you even know the day I've had?" She huffed. "Do you even care?"

He popped the trunk. Inside, rested a treasure chest the size of a beer cooler. The mahogany shell was hand-stained chocolate brown, warped and bowed by centuries of wear and tear. Rust-eaten straps and hinges that were once antiqued brass were now corroded beyond recognition. Daphne didn't know where the chest had come from, but it was clear the thing had seen better days. She was surprised the wood hadn't completely rotted out; whatever finish its makers had used to coat the wood had proved its worth. Other than those blemishes, the chest looked sturdy, in good shape. Stable. Able to withstand time and complete its task: protect the valuables within.

"What the hell is that?" Daphne asked, though the answer was obvious.

"It's a treasure chest."

"Where did you get it?"

Rick kept quiet and swayed on his heels the way a drunken pirate might after too many shots of rum.

"You're not going to tell me. Great. How about I march back inside and grab that lovely officer who escorted me to my dead husband's body? Maybe he'll be interested in how this thing came into your possession. What do you think about that?"

"You're not going to do that, Daph."

"And why the hell not?"

Rick popped the chest's latch and shoved open the lid.

The trunk brightened, the contents glowing preternaturally. The treasure cast a rich shadow on Daphne's face. She opened her mouth to speak but was hit with a sudden daze, and the words became lost in her stupor.

"Beautiful, isn't it?"

His question barely registered. She was transfixed by the trunk's radiant shimmer.

"Yes..."

For a moment her mind blanked out, her thoughts wiped clean by the presence of ancient fortunes. She forgot why she was there, why she was standing in the middle of a parking garage in some South Jersey town. Thoughts about her husband and his not-so-surprising demise were lost. She forgot about Jake, her sweet, beautiful boy, and she couldn't recall who was currently watching him. She mentally abandoned the years she'd spent with Donny, the good and the bad. She couldn't remember why she married him in the first place.

Then it all came back, arctic wind on a cold winter day.

"Are you okay?" Rick asked.

She didn't realize she was shaking until she heard the chattering of her teeth.

"Jesus, Daph." Rick placed a friendly arm around her, but she backed away. "It's okay, it's okay."

"Is it?"

Another question Rick didn't have an answer for. Once again, he avoided her gaze.

"Where did you get this?" she asked, her voice rough and uneven. "Did you steal it?"

"It's better you don't know the details."

"Why's that? In case I'm questioned?"

Rick blinked twice, and she understood that meant "yes."

"Jesus fucking Christ, Rick." She pointed at him, her finger trembling. "Did Donny die over this? Was he killed stealing this thing?"

He raised his hands. "No, it wasn't like that. We lifted this a week ago."

She wasn't sure if she believed him. Rick didn't have the best track record when it came to telling the truth. He was as bad at lying as Donny, and Daphne had always wondered why the two schmucks weren't pros given so much practice. She could always sort through their bullshit effortlessly. For her, it was hardly amusing. More like a chore, another constant on her never-ending to-do list.

Item number nine: Sort through Donny's lies today.

Her intuition confirmed Rick was telling the truth. Donny hadn't died during their heist, or whatever it was. Something else had happened to him.

"Honest, I swear to God." Rick pressed his back against the car, hands still up, prepared for her to take a swing at him. "I don't know what happened at Wilson's, but I know damn sure I wasn't around when it went down."

"Then why are you here?"

"Because I feel bad." He swallowed as if something had been lodged in his throat, something that wouldn't go down. "And I want to make things right."

"How so?"

"The chest..." he said, nodding to the trunk. "It was a contract job. I'm meeting with the buyer tomorrow night."

Something gnawed its way through her stomach. "How much we talking here?" she asked, trying to sound bemused. She even looked away, pretending the elevator doors were more worthy a look than the chest and what lived inside it.

"A million. Split four ways between me, Kevin, Barry, and... well... you."

"Why me?"

"Because it was Donny's share."

"No, I mean, why cut me in at all?" With her eyelids half-closed, she surveyed Rick's face, waiting for his nerves to betray him.

"Told you. I feel bad."

"Don't bullshit me."

His gaze hardened. "Okay, look. Word is that the cops are looking into his death. We don't want anything pointing back at us. Kevin and Barry are shook. They think you're gonna squeal like a sick piggy once they start asking questions."

"But I don't know anything. And like you said, the less I know the better."

"Well, yeah, but they don't know you like I do. I know you won't say anything but they aren't convinced. Look, I told them I'd talk to you. Told them I'd give you Donny's bit. They aren't too happy about it, but if it keeps our names out of your mouth, then they're willing to pay." He corrected himself. "*My* name, actually. One word about me is all it'll take for them to come knocking on my door, and I can't have that." He stopped long enough to breathe. "Now, do I have your word?"

A tug on her heart. A phantom explosion of pins-and-needles throughout her body. A spell of dizziness. Pressure on her temples. She wasn't sure if she was getting sick or on the verge of passing out.

"Daph, you still with me?"

She swallowed. "Yeah."

Nothing about this eased her mind. She couldn't think straight. All she wanted was for the nightmare to end. Fast forward to six months later. Maybe a year. Whenever the aftermath of her dead husband's fuckery concluded. After Jake had moved on. Maybe she'd get lucky and in ten years, forget he even had a father. Or better yet, maybe she'd find someone new to replace the void Donny left in their family.

Is it too early to find someone else? To have a boyfriend? She was stalling. Distracting herself from the real-world issues at hand. Stupid thoughts at stupid times.

"Do I have your word?" Rick asked, louder than before, snapping her free from twisted reveries.

She blinked and it was gone. All of it. The senseless thoughts, the odd pains, the feeling that she was on the verge of death. Vanished like a hazy dream.

"Yes," she said without further delay.

"Good. I'll reach out tomorrow night after the deal goes down. We'll meet up and settle things."

She opened her mouth to say "okay," but no sound came out.

Something about the way the treasure glowed, that unnatural aura, filled her with dread, seized the words from her throat.

Run, something inside her urged. *Leave this town and don't look back.*

Powerless, she watched Rick close the trunk, limp inside, and drive away.

In the shadows of the parking garage, she stood frozen until her cell went off. She dug the phone out of her purse and read the message from MOM: WHERE ARE YOU?

ON WAY HOME, she responded.

The entire ride back to the apartment, she cried.

CHAPTER FOUR

Without warning, a rusty pickup truck drifted across the left lane and cut in front of Eric. He blared the horn and the driver slammed on his brakes, causing Eric to do the same. Behind him, he heard more horns and narrowly escaped a five-car pileup. The truck eventually sped up but not before the driver threw his fist out the window and proudly displayed his middle finger.

In the distance, a sign appeared along the side of the road.

Welcome to New Jersey.

Eric Jordan hadn't been home in a little over five years and it'd been even longer since he'd seen his brother. The two boys, born exactly one year and three days apart, had never gotten along. It began as a harmless sibling rivalry but grew more serious as they became adults. Their lives had traveled in entirely different directions. Eric left home at eighteen, putting himself through college and getting a teaching job at a community college in Pennsylvania. The pay was slim and the benefits were nonexistent, but it was a step in the right direction. He made ends meet, was engaged to a beautiful and supportive woman named Anita—former student nonetheless—and he had a promising future ahead of him.

But Donny...

His brother had never dreamed of leaving his hometown. Donny had gotten mixed up with the wrong crowd for as long as Eric could remember. He'd started smoking weed in eighth grade and was snorting coke and dealing harder stuff by his sophomore year of high school. Until he got himself expelled for selling to an undercover in the boy's locker room.

He'd been clean on and off again since—mostly off—but that didn't matter now. Now he was dead and Eric was on his way home to help his mother after being absent for all those years, the only Jordan to escape the soul-sucking clutches of Lea Bay.

He turned on the radio but every song seemed auto-tuned and synth-laden, so he settled on a local news station where the anchor discussed Jersey's current heat wave and some disturbances a few miles out to sea. *Some sort of seismic activity,* the man's pitch-perfect voice stated.

They cut to a pre-recorded expert who'd been interviewed earlier that day. "There's no need for alarm just yet. Believe it or not, this sort of disturbance happens quite frequently. Platelets shift often and most of the time they cause no activity whatsoever."

A different voice than the male anchor, this one female and nasally, asked about any threat to the coastal towns.

"Not at this time," he said adamantly. "Tsunamis are extremely rare in this part of the world."

For a frightful moment, Eric imagined a wave the size of a skyscraper appearing on the horizon, carrying with it cars and homes and thousands of screaming victims. The ocean would run red with their blood and it would take him with it. The world seemed so fragile at that moment. Mother Nature could come undone in the time it took for a disgruntled driver to tell you to fuck off.

The moment passed and he shut off the radio, chocking the daydream up to nerves. Assuring himself there was nothing symbolic about it. He'd be safe in Lea Bay. It was home. It was where he was meant to be.

Thy business will be done.

A few minutes later, the exit appeared on the right and he pulled off the highway. His hometown hadn't changed much, though it had been gentrified some. Upscale restaurants appeared where there'd been dive bars a decade earlier. And he hadn't remembered so many corporate chains. A Home Depot had replaced the local hardware store and the small cinema had been torn down in favor of an IMAX. Unsurprisingly, the Blockbuster was also gone. A 711 had taken its place, fully equipped with a double-sized Redbox.

In the distance, the boulevard came into view and he fought a wave of nausea. This time, he didn't think about tsunamis or natural disasters.

This time, he thought about something living in the harbor.

It seemed silly now, of course, but as children he and Donny had been certain there were monsters out there, under the ocean. Their childhood home had been only a five-minute walk from the water. The house had been in the family for two generations and was in desperate need of repairs. Once their father died, the Jordan boys had been tasked with fixing it up. Karl Jordan had left behind a nice chunk of change for the repairs, but Donny had stolen most of it for drugs. Another reason for Eric to hate his brother. Their mother had hired handymen here and there, and Eric helped out financially when he could, but the structure hadn't exactly been a model home when Eric left, and there simply weren't enough funds to keep up with the work.

He felt a surge of guilt for not coming back sooner, not visiting more often.

But the guilt faded as he thought of the stories their father used to tell. Urban legends about sea creatures inhabiting the shore, sightings of them throughout the ages, a blurry picture here, a poorly drawn sketch there.

"What do they want?" Eric always asked when his father corralled him, forcing him to listen to the legends of Lea Bay.

Karl Jordan, holding a flashlight beneath his chin, would scowl. "Us, buddy. They want us."

Eric had been plagued with nightmares these last few months, all of them nearly the same. They started out innocently enough. He was back home, an adult now, living two streets over from his mother, and he was taking his future son, a boy who looked strikingly like Anita, for his first fishing trip. They sat on an unfamiliar dock, surrounded by tourists. The strangers' faces were distorted in the way dreams often hide insignificant details, as if the dream's architect had rubbed out their identities with an eraser. Their voices were hushed and harsh, spoken in languages Eric could not decipher.

The only words he could understand were those of his unborn son, asking his old man for help. "How do I get the worms on?" He held up the hook.

"Like this." Eric pushed the earthworm through the sharp metal, impaling it. Then he showed his boy how to cast a line. It landed far in the distance, much farther than he'd ever cast in reality.

"Now what do we do?"

"We sit and wait."

"Sounds boring."

"More like relaxing."

They sat like that, father and son, holding their rods. It was at this section of the narrative that Eric began to suspect he was dreaming each time. The nondescript beach, busy moments before, stood empty. The sky was no longer sunny. Dark storm clouds, the color of ancient ash, tumbled into view.

And the water was far from calm. The waves grew choppy, moving in a circular pattern. A half-mile out to sea, a black hole formed in the water, the size of a bus, sucking everything within its path into pure, utter darkness.

"Dad!" the boy said, pointing. "Your hook!"

Eric followed the boy's line of sight and saw the newly-formed hole was taking the bait. As the rod bent, the line wrapped around his hand, cutting the flesh and slicing through several fingers as it was pulled from his grip.

When the severed digits fell into the whirlpool, something roared.

It sounded huge and old and grateful for the offering.

And it sounded hungry.

The dock came apart as the waves increased. His son fell into the water.

Eric dove after him, screaming the boy's name, though the word was indecipherable. He swam toward the hole and just as something large and cylindrical appeared at the edge, he woke screaming in a pool of cool sweat.

Anita insisted he see a therapist after each occurrence. He was inclined to agree but never got around to making the appointment. Work and life were happy to interfere. At least, that's what he'd told her. In reality, he had no intentions of going. He had other ways of combating the night terrors.

Confront them. Head on.

He passed a handful of strip malls before finally turning onto the street on which he'd lived for the first eighteen years of his life.

The house looked better than he'd hoped, but that did nothing for his nerves as he pulled into the driveway and cut the engine.

Because the house was still only minutes away from the ocean.

And the nightmare seemed even closer.

He stepped out of the car and saw the front door was already open. His mother stood on the front steps. Even from here he could tell she was crying.

CHAPTER FIVE

The scalpel drew a vertical red line down Donny Jordan's chest, over his stomach, and stopped just above his pubic bone. Franklin Weiss, the county medical examiner, set the tool down on the metal tray next to the dissection table, cracked his knuckles, and grabbed the pruning shears.

"What the hell are you using those for?" asked Harold Tripps as he pushed his glasses against the bridge of his nose.

"The sheers?" Franklin shrugged, a casual gesture, and looked at the garden tool with no more admiration than he would a ham sandwich. "Heard they were good for cracking ribs. Google said so, anyway."

"You idiot. Don't you have a bone saw?"

"Yeah, but what do you know about it, old man?"

"Listen." Tripps shook his finger at him. "You may be my nephew and about half my age, but that doesn't mean I still can't put my boot up your ass."

The medical examiner shuddered with laughter. "I'd like to see you try."

"Just remember who got you this goddamn job."

"Yeah, yeah. How could I forget, Uncle Harry?"

"Least you could do is pretend you're a professional." Tripps pointed to the cadaver, then to each individual bruise on the body. There were many, some big as fists. There were also small pockets of absent flesh and what looked like bite marks surrounding them. "Okay then. Let's stop dicking around and get to work, shall we?"

Franklin let out a deep sigh. "I don't know why we're going through all this. I mean, look at the back of this dude's head. I thought you were pretty conclusive with your initial assessment."

"County sheriff's office suspects foul play. It's mandatory we perform a full autopsy. We need to be thorough here, Franklin. Lotta eyes on us. So get your head out of your ass and let's do this."

Groaning, Franklin tapped the blackened flesh on Donny's arm, the soft veiny part near the elbow. A hole the size of a dime had been opened there, the surrounding flesh badly decayed. "I mean, what's the point? The guy was obviously a junkie. Who cares what happened to him? Why are we wasting the taxpayer's money with this horseshit?"

"I know you haven't done a ton of these, boy, so let me explain. A criminal investigation automatically warrants a full forensic autopsy. Simple as that. No way we're getting out of this one, so shut that flapper of yours and we'll get on just fine."

Franklin began to peel back the skin. This wasn't his first rodeo; he'd done a total of twelve autopsies since becoming the county medical examiner about a year ago. All of them routine and mundane and not the least bit out of the ordinary. He wasn't the only M.E. in the county but since he was the newest, he got handed the simple cases; the accidental pill overdoses, the intentional pill overdoses, the occasional slit wrist. Most of the interesting stuff took place north in the county, not in the small, picturesque, and boring as shit seaside town of Lea Bay. Not in his hometown. Although, about a month ago he dissected a local who'd clearly blown off his head with a shotgun. Needless to say, there wasn't much interesting happening inside him, nothing that told a different story other than the one written on the remaining half of his skull.

Nothing interesting ever happened in the Bay.

Until tonight.

Donny Jordan's case was kind of neat. Mysterious. The man had been found washed up on the shore near Wilson Rhodes's Marina, the back of his skull caved in, all sorts of strange bruises on his body and a few areas of missing skin that suggested he'd been chewed on by some ocean critters. The latter had been done post-mortem, so Uncle Harry guessed, but Franklin wasn't so sure. Only the lab results would shed some light on that mystery, and they weren't due back until tomorrow afternoon.

Donny's skin folded back like an open tuxedo. Franklin peeled both sides, allowing them to hang open until he pinned them apart, exposing the raw muscle and tissue mass. He sighed and sunk the sheers into the tissue, cutting through the area covering the heart. Once finished, he separated the outer layer and exposed the heart and lung.

"How we looking?" Tripps asked.

"Just dandy, thanks for asking. Sheers worked like a champ, by the way."

Tripps ignored this. "Heart and lungs look okay?"

"For a ninety-year-old man who smoked three packs a day since the day he turned twelve—yeah, sure."

"Donny Jordan was thirty-two."

"My point exactly."

Franklin waved his uncle over. The old man hobbled for ten feet and stopped when he was close enough to lean over and have himself a look.

"Well, I'll be goddamned," Tripps said, breathing heavily. Franklin didn't know if the short walk or the hideous condition of Donny's organs caused the old man's respiratory issues. "Looks black as tar."

Franklin ran his fingers over the greasy onyx lump that was Donny Jordan's heart. "Disgusting." But that wasn't all. He noticed something else odd about the cadaver's interior décor, less obvious than the heart and lungs' advanced stages of decomposition. On the inner right flap of Donny's skin, something had been scrawled. Leaning in, getting a closer look, Franklin saw what it was: ink. *A tattoo*. A drawing. No, not a drawing, not exactly. They were tiny symbols printed in the tissue.

With a flat metal blade, he scraped away the thin layer of yellow fat buildup that clung to Donny's epidermis. Once cleaned, Franklin saw three boxes, each touching, overlapping, forming a triangular pattern. X's running through each of them.

If he didn't know any better, he'd say it was a map. That, or some ancient hieroglyphics. Honestly, he didn't know what it was, only that it didn't belong underneath the man's skin.

"I'd say more like *impossible*," Tripps said.

Franklin averted his eyes from the markings, let the image fade from his mind as his concentration fell back on the tar-black heart. "Well, shit, Uncle Harry. What could cause such decay?"

Tripps had no response. Instead, he raised his finger in the air and announced, "I have to use the lavatory. I'll be right back."

"Going to throw up?"

"I just might."

"Your stomach is getting weaker with old age."

"Fuck you kindly, nephew."

Franklin winked as Tripps turned and limped toward the exit. Once he was gone, the youngster returned to his work.

His heart thudded when he looked back and saw Donny Jordan's eyes were open, glaring at him. Staring. Two cloudy ovals.

"Jesus fuck!" Franklin shouted and jumped back, knocking the tray of tools aside, causing them to spill across the concrete floor. The clatter echoed in the almost-empty chamber.

The doors to the room swung open and Tripps burst back in, drained of breath. "What is it?" he asked, between heavy, chest-heaving gasps.

Franklin pointed at the cadaver. The *still* cadaver, the cadaver with two eyes, both shut. Forever sealed.

"It... it..."

Tripps waved him on. "It *what?* Spit it the fuck out!"

"It opened its eyes."

For a moment, Tripps's face was a blank slate, as still as the body resting on the metal slab. Then, unexpectedly, he began hacking with laughter.

"What?" Franklin asked as a tingly-numb feeling ate its way through the nerves in his face, neck, and chest. "What the fuck is so goddamn funny?"

"You're fuckin' with me." Tripps pointed at him and laughed harder. Franklin feared the old bastard's ticker might not be able to handle the vibration. "I might be old, but that doesn't mean I'm falling for this shit."

"*Mītūtu šurrâtu,*" a raspy voice said, barely audible.

Franklin froze. His face blanched. "D-did y-you he-hear that?"

"Hear what?"

Franklin's head rotated toward the cadaver. No movement. Not a single twitch.

"It spoke."

Tripps shook his head. "Now, now. This has gone on long enough."

"*Mītūtu šurrâtu,*" the voice repeated, louder this time.

Franklin swallowed what felt like an entire apple. "You... you d-didn't h-hear it?"

"Boy, don't make me—"

Donny's arm shot out, fingers gripping Franklin's windpipe. He used the man's throat as leverage and hoisted himself to a sitting position. The dead man's eyes were milky white, void of life. His cracked lips split, displaying yellowed teeth and blackened gums, which didn't seem possible for a man less than twenty-four-hours dead. The corpse snarled, blowing hot breath in Franklin's face. The foul gust of air turned the medical examiner's stomach. It reeked like a deck full of dead fish left to spoil underneath the summer sun.

(a tilted horizon. A ship going down, sinking beneath ashen waters. Eyes in the murk. Green, glowing ellipticals. Pain. Death.)

Tripps's jaw dropped open, hung agape. "Jumping fucking fish sticks," he muttered, before stumbling backward through the swinging double doors.

(a cosmic map. An old wooden chest. Several gathered around a fire, every inch of their skin covered in grime and filth and blood. Singing. Chanting. Dancing. Sacrificial offerings for ye foreign ones.)

Tripps had collapsed, probably died of a heart attack right then and there. Franklin couldn't blame him. His own heart kicked wildly against his chest, adrenaline spiking off the charts.

(a trail through the woods. A hole in the ground. Shovels. Dirt. Bodies. Eyes in the murk. The ship going down. Screaming. Fire. Scaly skin. Eyes in the murk. A rush of cold water. Collapsing black waves. Oxygen bubbles rising to the surface. Campfire chants. EYES IN THE MURK.)

Donny Jordan tightened his grip. *"Tell me where it is."*

The voice was gruff and hardly human. When Franklin didn't answer, the cadaver toughened his hold, making it even harder to breathe, let alone answer the question.

"I won't ask ye again."

Slight reprieve as Donny relaxed his fingers, but not much. Enough to breathe a syllable or two. "Wha... talk... about?"

"Useless!" Donny heaved Franklin aside, shoving him to the ground.

On the way down, Franklin knocked his head against the table, splitting open his forehead. Runnels of blood trickled down his face, off his chin, and puddled on the concrete below. He threw himself onto his back and looked up in time to witness the dead man's shadow drape over him. The two gray flaps of skin flopped around like an open vest, proudly displaying his rotten stock of human organs.

Human?

Whatever was standing over him definitely wasn't human. At least, not anymore.

Franklin noticed two things, almost simultaneously. First, the peculiar markings on the inner flap of Donny's skin caught his gaze. The collection of boxes, triangularly-placed, the X's running through them. They were alive, glowing a bright shade of green. Pulsating. Letting the world know that Donny Jordan was alive and fully charged.

The second thing Franklin noticed was the light glinting off the sharp metal object in Donny's hand. *The scalpel.*

The goddamn scalpel.

Donny lingered over him. Snarling, he bent down.

Franklin couldn't react. Fear had paralyzed him, twisted his body into permanent knots.

Donny plunged the scalpel into the softest part of Franklin's throat. A warm splash of blood erupted from the wound, freshets of sticky crimson coating his neck and chest area. The room went fuzzy, grew hazier as the dead man carved. The flesh opened like a cheap wedding dress. Franklin felt his entire throat empty, slicking his body with a surprising amount of warm fluids.

"Useless," Donny Jordan said again, and the last scent Franklin Weiss took in was the salty ocean air and the several centuries of death that came with it.

CHAPTER SIX

Rick paced his studio apartment, knocking over a half dozen empty beer cans in the process. The place was a mess. Half-eaten Chinese food littered the table and a cloud of blowflies helped themselves. The windows stood open, which helped the smell some. From somewhere nearby, a radio blared and teenagers laughed.

A party.

Rick longed to be with them, drinking (though he'd done plenty of that tonight already) and smoking and pretending his life wasn't turning to complete shit.

His gut twisted each time he recalled his conversation with Daphne. Telling her had been a grave mistake, though he couldn't pinpoint why. He'd already spoken with the boys and though they'd been royally pissed off at first, he'd been able to talk them down. It didn't make a difference where Donny's cut of the profit was going, so long as Daphne didn't run her mouth to the cops.

Assuming, of course, she accepted his offer.

That was to be determined.

Part of him thought she'd come around eventually. Donny (most likely) hadn't taken out a life insurance policy and funeral costs alone could reach ten grand. It was simply a matter of waiting for her call, fighting the urge to contact her himself.

Until then, he'd pace his apartment and finish the thirty pack of PBR he'd bought earlier that night. He opened the fridge and saw he'd already made a sizable dent in the box. His vision blurred in spots and the room spun. Another few beers and he might just be able to forget about this whole mess. Maybe even get some sleep.

He cracked open the can, grabbed an egg roll off the coffee table, and chewed on it on his way to the couch. The shell was hard and stale, cold beyond comfort, but it helped with the hunger. Most people lost their appetite when faced with incredible amounts of stress, but Rick had always been the opposite. He ate and ate until his stomach felt ready to burst. A coping mechanism no matter how unhealthy. After dropping out of high school, he'd double in size but shooting up had solved that problem, shedding a hundred pounds in the last two years alone. He was only an occasional user, nothing close to Donny, but he was heading down a similar path.

He polished off the egg roll and turned on the television. The local news played more coverage of the seismic activity the town had experienced recently. Kind of creepy if you asked him. Some scientist was going on and on about how there was still no need to panic.

He changed the channel until he found an old episode of *The Night Gallery*. He used to watch it with his grandmother whenever she'd come over to babysit. It brought back a series of pleasant memories that, combined with the booze and the stomach full of fried food, made his eyes heavy. He woke two hours later, unaware he'd slept at all.

His heart pounded and his skin was covered with a layer of cool sweat. A nightmare, though he couldn't remember the specifics. All he knew for certain was that something had been chasing him. Something horribly deformed. That feeling of being watched, of being hunted, remained even after he woke. He got up, poured a glass of water from the faucet, and gulped it down greedily. His stomach was sour and he burped acid.

And dropped the glass on the counter when he saw the face outside the window.

He lived on the third floor of his apartment complex. The back porch where he smoked weed and shot up was more of a fire escape, only big enough for one body. Whoever was out there seemed in no rush. Rick hadn't turned on the back light and the face was mostly obscured by the late-night shadows. He couldn't make out any specifics, only that the skin was dark grey and the person—if it *was* a person—had eyes that seemed all white and nothing else.

"You best get the fuck out of here," Rick said loudly, hoping to wake his neighbors. "I've got a gun in the other room."

It was partially true. He did have an ancient 9mm. He'd bought the thing off a dealer ages ago. Its serial number had been scratched clean and much of the metal had rusted. He wasn't even sure if the thing fired, being as he never had to use it.

Until now.

He turned toward the bedroom but froze halfway across the kitchen when the voice spoke.

"Where is it?"

He turned back. "W-w-where's what?"

"The treasure. Where is it?"

The voice sounded both familiar and foreign and he could've sworn it belonged to—

"Donny?"

The face did not move. The eyes did not blink.

"Donny? Am I still dreaming?"

The doorknob jiggled as the thing outside stepped away from the window and tried to gain entry.

Rick was glad he'd locked it earlier. He was usually careless with such things but, recent events considered, he'd been on edge. More cautious than usual. He reached for the outside light and turned it on, immediately wishing he hadn't.

Donny stood on the fire escape.

But not the Donny he remembered. This was a grey-skinned, blue-lipped Donny, whose cataract eyes reminded him of dull pearls.

He could've screamed but his throat suddenly tightened. The night's air seemed charged, as if a thunderstorm approached. "Donny, you're dead. This isn't real. Daph identified your body yesterday."

Donny didn't respond. Instead, he tried the knob again, then began pounding on the glass door, trying to smash it in.

Assuming what stood outside was real and not a product of his anxiety, Donny should have known where the treasure was. They'd hidden it, together, in plain sight: in the trunk of Rick's Honda Civic. It weighed the car down and when he took turns too sharply he could hear the metallic jangle of coins.

Donny brought his fists against the glass one more time and there came a shattering sound. Shards of glass exploded onto the tiled floor, scaring away the parade of flies in the process.

A desiccated hand reached through the opening and unclasped the lock.

The door opened.

Donny stepped in.

His stomach was flayed, curtains of flesh hanging down, offering a view of what was left of his organs. On the interior of his skin, Rick could've sworn he saw something. Words of some sort. No, not words. Something else. *Symbols*. Drawings. A sketch.

An emblem, like something you'd see stitched on a flag. *A brand.*

He didn't have time to analyze it. Didn't have time to do anything but grab his keys off the hook and spring through the hallway, through the other door, down the main flight of stairs, and into the humid night. He looked back only once, and staring through the broken window was the corpse of his former partner and perhaps his best friend. Rick and Donny had never been the best at showing their emotions but they were as close as brothers. He felt a pang of sadness to see Donny like this. It tore at him harder than the news of his death. But this... this *thing*, however it had happened, defied all logic. The longer he watched and thought of the logistics, the more the sadness turned to something more akin to fright.

He jogged for his Civic, got in, and drove off, his foot heavy on the gas pedal.

A few miles later, he tried Daphne's cell. He owed her a warning.

He was hoping for a voicemail until she answered. "Daph, it's Rick. Look, I'm sorry for everything. You can have the treasure, okay? You can have all of it."

She cut him off. "Rick. I already told you. I'm not interested."

"But you don't understand. Donny... he's—"

"I understand perfectly. Call this number again, *I* call the cops."

She hung up.

Rick tossed his cell phone and bashed the steering wheel with a clenched fist.

From the trunk, he heard the treasure settling, that soft jingle.

Fuck it. He no longer wanted any part of this. Everything he thought he knew about the rational world had come undone in the time it had taken to eat a stale egg roll. He couldn't stay in this town, not after what he'd seen.

He drove aimlessly for a few hours, waited until well past midnight to park outside of Daphne's house and lug the treasure up her drive, setting it down outside her front door. He thought of ringing the bell, then decided against it. He was afraid of her almost as much as her dead husband.

He sprinted back to his car, peeled out of the driveway, and gunned it down the street.

A few minutes later, something caught his eye to his right. He almost screamed when he saw the coin on the floor in front of the passenger's seat. He wasn't sure how the treasure was connected to Donny and he didn't care to find out. All he wanted was to be rid of every last piece of it.

He pulled onto the state fishing pier, made sure there were no idling cop cars looking for late-night drug deals. Certain he was alone, he climbed outside, took one last look at the coin, and tossed it into the ocean. He felt a brief moment of relief that ended quickly when something broke through the surface of the water.

Something large and long and slimy.

Something that reminded him of a worm or an eel or a—

A snake.

It was an impossibly large snake, reaching the height of his apartment complex and then some. It watched him with obsidian eyes and though he should have disbelieved what he saw, he was able to suspend that reaction, all things considered.

He backed away slowly until his ass bumped the front fender of his car. If it wanted, the snake could kill the distance between them before Rick could scream. But instead, it simply watched. As if this were a warning. And suddenly, staring the thing in its lifeless, demonic eyes, he had an idea what happened to Donny and what might be behind the recent seismic activity.

But he didn't dwell too long on the matter. Instead, he ducked back inside the Civic and cruised toward the highway, not blinking until his hometown was in the rearview.

He pulled over at the first rest stop and searched his car for gold coins. He didn't find any, but clinging to his soul was the phantom sensation that something had followed him the whole way.

CHAPTER SEVEN

Detective Andy Striker looked down his nose at her.

"I'm telling you the truth." Daphne sipped her coffee. In the background, Jake was playing *Fortnite* while his grandmother watched. She wasn't exactly happy with the cartoon violence that was being displayed, and sat in the shadows of the room, her scowl illuminated by the television's blue-ish glow. "I don't know how the chest ended up on my front porch."

About an hour ago, two men in black suits, who claimed they were from the historical society, swung by and picked up the chest. Striker had called ahead and verified they were coming, so their visit hadn't seemed completely unorthodox. But their presence left Daphne slightly shaken. She couldn't help but think of *The X-Files* during their visit, especially while they conducted their interview. *Did you see anybody? Hear anything? Suspect anyone?* She answered "no" to all of it, and their exit was like she'd gotten rid of an overaggressive in-home salesperson.

She didn't feel that way with Striker in the room, though he was beginning to wear out his welcome. Her patience had grown as thin as his hairline.

"And your husband's body?" he asked, for the second time, though it felt more like ten.

She rubbed her temples. "How many times do I have to tell you?"

"Two men are dead, Mrs. Jordan. The county medical examiner and the city coroner. I'll spare you the crime-scene photos, but let me tell you—it's about the worst I've ever seen in Lea Bay, and I've been doing this shit for twenty-five years. This has been a relatively safe community. We hardly see murder here. The occasional drug dealer gets himself scratched, but that's about all. This..." He thumbed the flap of the envelope that contained the photographs. "This is on another level."

"I don't know what you want me to tell you." She checked the clock. Already fifteen minutes late for work. "I don't know who killed those men and abducted my husband's body. Really. Now, if you don't mind, I have to leave for work and I'd like to kiss my son goodbye. It's been a traumatic day."

His eyes fell on the name tag above her left breast, lingered there just long enough to make her feel uncomfortable. "You're a nurse, isn't that right?"

"Yes."

"You have access to certain medical supplies? Drugs?"

"I mean, yeah, but—what does that have to do with anything?"

He jotted something down on his notepad and shrugged.

"Your husband has a well-documented history of drug abuse." It wasn't a question.

"Yes," she said, her frustration now bleeding into her words. "Look, Detective, I'm late for my shift, should have left a half hour ago. I've been very cooperative for you and the other..." What were they? Agents? Secret Service? *Men in Black?* "...other detectives. I really can't afford to miss any time."

"Yes, of course. Please. Just a few more questions." Striker didn't wait for her protest. "Did Donny meet up with anyone prior to his death? Did he mention a job, anything like that?"

Daphne shook her head. "He hadn't been around much over the last few weeks. Months, even. He'd disappear for days. Weeks, sometimes."

"I see." He scribbled more notes. "One more question: do you know where I can find Eric Jordan, Donny's brother? Your brother-in-law," he added, as if she didn't know how the family tree worked. "His last known address is Wyatt, Pennsylvania. I had the local PD send a few officers to his home, but he wasn't there. Place was all packed up, mostly empty, as if he was ready to move out. No sign of his fiancée either. Like they rushed out in a hurry, maybe left a few items behind. Wondering if you'd been in contact with him. I suspect he's here, in Lea Bay, considering his brother's death. I assume there will be a funeral?"

"Haven't scheduled it yet. Might be hard without a body, right?"

Striker nodded slowly. "We're working on that, Mrs. Jordan. Anyway, have you seen Eric Jordan? Has he called?"

Daphne shook her head.

"When was the last time you two spoke?"

He was starting to tear through the last of her patience. She didn't know how Donny's never-present brother factored into his death, if at all. Didn't care either. She hadn't spoken to Eric since... when was it exactly?

"Probably our wedding day," she said, squinting, trying to remember. "Or maybe when Jake was born? I couldn't tell you. Honestly, I don't think I'd recognize him if we passed each other on the street. Come to think of it, I don't even think he's on Facebook."

"He's not. We checked. No social media at all."

She nodded. "I'm sorry, Detective, but what does Eric have to do with Donny's death?"

The detective stared at her as if he were about to divulge a secret. Something big. Something important, not meant for her ears.

Then, plainly, he smiled. "We're just exploring all angles. Thank you for your time. Sorry to keep you from work. I'll be happy to call your supervisor and excuse your absence."

"That won't be necessary."

"Have a great night." He stood and showed himself to the front door.

She walked him out and closed the door behind him. The uneasiness sat in her gut like lead as his unmarked cruiser vanished around the corner of Maple Street. Her anxiety crawled inside her, slithering through intestines like a never-ending snake, eating as it went.

* * *

"Supper?" Sally Jordan asked, holding up a container of leftovers that may have been hunks of some slimy, unknown meat. It was probably turkey and gravy, but the fact that he couldn't tell for sure didn't sit well with Eric's stomach.

He winced. "No, Ma. I'm good."

"You sure?" She shook the contents as if that would make it appetizing.

He gave the Tupperware a second glance. "Positive."

"You're not on one of those vegan diets again, are you?"

He laughed. "That was just a phase in high school."

Her eyes bulged. "To impress Susan Walters!" She threw a finger in the air as if announcing some great discovery.

"That's right. And it worked too. For a while."

She placed the leftovers back in the fridge and sat at the kitchen table across from her son. Taking Eric's hands into her own, she frowned. "Your brother..."

Eric nodded, already knowing where their conversation was headed.

"...he was always troubled."

"I know, Ma." *We both were,* Eric thought. *In different ways.* He closed his eyes, kept them shut for an incalculable amount of time, and then reopened them. A part of him expected to wake from this nightmare.

Troubled, he thought, echoing his mother's words, recalling the *real* nightmares that had plagued him, the night terrors that invaded his sleep of late. *Shit, I still am.*

"He ran with the wrong crowd since I can remember," his mother mused. "Got all messed up on drugs. We tried, your father and I, but it got harder as Karl got... as he got *sicker.*"

Sicker. That was one way of putting it. The *gentle* way of putting it. What she really meant was *"as your father lost his fucking mind,"* but that was the harsh reality of it, and Sally Jordan didn't deal in harsh realities. Even though much of what had happened to the Jordan family, their falling out or—as Eric called it—falling *apart,* was mostly his mother's fault for turning a blind eye to certain things and sugar-coating certain truths, he never blamed her too much. He might have fought with her on the subject, might have called her names and called her out, but in the end she was his mother and he couldn't hold the past against her. Not with his father and brother both gone.

They were the only ones left, the two of them. The ones who had survived.

"Mom, I'm not pointing any fingers here. What happened, happened. But I need to know...Did Donny mention anything strange over the past several weeks? Something he saw, maybe?"

Sally tilted her head like a confused canine. "No. Why do you ask, sweetheart?"

With his gaze falling on the peeling wallpaper, Eric shrugged. "No reason. Just thought I'd ask."

"Eric..." she said in that motherly tone. "I know when something's eating you. What's going on?"

It took a moment for his eyes to settle back on hers. "Things have been odd lately. I've been getting those nightmares."

"You always had nightmares." She glanced up as if the past were scrawled on the ceiling. "That's why the doctors used to give you medicine."

He didn't have the heart to tell her that the pills never worked. "These are different. More frequent. Have you heard about the seismic activity off the coast?"

She shook her head. "You know who you're starting to sound like?" Her smile began to fade.

"I know," he said, laughing, although he didn't find any of this funny. Sounding like his old man terrified him, but not in the ways he'd expected. "But, you at least know about the chest..."

"The chest?"

"The one Don—" He stopped himself, started over. He didn't need to burden her with that now. She'd find out soon enough. "The one that someone stole from the historical society?"

"Haven't been much of a *current events* person lately." She located her smile. "I only log onto Facebook to play Candy Crush."

He could see this would require a more direct approach. "Mom, do you have any of Dad's old things? Journals? Articles he wrote? Books he owned? Anything?"

"I think the hospital and the police confiscated most of his materials. For *obvious* reasons. But if there is anything left, it would be in the attic."

"Mind if I poke around?"

"Not at all." With growing concern, she leaned over the table. "Should I ask what this is about?"

"Probably not."

He stood, made his way over to Sally, and pecked her on the cheek. Then he strolled down the hallway, locating the pulldown attic stairs. Grabbing the dangling string, he yanked down.

Once in the attic, he tugged on the pull-chain light, which gave very little luminance. For twenty minutes he sifted through cardboard boxes that had been chewed through by resident rodents. He handled framed photographs that Sally Jordan hadn't deemed worthy of public display. Most of them captured their family, together in one place, when he and Donny were little, before things went wrong.

Before their father tried to murder them in their sleep.

He pushed back the memory of that evening and kept searching, cleared away totes full of seasonal decorations, mostly Christmas and Halloween, the only two holidays the Jordans had ever celebrated. In the end, he discovered nothing, not a trace of his father's old notebook and texts, the items that had once taken up entire bookcases in their study room.

Nothing.

He felt lost. Confused. Disheartened. He'd been sure he'd find something here. Something told him to keep looking, but as he glanced around he knew he'd overturned every stone.

Overturned, he thought, and then began to search the plywood that covered the ceiling joists, hoping to see a loose board sticking up. A quick five-minute glance around proved that theory wrong. There was nothing up here. He supposed there could be something his father left behind underneath the plywood, but without taking a crowbar and making a project out of things, he couldn't know for sure.

Something wet smacked his forehead. He touched the warm liquid and his fingers revealed a dark substance, almost black. Probably dirt and rainwater. He looked up. There weren't any visible faults in the roof, no light entering where it shouldn't. Upon closer inspection, he still couldn't see what had dripped on him and where it had come from. The house was built a hundred years prior. Old houses have their quirks. His father's words.

Crouching, Eric noticed something in his periphery. Something palm-sized had been resting on a horizontal beam at eye-level. The way the evening filtered in through the roof vent gave the item an ominous glow. He made his way across the attic, dodging trusses and other wooden obstacles. The object became clearer as he neared it. A small book. The pages, bound by three loops of string, didn't contain a story, not in the linear sense. The cover was white and on it, written in cursive, was the title.

The Lords of the Deep. Where had he heard that before? The term had come from his father's brain, penned by his father's hand, and quite possibly—at some point—spoken by his father's mouth, but at the moment he couldn't recall a single memory of his father uttering those words.

The Lords of the Deep.

He opened the book and out spilled several newspaper clippings. Karl had glued articles to the pages as well, some dating back almost a hundred years. They all contained a similar theme—peculiar changes in the weather, unexplained shifts in the tide, and the fabled appearances of a large sea monster. A snake-like beast that prowled the local coves. There were even a few articles on local hauntings on the Jersey Shore, including the famous Ghost Ship sightings of Cape May. All things Karl Jordan researched as a hobby before it became his obsession.

Here it is. Exactly what I've been searching for.

After he scrounged up the fallen newspaper articles, he tucked the scrapbook in his back pocket.

The truth.

A phantom knife ran its blade through his abdomen. He bent over and cried out in pain but after a few seconds the sudden torment was gone, if it had ever been there. He pulled up his shirt and checked his flesh just to be sure. Only an old scar from his childhood. No new markings. He rubbed the area, skeptical of his own sensory receptors.

Sometimes, old wounds continue to hurt, Karl whispered in his ear.

Old wounds hurt too.

A fact Eric Jordan knew better than most.

CHAPTER EIGHT

"I'm sorry," Officer James Holbrook said, even though he wasn't. He pointed at the treasure chest with authority. "I'm going to have to take it back to the station."

"I'm afraid I can't let you do that." Horace Dweyer stepped in front of the young officer, blocking his exit from the historical society.

"It's not your decision to make," Holbrook said.

"Then whose is it?"

"The chief. This is evidence, Mister."

"*Doctor*," Horace corrected. He held a PhD in history and was working on his Master's in business administration. Not for a pay rise or promotion. Horace Dweyer didn't care about those things. Working at the historical society brought in a laughable salary but he scraped by just fine. He was a man of action, whose mind wandered if left unstimulated. Idle hands and all that. So he'd dedicated his life to knowledge, wanted to stay in school in some capacity until the day he died.

Holbrook smirked. "No offense, *Doc,* but you're not a surgeon and I don't see a stethoscope anywhere. I'll stick with mister."

The boy really was stupid. Horace had attended high school with James's father, Gary, a man whose claim to fame was that he'd led the football team to a near-perfect season during his senior year. All the boys had envied him. All the girls wanted to date him. When he'd dropped out of college and taken a job at the foundry, Gary Holbrook grew bitter. So he'd lived vicariously through his son's football glory days. Except James wasn't a fraction as talented on the field. If rumors were to be believed—and in small towns, they often are—Gary took to whipping his son with a sturdy, metal-studded belt. The boy supposedly had several worm-like scars on his shoulders and back to prove as much. He was known to brag about the abuse after a few drinks. And a few drinks after that, he'd move on to crying.

Horace would've felt bad for the kid if he wasn't such an insufferable asshole.

He tried blocking the way once more.

Holbrook stopped and sighed, setting the chest on the tiled floor. "Look, are you really going to make me cuff you and bring you in? I've got orders to bring this to the evidence room at the station and that's final. I'm sure they'll give it back once the investigation's over."

"And when will that be?"

"Hell if I know. So do me a favor, will you, and get out of my way."

Before Horace could protest, the boy was picking up the chest, grunting from exertion, and walking down the front steps of the historical society.

Horace's blood ran cold. The boy had no idea what lay within that splintered wood. He needed to call the board and let them know immediately.

When he turned to head toward the phone, two men in black suits blocked the way.

"Where are you going?" asked the man on the left.

Horace tried to walk around them but they cast a wide net. "To let the others know about this. The cops can't just walk out of here with an artifact like that. Its worth is priceless and it was already stolen from us once."

"Not to worry, Dr. Dweyer," said the man on the left. He wore sunglasses even though it was well past sundown.

"What're you talking about?" Horace asked.

The one on the right held his ear-piece, nodding at something. "It's been taken care of. The chest that Officer Holbrook just removed was a decoy."

"A decoy?"

They nodded in unison.

"Does someone want to tell me what the hell's going on here?"

The men in suits had shown up earlier that day, returning the *supposed* treasure chest to the historical society. The employees had probed them with questions but the men didn't seem all that talkative. Their faces remained emotionless. They could've been FBI, he supposed, but wouldn't they be working with the local police? Their jurisdiction seemed separate somehow. As silly as it sounded, Horace thought they looked more like secret agents.

The one with the ear-piece spoke softly into his watch, then whispered something to his partner. They conversed in low tones, concealing their words from interested parties. Horace considered escaping, sneaking out and following Holbrook. He didn't feel like getting arrested but it was surely better than facing those stoic stares. And besides, the guys had to be lying. He'd examined the chest an hour ago and it seemed quite genuine. The wood was ancient and rotting and the marks, both inside and out, had been just as the legend foretold.

Sunglasses finally spoke up. "Frazier Wilton would like a word with you."

"What does Frazier have to do with anything?" Horace had tried his best to forget the man existed, but it was difficult considering he was the mayor of Lea Bay, the face of his hometown. The two did not get along, mostly because Horace had bedded Frazier's second wife, Amelia, some ten years ago. The two had divorced soon after and he'd moved onto a younger trophy wife. But Frazier never let the infidelity go. He'd made Horace's life a living hell whenever he could, which was often. Slashed the historical society's budget a half dozen times this past decade and converted one of their oldest buildings into a parking lot for tourists.

"He'll explain everything," Ear-Piece said.

I'm sure he goddamn will, thought Horace as they led him out of the building, down the long stretch of front steps, and toward a nondescript black Ford Explorer with windows so tinted they matched the night sky. When the door opened for him, he thought again of fleeing. There was something off about these men, this whole situation. He trusted them as much as he trusted Frazier Wilton. But he had a feeling he wasn't being *asked* to follow their orders. Something told him that he'd be headed to city hall with or without his cooperation. The thought chilled him. He had enough to worry about as it was. He decided to bite the bullet and step into the Explorer.

They closed the door behind him and a moment later, the doors locked.

* * *

Fifteen minutes later, they slowed to a stop out front of city hall, parked in a fire zone, though neither man seemed worried about a ticket.

Ear-Piece stepped out of the passenger's seat and opened the door for Horace, gesturing toward the entrance. It felt like he had a personal driver, then remembered he'd been all but abducted.

Sunglasses told them he'd wait outside and keep the motor running.

Ear-Piece led Horace up the large front staircase and by the time they reached the top, Horace was winded. Sitting at a desk all day, reading through historical records and archival information, had swollen his midsection and rendered his lungs out of shape.

Janine, the front desk attendant, gave Horace a look of shock when they'd entered. She eyed Ear-Piece and looked away immediately. She knew something was up even if she'd only heard it through the grapevine. The suited man made no move to speak to her. Instead, he walked Horace down the main hall. As they waited for the elevator, Horace tried several times to get information from the man or agent or whatever the hell he was, but the guy was too tough a nut to crack. Eventually, they rode the elevator to the basement floor, which seemed odd considering there was only janitorial equipment and decades-old computers.

The hall was dim and there were cobwebs along the way. Horace wiped his beard just to make sure there was nothing crawling in it. At the end of the hall, they turned left and opened a door to what looked like a boiler room.

Ear-Piece opened yet another door but Horace did not spot any mops or brooms or tools of any kind. Instead, there was another elevator. A *hidden* elevator. It looked very much out of time, like something from the 1930s. It shimmered, gold-like, and the details were much more ornate.

"What is this?"

Ear-Piece gave him nothing.

There was a sole button on the right-hand panel. No numbers or letters to discern to which floor they were headed. Without understanding, Horace had a feeling they were going down.

To hell, he thought foolishly. *We're on our way to hell.*

He proved to be right—about the down part, not the hell—after they got on the second elevator and pressed the button.

When the doors parted, he saw not a boiler room or dingy hall, but an office. Again, the space seemed like a time capsule. Large oak bookshelves lined the walls and a desk that must have been a priceless antique stood on the far side of the room. There were no windows in this subterranean space but the lights did a good job of emulating natural sunlight.

There was only one person in the room. A man with a small scar under his left eye, given to him when he'd confronted Horace about fucking Amelia ten years ago. Frazier Wilton had won the fight but Horace liked to think he hadn't made it easy.

Frazier smiled, snake-like. "Horace. It's been a long time."

"Not long enough," Horace said, emotionless. "Will you please tell me what the hell is going on here? Why you've kidnapped me and brought me here?"

Frazier stood, waved at the seat in front of the desk.

"I'll stand, thank you."

"What I'm about to tell you is on a need-to-know basis and as much as I'd like to think you don't need to know, you're part of this now. Might even be of some use to us." He paced for a moment, thinking, choosing his next words carefully. "Have you ever heard of *The Lords of the Deep?*"

"I don't listen to heavy metal." Of course he'd heard of them—he was head of the historical society of Lea Bay, well-versed in the Lords lore, the famous cabal of pirates that once called this seaside town their home.

"They're not a band, you imbecile. They're... something very dangerous. A group of people—pirates, if you can believe such a thing—and many years ago, they made themselves home here at Lea Bay. I'll spare you the details, but suffice it to say, they were into some bad stuff. As in summoning things. Beasts from the nether. They may have been pirates, but they were so much more than that. They operated like a cult." He pointed to what looked like a vault on the eastern wall, next to a self-portrait of Frazier smiling for whoever was forced to paint the man. "Behind that door is the real treasure chest, and we hope to keep it there. It's safer for all involved parties. That means you too."

"What does this have to do with the theft?"

"Those coins in that chest are more than just priceless. They're dangerous. They predate the Lords, predate Lea Bay. Hell, they predate just about anything you can name. They hold more than just monetary power."

"It's my job to research this kind of stuff, Frazier. I know all about the Lords. All about the cult. You think I don't know the value of what's inside that chest?"

"You know very little. I'm not talking about whatever bullshit was recorded in history books or what you *think* you know on the subject—except one of course."

Horace studied his old nemesis. "What're you talking about?"

"Have you ever heard the name Karl Jordan?"

Horace nodded. Very few people who lived in Lea Bay *didn't* know Karl. "Sure, I knew him. What's this have to do with a crazy dead man?"

"Everything," he answered, voice raspy as if something had stolen his breath away. Frazier stared at the vault door again and for a moment so quick it might've been a mirage, he looked scared.

He wasn't sure what they were talking about here, but he trusted his gut well enough to know it couldn't be good.

CHAPTER NINE

As he surveyed the stock at Captain's Cove, Wilson Rhodes scratched his chin, wondering where to start. Moonlight, along with the solar LEDs fixed to the bulkheads, brightened the pathway along the boards. He walked down the main strip, examining the boats that had been damaged by whatever the hell had happened on the night Donny Jordan died. No one seemed to have answers, police included. They'd clammed up on the subject, told him nothing other than Donny's body had washed up on shore a hundred feet from the marina. Everything surrounding his ex-employee's death seemed hush-hush. Usually, when something newsworthy happened in Lea Bay, people talked. Especially when a member of the community was found dead from unnatural causes, which didn't happen often. It was odd that no one was talking about Donny's death. Nothing on the local news channel, no whispers at the grocery store. Rhodes couldn't even remember seeing a small, two-sentence obituary in the paper.

That's because he was a junkie, Rhodes thought. *And junkies don't deserve a shred of attention.*

Donny *had* been a junkie, sure, but he'd also been one of Rhodes's best and longest tenured employees. The man came in brain dead from time to time, but he'd always shown up. And worked. Which was more than Rhodes could say about three-quarters of his crew.

Now Donny was dead. Dead because he'd been here after hours, trying to break into the clients' boats, *probably* with the intent of pawning off expensive items for heroin money. That was the cops' summation and Rhodes couldn't argue with their logic. The wife, Daphne, had all but confirmed Donny's struggles with addiction and their somewhat volatile situation at home.

Rhodes had received the call on the second day of his North Carolina getaway, his annual trip with the wife and kids. Donny's tattered corpse washed up on the sandy shore. The news cut the Rhodes's vacation short, forcing the whole family back to their year-round home on the Jersey Shore. He hadn't been happy about that. Neither had Linda and the kids. But duty called, and a two-hour flight later, he was back home handling his affairs, meeting with insurance adjusters and outraged clients who sought alternative locations for their personal treasures.

It had been a week from hell.

He passed *The Kerplunk* and noticed tiny markings on the hull, pockets of exposed fiberglass where something had rubbed away the finish. It wasn't too noticeable. Nothing a quick coat of bottom paint couldn't cure. He'd put Mark Evans on it first thing tomorrow morning. *The Kerplunk's* owner, a wealthy, self-obsessed lawyer from New York City, was due to come down tomorrow afternoon and check on his precious luxuries. The less Rhodes had to show him, the better.

He couldn't see anything wrong with the rest of the Whaler, nor the other boats in that lot. He moved onto the next section, his eyes immediately drawn to the boat with yellow caution tape tied around its railing, completely roping off the bow. Even under the pale moonlight he could still see the faint red smears that stained the deck. Blood. Donny's.

This was the boat where the junkie had fallen and cracked his head. Rhodes folded his arms across his chest and exhaled. "Donny, Donny, Donny," he said with a mixture of sadness and disgust. "You really screwed me, kid. In more ways than one."

A shadow stretched across the boat's bow.

Losing his footing, Rhodes stumbled back, nearly stepping off the boards. He wrapped his arms around the nearest bulkhead, saving himself from taking a splash in the bay. The black, midnight water slapped against the dock, and a fine mist tickled his neck.

The figure stepped out from the cabin, entering the slab of silvery moonlight.

Rhodes's breath died in his throat. He tried to speak but his jaw locked up. Hands slipping on the bulkhead's surface, Rhodes managed a soft cry for help. No one knew where he was except for Linda, and she'd gone to bed several hours ago. Even if he somehow managed to grab his phone from his pocket and punch her digits, she wouldn't answer. She'd never know what her husband saw during his final moments, if these were indeed his last.

"Where is it?" the figure asked, its voice wet and guttural. Rhodes recognized it. The inflection. The tone. Despite its inhuman qualities, something about the figure's voice triggered Rhodes's memory.

Donny Jordan stood in the soft white glow of the moon, no more than twenty feet from where Rhodes cowered.

"Impossible," Rhodes squeaked. "Y-y-you're d-dead."

"Where is it?" Donny repeated.

"I don't know…" He trailed off, forgetting the rest of the words before they reached his mouth. Surveying Donny's appearance, his dinner—fresh Chilean sea bass—threatened to climb his throat. The man's pallid skin was thin, almost transparent, allowing a network of purple veins to be seen with absolute clarity. There was a thick red scar that started near his throat and ran vertically down his body, as if he'd been recently cut open and stitched back together. Only, Rhodes couldn't see stitches, and not because of the poor lighting. Because there *were no* stitches—the skin had melded, fused by what looked like some sort of natural glue. The rest of his flesh was covered in scars. The most prominent had been carved into his midsection, what looked like a tight cluster of ancient symbols, three full moons with X's through them. They seemed to glow in the moon's bright reflection.

Rhodes summoned his strength, which wasn't much, and rose to his feet. It was as if the lower half of him had died, grown numb. Like the upper half of him was floating on a cloud. Nothing about this night seemed real. He expected to wake up any moment, next to Linda. In their bed, bundled under the covers.

"Where are the tokens?" Donny hissed.

Rhodes puffed out his chest. If he couldn't be courageous in this moment, he thought he should at least pretend to be.

"You're not real," he said. "Just a figment of my imagination. That's it. A trick of the mind." He narrowed his eyes. "I must be going now."

He made for the main boardwalk that bordered the boat shop. He could lock the door and keep the apparition out.

Apparition? Is that what this thing is?

No other explanation for it.

I should have given the asshole the raise he always asked for!

"You're not real!" Rhodes shouted as he hustled down the walk, the boards beneath his feet flexing with each stomp. "You're just an apparition!"

He didn't turn around. A cold, shiver-inducing sensation touched his neck.

A hushed voice whispered in his ear, *"We're real... The Lords are real..."*

Before Rhodes could kick his legs into gear, something emerged from the bay. To his right, an enormous shadow rose from the water. Moonlight bathed the undulating shape, clearing away the veil of shadows that previously hid its identity.

Strength bled from Rhodes's limbs, affecting his legs the most, causing him to trip and tumble forward. He went down on the boards. Flipping over, he attempted to crab-walk toward the safety of the building. The massive sea serpent, at least forty feet tall, hovered over the dock, casting its stare down on him. Red eyes peered like twin beacons against the night sky. They drew closer. Closer. Until they stopped, hanging in the air a few feet from Rhodes's face. Hypnotized by the creature's magnificent size, Rhodes found himself unable to move. He broke the paralysis, craned his neck in Donny's direction. The apparition stood near the end of the dock, glaring at him.

The ghost's eyes glowed electric green, the color of toxic slime he'd seen in superhero movies. Donny's sunken eyes emitted smoke, drifting wisps of emerald fog. He shuffled toward Rhodes, his legs bending awkwardly as if broken at the knees. He moved with the grace of a marionette having its strings pulled by some drunken puppeteer.

As Donny neared, Rhodes could see other scars on his body forming, collecting on his skin as he grew closer. Keloids, the size of fingers, broke out across his flesh. Marks on his cheeks, a dull color compared to that of his eyes. The markings were more symbols, Rhodes noticed. Hieroglyphics, some primitive method of communication. Circles and triangles, shapes of varying length and artistic quality, occupied nearly every inch of flesh on Donny's ghastly face.

The ghost snarled. *"The Lords are real. The Deep will rise. And the beasts of the realm will come ashore."* A second later, the translucent-looking man—*man,* he could hardly call him that now—was face-to-face with him, nose-to-nose. Rhodes could smell the deepest depths of the ocean on his breath. *"Aye, but first we need our bloody tokens."*

If Rhodes had been able to scream, he would have.

The giant serpent lashed out, striking through the air with an unnatural swiftness, an attack Rhodes could hardly brace for. He felt the monster's mouth close on his abdomen, the two fangs it had previously flashed now piercing him. Rhodes finally found his scream, shouting into the slimy tunnel that made up the serpent's esophagus.

He could feel his body whip through the air, then crash on the watery surface below. Water flooded his eyes and mouth. The thing was dragging him under. Deeper beneath the surface. Into the black. Into the shallow depths of the Barnegat Bay.

CHAPTER TEN

Daphne was planning Donny's funeral when she received word that his body was still missing.

The phone rang several times before she answered. In the living room, cartoon sounds emanated, traveling straight down the hallway and boring a hole into her skull. She'd told Jake to turn down the television a half dozen times but the volume, if anything, had gotten louder. She couldn't summon the strength to discipline him, not at a time like this. His only experience with death had been a few years back when his goldfish, Skeletor, unexpectedly kicked the bucket. The poor thing had died just three weeks after they'd brought it home from the county fair. They'd held a small ceremony before flushing its orange carcass down the toilet.

"Where does it go?" Jake had asked, eyes wet with tears.

Daphne paused. "The ocean, I suppose." She'd looked around for Donny before remembering he was "out," which probably meant selling or scoring drugs. She'd taught her son about death all by her lonesome self.

Not much had changed.

"Hello?" she answered, finally. She held the crown of her nose with her free hand, hoping to rub away the pain that had taken residence behind her eyes.

"Mrs. Jordan?"

"Speaking." The voice sounded official, belonging to someone with authority. *What now*?

"I'm afraid I have some bad news."

She could've laughed at that. How much worse could it get? Her husband was dead. Her father had died when she was young, leaving her mom and her alone. The only man left in her life was two rooms down, watching *Gravity Falls* and trying to wrap his head around the fact that his father was dead, D-E-A-D, and not coming back. Not this time. "I'm listening."

"It's about your husband."

She pulled the phone away from her ear and stared at it for a moment, as if this were some crank call she didn't have time (or patience) for. "I'm sorry, who is this?"

The voice—a man with a low, gravelly timbre—did not identify himself. Instead, he delivered the news he'd promised. "Your husband's body is *still* missing. We have no solid leads yet, but we are doing everything we can to track him down."

"Jesus Christ. I'm literally on the other line with the funeral director."

"I know, I'm really sorry. This is... well, this is about the craziest damn thing we've ever seen. It's as if... as if his corpse just up and vanished."

"This isn't happening."

The man went on. "We're looking at all the possibilities, but it's important we receive your full cooperation."

"Of course," she said, thinking his choice of words odd. Of course, she'd cooperate. It wasn't like she had something to hide.

Like a body.

"Has anyone gotten in touch with you, aside from the men retrieving the chest from your residence?"

She shook her head. "No one." Unless you counted the pizza delivery man, no one had stopped by since. Not even to offer their condolences. Donny had been a junkie, light in the *friends* department. His other acquaintances had been fellow users and they weren't the type to stop by with a fruitcake and an *I'm-so-sorry-for-your-loss* card.

"Good," the nameless man said. "Please let us know if you... uh... have any uninvited guests."

"Is there something you're not telling me?" she asked. "Who is this again?"

The line went dead with a hard click.

She set down the phone on the kitchen counter and poured herself a cup of coffee with shaking hands. Her skin grew frigid. She couldn't seem to get warm even though it was well after dark and the outside temperature was already pushing eighty. Her mind sped in a thousand different directions. She wasn't sure which path was correct but one of them told her Donny's missing body had something to do with the men in suits. In fact, the voice on the phone had sounded just as calm and measured and lifeless. He hadn't said if he was police or FBI, which made her think it was neither.

She was too tired to cry but she shut her eyes nonetheless, trying to catch her breath.

The coffee tasted burnt and acidic. She was jittery enough as it was, and the caffeine would do her no favors. She'd been adding up funeral costs, had just finished making an appointment to look at gravestones when the stranger called. Now she wasn't sure what to do.

Donny, you son of a bitch. Even dead, you're still tearing me apart.

The cartoons seemed louder now, but she would not tell Jake to turn them down. She would not raise her voice or tell him how exhausted and broken she felt. He deserved his TV time. Deserved his childhood ignorance. Because one day, he'd be her age and no matter how well his life went, he'd still understand that no one gets out in one piece.

She sipped her coffee again, wincing as it slid down her throat, nearly choking when she heard the doorbell.

She froze.

The man's voice spoke between her temples.

Please let us know if you... uh... have any uninvited guests.

The bell rang again.

She craned her neck, tried to look outside but the angle was all wrong. Whoever stood on the front steps was hidden from her view.

She wasn't expecting company—not now or ever—and with the phone call in mind, she ought to call the cops.

But moments later she heard footsteps coming down the hall, skipping in uneven steps like there was nothing wrong in the world.

"Jake!" she called. "Don't!"

Then came the sound of the front door opening.

"Who are you?" Jake asked the visitor. *The uninvited.*

She didn't wait for a response. She set down her mug much too hard and ran for the hallway, where a man stood in the doorway. He wasn't wearing a suit or dark sunglasses or an earpiece. He wore a t-shirt and jeans and his eyes looked as tired as her own.

"I'm your uncle," Eric Jordan said. "Is your mom home?"

* * *

"Eric? What're you doing here?"

Daphne hadn't seen Donny's brother in years. In fact, she'd only met him a handful of times. He didn't travel to Lea Bay often, had found himself a better life away from the shore. He should've visited home more, especially to see his mother. But truth be told, she didn't blame him. Even envied him to some degree. Because Eric had *gotten out.* Daphne—she was trapped here. More so now that Donny was gone. The house was paid off, even if it was falling apart, and she'd never be able to afford a new place on her own, not on her nurse's aide salary.

"Donny," he said, as if that explained everything. And in some ways, it did. But his eyes told a different story. There was more to his visit than his brother's passing. "Can I come in?"

She nodded, waving him into the kitchen.

"You want some coffee?" she asked, remembering her own mug.

"That'd be great. Tired as hell. Haven't slept in days."

"I know the feeling." She poured him a cup and topped off her own.

"Daph... I'm so damn sorry. I mean it."

She shook her head. "You know, I could read you the riot act, tell you how goddamn selfish you've been not visiting. Or I could accept your condolences because I bet you didn't want your return trip home to be under these circumstances."

"I've been an asshole," he said. "No doubt about that. But I would prefer the second option."

"Thank you for coming."

"You don't look like my dad," Jake said, surprising them both.

"Shit," Daphne said under her breath. She'd forgotten her son was standing in the kitchen doorway, listening to every word they spoke.

Eric knelt down, eye level with the boy. "I don't, do I? Your old man got all the handsome genes. Had his pick of the girls in school." He turned to Daphne. "I'd say he chose well."

"What gene did you get?" Jake asked.

"I guess I'm the brains of the family, though it hasn't gotten me very far."

Jake grew quiet, unsure of what to say. Eventually he excused himself back to the living room and resumed his *Cartoon Network* binge.

"Looks just like Donny," Eric noted. "It's uncanny."

She watched the doorway to ensure her son wasn't coming back. "Spitting image. Let's hope he doesn't make the same bad decisions as his dad."

"I would've come sooner," he said. "But I was tied up with mom. And, well, I found something I thought you might want to see. Something I... something I don't fully understand."

"What are you talking about?"

He pulled a book out of his pocket and set it down on the kitchen counter, slid it across to her. It looked important, journal-like, and the white exterior was covered in a layer of dust. Four words had been written in shaky cursive on the cover.

"Lords of the Deep?" she asked. "Sounds like a bad movie."

"It's my father's. He wrote it."

"What's it got to do with me?"

"I haven't had a chance to read the whole thing and believe me, a lot of it doesn't make any sense. See, I tried to stop by earlier. Yesterday, actually, when I first got in. But I saw these guys in suits out front."

"Oh, them. Yeah, I think they're from Area 51." Though she'd meant it as a joke, she wished she'd chosen her words more carefully. A shiver ran along her spine and she looked outside just to make sure there weren't any unmarked vans. She was probably just being paranoid.

He nodded. "That chest they were carrying—I'm willing to bet it was filled with coins."

Her eyes widened. "Hundreds of them. Looked like something out of Indiana Jones."

"It's pirate treasure," he said.

"How'd you know that?"

He tapped a finger on the book. "Because I read it in here. I think there's something big going on. I think Donny accidentally got himself wrapped up in more than just drugs. That chest, those guys in suits— even the seismic activity—I think it's all part of something bigger."

"That sounds crazy."

"You don't know the half of it." He lifted the book, opened it to the first page, and handed it to her. "Here, read it."

A half hour later, he didn't sound so crazy.

CHAPTER ELEVEN

Kevin Kane and Barry Dillinger paced their apartment's living room, trying not to let their anger boil over. The words *kill* and *revenge* were at the forefront of their thoughts, but each time things got a little too intense, a little too heated, one had been there to mitigate the other's murderous intentions. They'd talked each other down from many ledges over the years, but none quite as high as tonight.

"That motherfucker," Kevin spat as he fixed his trucker's hat, pulling it tight against his scalp. He snatched a can of PBR from the couch's cup holder, gave it the sniff test, deemed it drinkable, and downed the entire beer in four gulps. He let out a loud, drawn-out burp that echoed across the sparsely decorated apartment. "Rick screwed us. Big time. We're not going to see a fucking cent for that heist."

Barry stomped his feet on the raggedy carpet and pulled at the ends of his curly hair. His gold-chain necklace—sporting a worthless, gold dollar-sign pendant—clanked around wildly. "Never thought he'd do us like that, man. Never in a million years. Just pick up and ghost like that? That bitch better hope we never see each other again."

"He was our friend."

"He was our *best* friend."

"And Donny? Man, what about Donny?"

"And his wife?"

Kevin didn't want to say *fuck his wife,* but at the same time—he did. When Rick had presented the idea of giving Daphne Donny's share, he hadn't exactly been on board. Over the span of a few hours he had come around and reluctantly agreed to give the widow a nice chunk of change, but only under one condition. In return, she'd clam up about Rick, about what she thought she knew.

About their side work.

"I don't like anything about this, man." Kevin leaned against the wall, hugging himself for comfort. "First Rick turns on us, then someone snatches Donny's body from the morgue. Something ain't right."

"Well, what do we do?" Barry continued to pull harder on his hair, so much so that Kevin thought the remaining brown tufts would rip out.

Kevin shut his eyes. Breathed. Mulled over their limited options. On one hand, they could do what Rick had done: get the hell out of Lea Bay, undoubtedly the wisest of the two available choices. The other was to sit tight, hope this whole disaster would blow over, hope the cops would see no need to investigate the missing treasure chest. But if it was worth what Rick had said it was worth, surely *someone* would come looking for it.

Run, Kevin thought to himself. *Get out and leave this miserable town, once and for all.* An overwhelming rush of emotion, the result of his anxiety manifesting itself, pumped steadily throughout his body. His veins flooded with adrenaline and he suddenly felt like hurling himself through the second-story window. *Run. Just like Rick. Run and don't look back.*

"We should find him," Barry suggested. "Rick. That piece of shit. We should track the bastard down and snuff his ass."

There went Barry, climbing up that ledge again.

"We went over this," Kevin said, pinching the bridge of his nose. "We have no idea where he went. We'll never track him down. He's gone, man. He ghosted."

Barry nodded in agreement. Of course Kevin was right. Rick was gone. Poof. Just like that. Never to be seen or heard from again.

Smart motherfucker.

"Unless we already know where he's going," Barry said, rubbing his chin, deep in thought.

"And where's that?"

"To sell the chest."

"We don't even know who the buyer is." Kevin clamped his temples with the palms of his hands. "We don't know shit. We're completely in the dark. Man, we trusted that fool with everything. How fucking stupid are we?"

Barry smiled. "Not *that* fucking stupid."

Kevin stared at him blankly. "What are you talking about?"

Barry's face beamed as if he only just realized he'd been holding a winning lottery ticket. "We head over to Rick's, break into his lame-ass apartment, and find the buyer's information."

Kevin glared at him. It took everything in his power not to waltz over and smack him upside his potato-shaped head. "Oh, yeah. We'll just go right over there. Maybe he'll have the information pinned to his refrigerator."

Barry snapped his fingers. "Exactly."

"That's the dumbest shit I've ever heard."

Before he could talk about things that actually made sense, like where to go before the police came sniffing around, a knock sounded at the door.

The men exchanged glances. They waited it out, hoping the knocker would identify themselves. Or better yet—leave silently.

Shit! Kevin thought. *They found us! The pigs found us!*

Their mystery guest rapped his knuckles on the door again, impatient. "Mr. Kane?" a deep voice spoke. "Mr. Dillinger? I was hoping to have a word with the two of you."

"Wh-who, who's there?" Kevin asked, limbs trembling, he crept toward the front door.

"Not the cops, I assure you."

Not the cops? What kind of answer is that? He glanced over at Barry, and his partner shook his head as if he'd been hit with five thousand volts of electricity.

"Just fucking identify yourself," Kevin said, arriving at the door. He closed one eye and peeked through the peephole. A man in a black suit swallowed up most of the view. Two other guys stood behind him, dressed similarly. Their black sunglasses made them look like secret service agents, and it was because of this Kevin recognized their unexpected visitor.

He turned to Barry and mouthed, *The mayor?*

Barry shrugged, his forehead bunching with uncertainty. He didn't know the mayor's face let alone his name. Barry wasn't exactly tuned into local politics. He wasn't even registered to vote.

"My name is Frazier Wilton and I would like a word," claimed the voice.

"The mayor?"

"That's right, Kevin. The goddamn mayor."

"What... what are you doing here? How do you know who I am?" Sweat beaded on his hairline. A furnace burned inside him, and the room dimmed a little, throwing off his equilibrium. The floor felt unstable. He thought he might lose consciousness, he put a hand on the wall and steadied himself.

"Maybe we should discuss this inside, and not in the middle of the hallway."

Before Kevin could think about hiding the ounce of weed on the kitchen table, he reached for the handle, turned it, and let Frazier and his two goons inside.

"Thank you kindly," the big man said, entering the apartment, immediately having himself a quick glance around. He spotted Barry and said, "Evening, Mr. Dillinger."

"How do you know me?" Barry asked, awe-stricken.

"I'll cut right to the chase," Frazier said. The two men stood absolutely still behind him, like stone statues representing prominent historical military leaders. Kevin felt the heat storm burn its way throughout his body and stop when it reached his face. His entire frame had become a three-alarm fire, and the people on the top floor were jumping. "You knucklefuckers aided Mr. Ricardo Lopez in procuring some very important artifacts."

Before they could deny their involvement, Frazier put up his hand.

"Now, now. What's done is done, and I'm not here to break your balls about it. If you tell me what I want to know, I don't see why we can't let this little transgression slip. Sound agreeable?"

The men looked to each other, then back to Frazier, nodding feverishly.

"Good." He paused, lost in his thoughts, as if he wasn't sure he should continue. "We recovered the chest."

"Where's Rick?" Kevin blurted out.

"I don't know where Mr. Lopez went off to, and quite frankly I don't care." He shot them a stern look, encouraging them to remain silent. The mystery men took a step forward. "There seems to be some items missing from the chest. Important items that we need to locate before... well, before something very bad happens to Lea Bay and the good people who live here."

The two low-level criminals exchanged dumb glances.

Kevin spoke first: "Rick was in charge of the exchange."

"Did you try to open it? Be honest now."

Again, the two thugs looked to each other, hoping the other would provide Frazier with the answers he was looking for.

"We tried," Barry admitted. "But we couldn't get it open. It was locked. And we couldn't break it. Tried bolt cutters and everything."

"It's a lock that cannot be opened without the key." Frazier shook his head. "But alas, something is missing and *someone* opened it. Someone who knows a thing or two about it. What I want to know is—where are the other items?" He paused, his eyes narrowing, shooting them a look that burrowed into them, into their souls. "The tokens? Where are the goddamned missing tokens?"

"We don't know, man," Kevin said, hating the tremble in his own voice. He wasn't accustomed to being intimidated. To being scared. "We don't know anything."

Barry wiped his brow with his forearm. "Nothing. Not a damn thing. Sorry we're so useless to you."

Frazier hung his head. "Me too."

Ear-Bud stepped forward. Kevin had no time to react. A muffled gunshot, like a quarter falling into an empty pail, went off. A cloud of crimson misted behind Barry's head. The red vapor vanished as quickly as it had appeared. Kevin turned for the door but got no closer. No pain registered when the bullet punched through his skull and painted his world with infinite darkness.

CHAPTER TWELVE

When she'd finished reading the book, Daphne could hardly breathe. Eric watched her for a while, reminding her now and then that this wasn't some nightmare, some horrid dream from which she'd wake. This was reality. This was her life now.

Eventually, he left, promising he'd be back when she'd had enough time to digest its contents.

Daphne canceled the appointment with the funeral home, giving vague answers when they asked what had happened. Nothing, she'd insisted. She just needed more time.

Because my husband's body is gone and I'm not sure when or where it'll turn up.

If *it turns up.*

She read the pages again in bursts, Jake taking away her attention throughout the day. Asking questions about his dad, mainly when the man was coming home. After all the conversations they'd had, Daphne patiently explaining that Daddy was gone for good, the boy still didn't fully grasp it. Maybe she should've been more direct, but she couldn't bring herself to crush him like that. He'd clung to hope for months after they'd flushed Skeletor, insisting there'd been some cosmic mix-up. That'd he'd rise up through the sink one day.

Finally, when Jake had fallen asleep in his room watching more cartoons, she turned off the television and pulled the blankets up to his chin. He looked so peaceful, snoring softly. She fought the urge to crawl into bed beside him. Hold him close until they rode this out together.

She drank more coffee but it did nothing for her nerves, so she poured two generous shots of whiskey into her mug. Then she pulled up a chair near the living room's sliding door and finished reading through the book for the second time.

She found herself coming back to the title every few pages.

Lords of the Deep.

What did it mean? Who were these Lords?

Half of the manuscript consisted of newspaper clippings, things that would've seemed strange under other circumstances. The headlines often spoke of seismic activity, something that had been in the news plenty over these last few weeks. It got stranger from there. Back in the early eighties, a group of college kids, after drinking on the beach, had allegedly spotted something moving in the bay. They claimed it had an elongated neck, a snout with two large holes for nostrils, and one of the teens was quoted saying the thing had "red eyes like the devil."

She tightened her robe until it nearly choked her.

Sipped her drink and waited for it to calm her.

A sea snake.

That was what the kids had seen that night. A giant snake that had come out of the bay and scared them shitless. She wanted to believe they'd just been high out of their minds. She'd smoked a bad batch of weed as a teen, laced with who knew what. For three hours, she'd been certain something was watching her until the feeling faded and she'd given up smoking altogether. But the way these kids had described what they'd seen—it was far too particular. Far too detailed. *Red eyes like the devil.* And after the week she'd had, she was more inclined to believe they'd seen *something.*

There were pages of handwritten text sandwiched between the articles, but not much of it made sense.

From what she could piece together from Donny and Eric's father's shaky handwriting, Lea Bay was once home to pirates. It wasn't something often discussed in textbooks, had seemingly been erased from history completely. But there was evidence if you looked hard enough. These pirates had murdered several locals, pillaged their way through town, leaving behind a trail of rape and murder and torture. Eventually, mob justice prevailed. The villagers chased away the band of pirates, losing half their militia in the process. A bloody, violent clash, but Lea Bay had persevered and won back the rights to their freedom.

The pirates—what remained of them—had sailed into the distance, but they'd left something behind. Something important. Something the town kept for itself.

She gasped. Read the words several times just to make sure she wasn't losing her mind.

The treasure chest.

During their escape, the pirates had left behind a chest full of cursed tokens. More valuable than anything they could've pilfered from Lea Bay. But the further she read, if the chicken scratch was to be believed, the more it sounded like the chest wasn't stolen by the townspeople—the Lords had *deliberately* left it here along with a group of their own to watch over the treasure. They'd taken to the woods and were never seen again.

From there, the book went back to earthquakes and sea snake sightings up and down the east coast, the occasional ghost ship spotting. There was mention of the Lords' treasure being lost sometime in the nineteenth century, never to be seen in Lea Bay again.

Until now, she thought. *I've seen it with my own eyes.*

She closed the book, feeling another intense headache coming on. Advil and sleep sounded like heaven.

Through the glass panels, she watched the bay. The waves were calm tonight, the water nearly flat. The only sound, aside from the fan down the hall, came from the seagulls. She'd always loved their calls. Most people in town considered them pests, but not Daphne. There was something lovely about their voices. Something beautiful even.

She yawned, stretched, leaned back in the chair. Maybe the whiskey was working after all.

Her mind spun but she couldn't seem to form coherent thoughts. All she knew for sure was that tomorrow she'd speak to Eric and they'd figure this all out. Donny's missing body, the book, the Lords of the Deep—all of it. Eric had been right. There was something big afoot, though she was too tired to piece together the information and assess what *it* was.

So she watched the bay, feeling lucky for living so close to the water, even if the house wasn't all that glamorous. Even on her worst nights the view had always been there for her. A foghorn cut through the gulls and the fan and she began to drift off when she saw a shape appear on the tide.

Her eyes opened wide.

She tried to stand but her legs had grown paralyzed. Her heart thudded much too fast.

There was something out there, across the way. Something rising from the water, a gargantuan form taking shape beneath the bay. Aside from the crescent full moon, there wasn't a light to be seen, but as her eyes adjusted, she discovered more details of the dark presence. It was a shadowy mound at first, but quickly its size doubled.

This is a dream, she thought. *This is a dream and you will wake up soon to the real nightmare.*

She'd read too much of the book, nodded off in the chair and now she had sea snakes floating through her subconscious.

For that was what she'd seen out there, drifting in the bay. The elongated neck confirmed it. As did what appeared to be a mouth she was certain bared long, jagged teeth. It peered slowly as if combing the coast for prey.

She was suddenly reminded about the strange pockets of flesh missing from Donny's body.

Her breath hitched.

From her pocket, she pulled out her phone and brought up her camera. She pressed record and began taking video, zooming in as much as the cursor would allow.

The thing stood still, surveying the beach and the pier and the roads beyond. It seemed to be in no rush and that realization chilled her blood. She thought back to those college kids on the beach, how scared they must have been, how foolish they must have felt when no one believed them.

The thing turned toward her.

It was much too dark to make out a set of eyes but she could *feel* them, crawling over her, peering deep within her.

Red eyes like the devil.

Surely it couldn't see her from this distance.

Surely it wasn't taking note of where she sat.

Her hands grew shakier until she fumbled, the phone dropping to the floor. She cursed and reached down, finally finding the strength to move. When she sat back up the water was empty, no sign of anything with scales or teeth. No sign of anything there to begin with.

It's all in your head. You've been through so much that you're finally starting to crack. Next it'll be Bigfoot and leprechauns.

Except when she looked at her phone and pressed play, she saw the moon and the group of cawing gulls and the lighthouse. And among all of that normalcy was the serpent, turning toward her. Watching. Waiting.

Plotting.

She stopped the video halfway through and called Eric. It didn't matter how late it was. There were more pressing issues.

"Hello?" he answered a few rings in.

"Eric, we need to talk."

"What time is it?"

"Never mind that, just get over here. Quick. It's about your father."

"My father?"

She looked at the water again. Still empty, though it felt anything but. It felt full, pregnant with an ancient, hidden evil. Something brewing for centuries, some malevolent force ready to rise, ready to tear this town apart.

She felt its touch on her skin and shivered.

"Yes," she said. "Turns out you were right. He wasn't as crazy as he seemed."

Eyes. Red like the Devil's.

57

CHAPTER THIRTEEN

Jake woke to something tapping on his window. He waited nearly a minute for his eyes to adjust to the darkness, rubbing the blurriness away with his knuckles. At first he thought he was trapped in a dream, the moon-projected shadows of swaying branches suggesting this was the onset of a terrible nightmare. He could feel dread climbing into his body, seeping into his bones. The nightlight flickered. Despite the closed window, a cold breeze swept through the room, chilling his blood. Somewhere down the hall, a floorboard creaked.

Again, something rapped on the window. His seven-year-old brain cast an image of a witch, green skin and bent nose, riding a broomstick and knocking on windows belonging to delicious children.

He shook his head. With his eyes adjusted, he peeled off the comforter and planted his bare feet on the floor. Slipping his *Teenage Mutant Ninja Turtles* slippers on, he listened for a break in the eerie silence.

"Hello?" he asked the darkness. In the background he heard his mother downstairs, talking to someone. He didn't want her to hear him skulking around when he was supposed to be sleeping. She wouldn't get mad if she caught him up and about, but she *would* be disappointed and sometimes that was worse. Between his father not coming home *(dead)* and the other daily problems she complained about *(bills, food stamps)*, the last thing he wanted to do was add to her stress.

He heard it again, that tapping. Concentrating on the window, he saw nothing but the dark and the swaying branches.

Half-expecting to come face-to-face with the witch from his worst nightmares, Jake crept toward the window. He pictured the dreadful hag with yellow eyes. Gnashing teeth. A crooked nose, perfect for sniffing out bad little boys who stayed awake against their mother's wishes. A mouth packed with rotten shards of teeth, leaking juices, dribbling with infectious disease.

But there was nothing. Nothing but the tree being pushed around by summertime zephyrs. The empty street and the small cluster of trees that separated the road from the narrow beach bordering the bay. The empty street.

Except it *wasn't* empty. Not completely.

A figure stood rooted in the middle of the road, shrouded by shadows and green mist. The dark outline of a man, unwavering, frozen stiff. A statue, maybe.

Then, jerkily, it began to turn and face Jake.

He stepped away from the window, not wanting to know the figure's identity. Then he stayed put and watched for exactly the opposite reason. Because he *did* want to see it. He wanted to know what was there, bathing amongst the shadows. Something kept him there, facing the view. Some deep intuition. He wasn't going anywhere. Parking himself in the small patch of moonlight, he stood. And watched.

The figure faced him, revealing himself.

Jake almost screamed but covered his mouth just in time. The cry was muted, a lessened version of what could have been the real thing.

Daddy?

It couldn't be, but it was. His father stood in the middle of the street. The moonlight painted his skin paper-white. There were bruises all along his body. A long vertical scar ran down his chest, bright red, the color of Santa's suit. His eyes were so sunken they looked like little black holes, miniature gateways into pure nothingness. His father's nakedness was the last thing he noticed.

Donny turned and started toward the trees.

"Daddy?" he asked aloud, softly though, so his mother wouldn't hear. "Daddy, come back."

The dead man did not stop, ignoring his son's almost-silent request. Even through the distance between them, Jake sensed his father could hear him.

The dead man kept trekking toward the bay. Toward the calm, waiting waters.

Without thinking, Jake grabbed his desk chair and dragged it over to the window. He stood on it and unlatched the security tabs on the top sash, allowing the bottom sash to open all the way. Once he slid open the window, a strong breeze bustled into the room. The sudden gust tossed aside photographs and finger-paintings from a nearby wall, scattering them across the floor. Jake didn't care about them; he only wanted to see his father again.

He knew his old man would come back. *Wait till mom finds out!* She'd be so happy. She'd smile again. Oh yes, she would. Having Daddy home would solve a heck of a lot of problems. Mom would stop moping, go back to being her fun, play-all-day self. No more hanging her head. No more staring out the window for hours, getting lost in her thoughts. She'd stop being sad. Grandma would stop being sad, too. So would Daddy's brother, Eric. Though he only just met his uncle earlier that day, he seemed like the saddest of them all. He'd put on a happy face in front of Jake, sure, but Jake could see through the man's mask as clearly as he spotted his father standing in the middle of the street. Yes, Daddy's homecoming would cure a lot of sadness, and Jake could help with that.

He could help by *bringing him back.*

He could convince his father to come home, maybe even entice him to "stay clean", that phrase his mother always threw around.

Jake climbed on the roof and spider-walked his way down the shingles, over to the Japanese maple that extended over the gutters. He was confident that the branches would support all fifty pounds of him. He *wasn't* confident that he could make it all the way down without slipping or falling, breaking an arm or a leg on the landing. He hadn't been the most athletic kid in phys ed, never once volunteered for after-school sports. Video games were more his speed. Cartoons and YouTube over kickball and shooting hoops.

But his father was waiting for him. Waiting to be told it was safe to come home. That his family loved him, needed him. That his son ached for his return.

Jake eased himself onto the branch and just like he'd predicted, it held his weight. He shimmied down the tree's flimsy extension, letting his knees do most of the work. He'd been taught this method on the playground while watching other kids climb up the fireman's pole. The same concept applied, only he was horizontal this time. Jake made his way to the trunk without incident.

Then his foot slipped on the wet bark. His slipper fell off and sailed to the ground. Heart leaping in his chest, he swung his leg over the branch and wrapped both legs around it. He glanced down and took note of the short distance to the ground. He could probably jump without busting his leg.

Probably.

It was that or risk falling while transitioning to the trunk. He decided jumping was his best option. He gripped the branch with both hands and shifted his weight to one side, allowing his feet to dangle freely.

Then he took a deep breath.

Let go.

He hit the ground with a thud and stayed in a crouching position for a long time. Hunched over, he waited to see if his mother came running out, screaming his name. She never did. He heard her voice again. And someone else's. Uncle Eric's? Yes, he thought so.

Good, he thought. *At least she's not alone.*

After that, he took off across the street and toward the bay, forgetting all about his missing slipper.

CHAPTER FOURTEEN

It was getting late when Horace Dweyer started packing.

He poured himself a glass of Dewar's. Then another. Then a third and fourth, though he took those straight from the bottle. His condo somersaulted and there was something beautiful about it. His eyes were heavy and if he let himself lie down, he would've slept for ten hours. But he couldn't afford to close his eyes, not even for a moment.

Outside, parked one street over, was a black Escalade. The engine was off. The windows were up. Tinted. But he didn't need to see inside to know the men in suits were staking out his place. They'd been there for two days. At first, he'd chocked it up to coincidence. But as he'd learned since this whole long-lost treasure debacle began: coincidences were getting harder to come by.

He needed to get out of Lea Bay.

It was risky, just about the dumbest decision he could make, but he wasn't exactly drowning in options.

If they caught him leaving, they might not kill him, but his life would surely take a turn for the worse.

But if he stayed behind, did what they told him, what then?

Escape would not be simple. He couldn't just saunter down his driveway. They'd be expecting that. But if he packed one bag, just enough necessities to hold him over for a while, he could sneak through his neighbor's yard and walk ten blocks to the bus station. Get a ticket for Boston and plan his next move. He had family there. An uncle and a cousin, both good people, the kind that would take in a man for a few nights even if he hadn't visited in far too long.

But first: he needed to make some calls.

He'd heard Eric Jordan was back in town, for obvious reasons. He didn't want to bother Eric's mother. Lord knew she'd been through enough. But he couldn't leave without warning them.

Then there was Daphne. Sweet, poor Daphne who'd drawn the short stick in life. He remembered her from the supermarket, where she'd worked in high school. She had the look of a movie star and was far smarter than she let on. She should have finished college, became a full-time nurse like she'd always talked about, and gone far, far away from this place. She too deserved the truth.

The truth.

He could've laughed at that.

The truth was relative as hell.

One day you were working your dead-end job at the historical society and the next, everything you thought you knew about the rational world came undone right before your eyes.

If what Frazier had told was the *truth*, then Karl Jordan had gotten close to revealing what those coins truly stood for. A pact of sorts. The worst kind of pact. He'd dedicated the last few years of his life to the matter. Studied resources you couldn't find in your local library. Conspiracy nut fodder. Except all conspiracies had some nugget of... well, *truth*.

Much like Horace this very moment, Karl had been watched closely.

Watched while he researched and prepared a manuscript.

Watched while he met with experts in local pirate lore.

Watched while he was murdered.

And his death had been for nothing. What he'd tried to expose—it was still a secret. And the consequences would reach far and wide.

But Horace wasn't like Karl. He didn't intend on exposing any of this. All he wanted was to right a wrong and be on his way.

He picked up the phone, dialed the number for Eric he'd found after a little online research. Karl would've been proud.

It rang once, twice, and a man answered. "Hello?"

"Eric."

"Who's this?" His voice was low, like he'd been awakened or he was trying to hide his voice.

"There's no time. I need you to listen to me."

On the other end, the man yawned, cleared his throat. "You have any idea what time it is?"

"I'm well aware. Now stop speaking and listen to me."

A pause. "What's this about? Are you...this better not be one of the suits."

Horace smiled. What he was doing did not come without risks but at least he'd never be one of them. "I won't tell you my name but I can promise I'm not wearing a suit. No more questions."

He took one last gulp from the bottle before he began.

"I knew your father. Knew *of* him at least. I also know about his research, about what he tried to uncover. I was sorry when he passed. He was a good man. So was your brother despite his problems. But your brother isn't dead. Not entirely. Part of him is still very much alive, except it's not really him." He paused, realized how crazy that must have sounded. He ought to just hang up and head for the station.

"Is this about the missing body?" The question came with no enthusiasm. "Listen, if you know something..."

"I'm afraid I know more than something. Donny is out there, in Lea

Bay, even if it isn't truly him. And you're in danger. You and your mother and Daphne. I can't save you or this town. Hell, I can't even save myself. But I can warn you before the end begins."

"The end..."

"It's as ominous as it sounds, Mr. Jordan. Now, please, get your mother and go. Pack as many bags as you can fit in your car and hope those bastards aren't watching you."

He looked again out the window, at the Escalade. Still unmoving, still as dark as the night, like some predatory beast waiting patiently to spring on its prey.

Were they listening in on him? Was that just simple static he heard in the background?

He didn't let Eric ask any more questions. "It's coming soon. Those coins your father researched? They're more than just gold. They're a means to that end. And Donny—or whatever's taken hold of him—wants them. The Lords of the Deep weren't just pirates, Eric. That's only part of it. Pirates don't cause seismic activity."

"Please," Eric said. "Let's meet and talk about this. A week ago, I would've said you were out of your mind. But I found some of my father's research."

Horace nodded. "Good. Then you know how serious this is."

"Maybe if we work together, we can stop it."

"You can't stop what's been beneath you all along."

He hung up.

The longer he spent in this condominium, this four-room, glorified apartment that felt more like a studio, the more he put himself at risk. He'd never even wanted this place, had been convinced by his real estate agent it was a sound investment. He'd wanted a house in the woods, far from the sea, used to worry about flooding. But now he was far more fearful of the things *behind* that flooding. *Beyond* it. Things that waited in the depths of the ocean, things that lurked in the impenetrable darkness, feasting on the soul of the sea.

Things that were *preparing*.

He would not miss this place. Not the condo or the town.

If the Lords have their way, he thought, *it will all be gone soon anyway.*

He picked up his phone to call Daphne just as the front door slammed open.

CHAPTER FIFTEEN

Jake burst through the tree line and found himself skidding in the cove's soft sand. He fell back on his rear, attention immediately turned to the black, starlit expanse above. The glow of the full moon bleached the entire clearing, but the bay water held onto its inky ambiance. In the night sky, a green vapor drifted through the air. To Jake, the passing cloud looked like something from a dream, and he pinched himself to make sure the scenery was real.

When he didn't wake up in his bedroom, he stood up and faced the bay. Surveying the area for his father, he put one cautious foot in front of the other and moved down the beach. The night was quiet save for the sounds of waves lapping the shoreline. The noise from the bay captured his attention, stealing him away from his search for his father. Jake found himself gazing into the small waves, like the bay was opening its mouth and waggling an endless run of black tongues. He stood there, staring into the water until something moved slightly beyond his vision. Something that splashed across the surface.

What was that? His whole body instinctively reacted, forcing him into a crouching, defensive pose. He was ready to run back home into the waiting arms of his mother. He didn't want to worry her. What if she came upstairs to check on him and found his bed empty? She'd probably call the cops, alert the whole neighborhood, phone each of his friends' mothers and ask them if they'd seen her precious Jakey.

He should head back. There was no sign of his father, and who was to say it had been *him* anyway? He could have hallucinated Donny Jordan standing in the middle of the road. Imagined the whole thing. Possible given the hour and the stress his young mind was under. The grime on the window mixed with the strange brightness of the moon could have thrown shadows together, merged darkness, making it *seem* like he'd seen the shambling corpse of his dead father.

But what about that floating green smoke? He saw it now, and it drew closer. This was happening. It was real. All of it.

He had to pee.

Turning to the trees, something grabbed his shoulder. He shrieked as loudly as he could. He wanted his mother to hear him, wanted her to come running. To save him.

Suddenly, he became aware that something awful was about to happen.

He turned and faced his father and screamed again.

"Quiet, boy!"

A clammy hand covered Jake's mouth, muffled his shout. The thing that looked like his father—but surely wasn't—wrestled him to the ground. Jake's head hit the sand hard enough to shower his vision with dark starbursts. That mutilated face hovered just beyond the black sky and the green mist. Within seconds, the star-showers dispersed. Jake faced his attacker. His father's ghost applied more pressure, making it impossible for him to scream again.

"Where is the map?" the ghost asked, white foamy spittle sputtering from his lips. *"I must have it."*

Jake's eyes gave him no answers.

"You know nothing? Aren't ye of the blood? How can ye be of the blood and know nothing?"

The words were as foreign as Cantonese.

"No matter. They will come for ye, aye? Those who have answers will come for ye."

Jake shook his head. He didn't know what this monster was referring to, but he wanted no part of it.

"Aye, they will. They'll travel deep into the Golgotha for ye. Deep into the Chamber of Lost Travelers. Down into the deepest, darkest circle of the Irkalla."

Tears began to run freely from the corners of Jake's eyes. His attacker leaned in and the overwhelming stench of death, of rotten fish, caused his stomach to ride up his esophagus. His dinner sat in the back of his throat, waiting to exit.

"You'll help me bring back the Lords of the Deep. Aye, ye will. You're of the blood, aren't cha? Aren't cha?"

Jake struggled in place.

"This body is failing. Won't be long before I need another. Yer daddy's a useless fool." The thing cackled, shuddering with mad laughter.

"But yer of the blood. Aye, yer of the blood."

Jake had no idea what that meant and he intended to keep it that way. Right now, all he wanted was out of here. To be home, in his mother's arms. He didn't even care if she was mad, disappointed, or flat out irate. He just wanted to be with her. To be safe.

Behind his dead father, something rose from the darkness. A long shape stood like a tower, reaching out of the water. Stretching. Gaining height until Jake thought the thing might touch the sky, tear a hole in the atmosphere.

It looked like the Loch Ness Monster he'd seen in a book down at the library. Only, this scaly creature looked less like a dinosaur and more like a...

Snake?

Yes. A snake. Mommy had said his father once owned a pet snake. A *python*. She'd made him get rid of it when they moved in together, claiming she couldn't sleep with that *thing* in the house. Until this moment, Jake had liked snakes. He'd wanted one of his own when he was older. Now, he would've rather had Skeletor back.

The massive serpent lowered itself to the beach and slithered toward him. His father stepped aside, allowing an unobstructed view of the sprawling creature. The clammy hand pulled away from his mouth, and Jake sucked in a deep, gasping breath. His dinner threatened to pay a return visit.

As the serpent neared, opening its mouth and revealing a dark, endless pit of suffering, Jake tried to scream again.

But no such sound came out.

Just a strangled whistle.

CHAPTER SIXTEEN

For a quick, blissful moment he thought he'd been sleeping. Thought he'd had a horrible nightmare that was behind him now. He saw the night sky, littered with stars, and thought: *they're infinite, those lights, filled with every answer to every question.* He wasn't sure what it meant but it seemed important in a poetic sort of way. He ought to write it down, hang it on his fridge.

He could hear the ocean nearby. Calm waves that moved slowly. Steady. It lulled him back toward sleep. His neck was stiff, his muscles filled with pins and needles. He turned to the side to get more comfortable.

And that's when the pain hurtled toward Horace.

A lightning flash of white-hot stinging pain that began in the base of his skull and seemed to emanate through his body.

He tensed.

He screamed.

He remembered.

The man with the sunglasses bursting through his door. Ear-Bud following closely behind. The same two suits from that day at the historical society. The day his world changed. They'd roughed him up first, tossing him around his place while they destroyed everything in sight. Coffee maker, television, stereo, a dozen different framed pictures—all of them in pieces now. This done without the slightest hint of emotion. Faces as blank as new canvases. Like they took no great joy in their demolition. Simply something that needed to be done. He would've preferred them smiling and laughing. At least that was a type of psychosis he could predict. This was something else entirely. No rhyme or reason or pattern. Just chaos.

After they destroyed all of his belongings, Sunglasses lifted what looked like a nightstick and bashed Horace into obscurity.

And now here he was, near the water, on a beach that seemed vaguely familiar.

With a headache that felt like murder.

"He's awake," someone nearby said.

"About time," a voice answered.

He did not like the voice. It hurt worse than the pain.

A pair of feet stepped inches from Horace's eyes. Two black leather shoes that had recently been polished. He managed to crane his head back, wincing against new agonies and wanted to scream again when he saw the face.

Frazier smiled. "Hello, Horace."

He didn't need to ask what this was about. It didn't take a rocket scientist—or a lifelong historian—to know where this was headed. He turned over, onto his stomach, and began to crawl away. He wasn't sure where, only wanted to distance himself.

There came the sound of more footsteps and he saw the men in suits in his periphery. They followed his progress along the beach. He followed the sound of waves, thinking if he could get into the water, no matter what the water may have been hiding, he could drift away from this whole mess. He wasn't certain the depth of his injuries. Wasn't certain he'd be able to swim. But the risk was preferable to what these men had planned.

"Where are you off to?" asked Frazier. "Little late for a swim, isn't it?"

Horace tried to ignore him. Tried to concentrate on the water. But for all the progress he made, it seemed the ocean still lay miles away. The pain in his head flared with his straining muscles. He was growing faint.

Frazier kept time with him. "I was hoping our working relationship would've lasted longer. I really was. But you gave me no choice. That was a very stupid move, calling Mr. Jordan like that. I should've known better than to trust you. You're not stupid, Horace. Never have been. You've kept your job—a very coveted job, I might add—for as long as you have because you've got the smarts to back it up. Yet, tonight, you made the dumbest decision of your entire life." He kicked sand into Horace's eyes.

Horace gasped but he did not stop moving. He was smart *and* stubborn.

"You don't know when to give up, do you?" Frazier asked. "I respect that. And this is coming from the man whose wife you once took to bed. I was angry at first. I'll admit it. But after a while, that faded. What's happening here, tonight, it has nothing to do with a personal vendetta. It's important you know that."

Horace was closer to the water now. Escape almost seemed possible.

The two suits followed him closely.

"We have the treasure in a safe place. Donny—or whatever force now resides inside him—may come for us but we'll be prepared. My hope was that Donny would think his brother or Daphne was hiding the coins. That they'd end up killing each other—*again* for Donny, of course—and this entire ordeal would blow over. But I see now things have become more complicated. It could be worse, I suppose. I could be on the sand, trying to crawl for safety."

"You bastard." Horace coughed, ribs burning from all the abuse they'd taken. He summoned all the spit he could, hoping to land a fat wad on Frazier's shoes, but mostly it dribbled down his chin.

Stop, he thought. *Don't feed into him. That's what he wants.*

"You can say a lot about Horace Dweyer," Frazier said, finally stopping, watching him go. "But you can't say he gives up easily. You should be proud."

One of the suits picked up speed but Horace heard Frazier tell him to hold up. "If he wants to go for a swim, let him."

A few minutes later, the sand grew cold and wet and his fingers sank into the mud. He felt the tide roll in. The saltwater washed over him. His tongue was sponge-dry and the salt would do more harm than good. Instead, he closed his mouth tightly, pushed forward a few more feet, and let the ocean take him.

He saw Frazier and the suits across the way, watching him intently.

He managed to wave to them, flip them off, and then he was pulled under.

His head felt better with the cold and he was able to move his arms and gain some control. He floated back to the surface and broke through, and he was swimming, *actually* swimming, around the beach, toward safety. Not more than twenty yards away lay a pier. It had seen better days, the wood splintered and weathered by age, but surely it could hold his weight.

He wondered if he could summon the energy to climb the eleven-foot pole and then he wondered what touched his foot.

It was light at first, almost a tickling sensation, but he was certain something had brushed the flesh.

Probably just a mackerel. They ran in schools. Quite harmless. Or maybe a crab, a blue claw skimming the surface under the almost-full moon.

The sensation came again, but this time something wrapped around both his feet *and* legs, and then he was positive it was not a school of mackerel or crabs. It was something much, much bigger.

It pulled him under.

The bay was dark and cold and as he clenched tighter, he felt first his ankles then his shins shatter. He screamed and the water rushed into his mouth, his lungs.

The darkness was all encompassing but he did manage to glimpse something impossibly tall and wide, and unless he'd passed out back there on the beach, he could've sworn it was a snake. A snake the size of a city bus and then some. It curled around him further until only his head was exposed and deeper down, beneath his captor, he saw other shapes.

Other snakes.

And they made a sick sort of sense, these things.

Everything that Frazier had told him. Old pacts and treasure and something inhabiting the water, something likely there all along. The truth (not so relative after all), every last word.

He thought of the condominium that he'd never wanted and who would replace him at the historical society, and he wondered if his bag was still packed and where it was, but mostly he wondered when the pain would end.

Mercifully, the answer came before he could think of anything else.

CHAPTER SEVENTEEN

For the second time that night, Eric Jordan found himself on Daphne's doorstep. She opened the door before he could knock. Stepping aside, she welcomed him in. Her face had paled several shades lighter since his last visit. Without wasting another second lingering in the humid air, he entered the house.

"Hey," he said, shutting the door for her.

"Hey." Her lower lip twitched between her teeth.

"Everything all right?"

"I don't think so."

He followed her into the kitchen. In the center of the table rested his father's book.

Together they eyed the collection of notes, newspaper clippings, and Karl Jordan's insane ramblings. It sat there as if it were just some mess that needed cleaning. Some ordinary household nuisance. They exchanged glances, neither of them knowing where to begin.

"I don't think your father was all that nuts."

"What makes you say that?"

"Sit down," she said, pulling out a chair. "You want coffee? I think we need coffee."

"Are we in for a long night?" He checked the time on the microwave. Already pushing one.

"I'm sorry I woke you." She headed for the Keurig. Plucking the K-cup off the pod tree carousel, she opened the machine and fed it. A black mug featuring a childish drawing of an owl with the words "Night Owl" etched beneath it was already waiting under the dispenser. She hit the power button, started the machine, and faced him.

"I was already awake. Sleeping hasn't been easy lately." *It's the nightmares,* he almost wanted to tell her. He wasn't sure how much his brother's widow should know about his terrifying dreams, the vivid images that derailed his sleep, how much to burden her. Probably best not to speak about it, to keep those things private. "It's funny, I just received the strangest call before yours."

"Oh?"

"Yeah. Someone who knew my father. He claimed to know about Donny's missing body. And he also mentioned..."

The Lords of the Deep.

"The pirates?" Daphne asked, as if she could read his thoughts.

Eric nodded. "Although he claims they weren't just pirates. Not really. They were... something else."

"Who was this guy? Did he give you a name?"

The Keurig finished its pour. She carried the mug to him, placed it on the table.

"Thank you," he said, bringing the coffee to his lips. It was too hot to sip but he did so anyway. The steam helped hide his trembling bottom lip. "No, he didn't. He made sure to hide his identity. Even used a website to scramble the call so I couldn't trace the number."

"Any guesses?"

"None." He set the mug down and stared into Daphne's cloudy-red eyes. She'd either been crying recently or she too had been deprived of sleep. He wondered if she dreamed terrible things. "Daphne, why'd you call me back here? What couldn't wait until tomorrow?"

"I saw something." She sat down and scrunched herself into a ball, rested her chin on her knees. "In the bay outside my window."

"What did you see?"

"*Something*... it looked like..."

Say it...

"Like..."

Say it...

"Like..." She turned her head.

"You can tell me."

Facing him, her brow twisted and arched. "It looked like a sea monster."

Eric didn't dispute her claim. He didn't argue. He didn't try to convince her she hadn't seen anything, that maybe the darkness had fooled her. Instead, he nodded slowly.

"The serpent," he said softly.

"Yes." She dragged Karl's book across the table. "From your father's journal."

She opened it to the exact page. On the cream-colored paper, stained with age and brown streaks that looked like spilled coffee, Karl Jordan had sketched his version of the sea serpent. Eric had been impressed with his father's artistic talent, a skill he never knew the old man possessed. If the situation had fallen under different circumstances, he might have enjoyed a laugh at this new discovery.

"The serpent," he said again, this time with more confidence.

"I saw this thing—this *exact* thing—in the bay. It was..." She shrugged. "It sounds silly, but I swear it was *watching* me."

"I understand." *Because I've seen it too,* he wanted to tell her. *I've seen the damned thing in my dreams. It's haunted me ever since I was a child.* "Have you heard about the seismic activity off the coast? There've been all sorts of reports. Platelet shifts. Possible tsunamis. Things that are quite extraordinary in our little nook of the world."

She nodded. "Saw something on the news."

"If what my father wrote in that book is true, then something very bad is coming to Lea Bay. All the signs are there. The treasure. Donny's missing body. The seismic activity." He gestured toward the front door with a nod. "The serpent."

"'The storm is coming. The storm of all storms.' That's what your father wrote."

"Yeah, the *perfect* storm. And I wonder what other monsters it'll bring."

She shuddered at the thought. She'd read the same tales he had, the same lore. Pirates and monsters, krakens and giant serpents. An entire underwater labyrinth that kept these monsters away from the modern world. Hidden in the abyss. Concealed in the void, where no man would ever travel. A prison for eldritch creatures.

"I think I better go check on Jake."

Eric sipped his coffee. "Mind if I come?"

"Sure."

They walked upstairs, down the hall, and hovered outside of Jake's room. Daphne put her ear to the door and listened.

"It's quiet in there. Hopefully, he's been sleeping better than us." She opened the door and poked her head into the room. "Jake?"

No answer.

"What is it?" Eric said.

She charged into the room. *"Jake?"*

Eric glanced around the kid's room. Piles of toys sat in the corners, everything from Ninja Turtle action figures to Nerf guns. A few stuffed animals. A deflated basketball. A small stack of books on his desk. Considering their financial problems, he was surprised to find so many playthings.

But no Jake.

Daphne called his name again. Nothing. Unless he was asleep in the closet, he wasn't there.

The lone bedroom window drew their attention. It was open, letting in a considerable amount of air. A hot, moist breeze, like dragon's breath, rushed the room. Despite the warmth of the wind, Eric shivered.

At the same time, they streaked toward the window and looked down.

All they saw was a sneaker.

No Jake.

Not another trace of him.

Daphne Jordan screamed into the summer night.

In the distance, storm clouds gathered. Something moved along the surface of the bay.

CHAPTER EIGHTEEN

The sun wasn't far off by the time Lea Bay sent its first officer to Daphne's house. She'd been crying so long her eyes were stuck half shut. She looked stoned and drunk and not unlike her late husband on so many nights. She remembered him now, looking as though he'd sleepwalked his way home. Rummaging through the fridge and grabbing a midnight snack, always cold and never heated. She latched onto the memories now. They seemed unimportant, pointless, but her mind kept them close just the same. A coping mechanism perhaps. Something to take her attention away from every mother's worst nightmare.

She stood out front, looking at the watermelon-pink sky and thinking: *I can't live without both of them.* Donny may have been a different man toward the end, promises to get clean aside, but he'd given her a sweet boy. And now that sweet boy was gone.

Not gone, she thought. *Just missing.*

A car appeared in the distance, seeming to take its time as it parked and killed its engine.

Eric stood closely behind, rubbing her back. Under other circumstances, she would've rejected this personal affection. Being touched in any way had been the last thing on her mind, but this was innocent. One human comforting another. And for that she was grateful.

A man stepped out of the cruiser. He looked left and right along the street as if some secret clue lay there. He closed the door and stepped through the front gate, into the yard, and up the steps to meet them.

She was prepared for an older officer, someone with a sizable gut, an unkempt mustache, and a painfully bored expression. A cardboard cutout of what an investigating officer *should* look like. Instead, the face was void of any stubble and her tired eyes widened when she recognized him.

"Hey," she said through strangled vocal cords.

The officer smiled. "Daphne."

"You two know each other?" Eric asked, keeping his hand on her back.

"Brendan and I graduated high school together," she said. "Right?"

"Yeah, we even had a few classes together."

Her face turned sour. "And you..."

He nodded. "I escorted you to identify—"

"—Donny. You led me to Donny's body. God, I was so out of it, I didn't even realize it was you."

She honed in on his badge. Officer Sawyer. How could she have forgotten? She thought back to that day in the morgue, though the memory seemed to belong to someone else. There was nothing good to be recalled, nothing aside from seeing Sawyer again, a face from her past. There was something different about him now, though. The longer she stared, the more she suspected he had changed in more ways than one. It was all in the eyes. She'd studied her own in the mirror plenty this last week. Dark bags surrounded the lids and miniature wrinkles had appeared.

It's always the eyes, she thought as she shook Sawyer's hand. *They're the first to harden in this life. The first exposed to the bad things.*

First on the crime scene.

"I'm very sorry seeing you again under such circumstances, Daphne, but do you mind if I come inside and ask you a few questions? I'm sure the dispatcher and officer with whom you spoke asked you plenty already, but it's procedure that I do so as well."

Eric stepped forward. "Shouldn't you be out there looking for him?"

"I don't believe we've officially met." He held out his hand. "I'm Officer Sawyer. Or, just Sawyer if you'd like to keep it casual."

Eric and Sawyer shook. From where Daphne stood, it looked like a tight grip. "Eric Jordan."

Sawyer's eyes widened. "Of course. You also went to Lea Bay High, right? You were ahead of us."

"Two years."

"Right. Sorry I didn't recognize you. I see the resemblance now."

"I'm nothing like him."

Daphne's eyes—wrinkles and bags and all—lingered on Eric then. Even now he tried to remind anyone who'd listen that he wasn't a junkie like good ol' Donny. And though that might've been true, he *was* a lot like his brother in other ways. Stubbornness included.

"Do you mind if we go inside?" Sawyer asked, eyes glued to Eric's. It wasn't a question.

She turned and studied the house. Above their heads, Jake's window still lay open. She didn't like the idea of going back in there. She'd spent far too much time within those walls as of late. Far too much time within her own mind. To think: she'd been reading that wretched book (though *book* seemed too kind a word) for hours last night before she'd noticed her son was missing.

How long had it been exactly?

She wondered for the thousandth time where he was and what kind of trouble had led him there.

Was he alone? Had he wandered off to look for his father?

Or was someone with him?

Had someone abducted him?

She found it hard to believe an intruder could've entered her home unnoticed but then again she was beyond exhausted. Hadn't slept for a long time and would likely remain awake for the foreseeable future. At some point, though, she would crash. She couldn't stay up like this forever. But as long as her son was gone—*missing, he's only missing*—she would fight off sleep with every ounce of her being.

"After you," Sawyer said.

Eric stepped in first and Daphne followed.

The house seemed different now. She couldn't explain but it felt more like a stranger's home. A sublet rather than the place she'd lived for years. The place where she'd grown her family.

And now her family was—

"When did you first notice your son was missing?" Sawyer said, sitting down at the table.

She studied her watch. "Going on three hours now."

"Three hours your cop friend could've been out searching," Eric reminded them.

For the first time, Sawyer's friendly veneer cracked. His annoyance peered through. "I understand your frustration, Mr. Jordan, but I'll have you know I searched the neighborhood after Daphne's call came through. That's not procedure but I did it anyway because I'm no stranger to this situation. I know what it's like to have something one moment and lose it the next."

She didn't ask him what he meant, found herself wondering what it could mean but then he began a long list of questions.

How old is your son?

How tall is he?

Do you have a picture of him I could make copies of?

Does he have any troubles with bullies at school?

It went on like that for the better part of an hour. He jotted down her answers on a notepad and she wondered why they still used paper instead of tablets. It seemed so archaic. She hoped their methods out there, searching for Jake, weren't so primitive.

The barrage of questions made her nerves sharper and her eyelids heavier. "Would you like some coffee?"

"Love some," Sawyer said.

She made three cups, giving one to Eric as well without asking.

"Where do you think he went?" she asked. "I mean, where could he possibly go?"

Sawyer reviewed his notes. "Hard to say, but we'll do everything in our power to find him. I give you my word. Normally we'd wait forty-eight hours to officially consider him *missing,* but since Jake's so young, we'll get moving as soon as possible. We have two officers driving around the neighborhood and we'll widen the perimeter if need be."

"I appreciate that," she said, cutting Eric off. He'd started to say something, but it was likely better left unsaid. She didn't need him antagonizing Sawyer more than he already had.

The officer studied his notepad again. The pages were wrinkled and some old stain left a Rorschach test on the bottom left corner. "Aside from the playground and the toy store, is there anywhere your son would've gone off to?"

She thought again of Skeletor, the poor fish who'd lived only a month. Jake had refused to believe his beloved pet was truly gone after such a short time together. Just as stubborn as his old man, he'd done the same when it came to Donny. That Jordan gene had been passed on without question.

"His father," she said. "He's only a boy and he still doesn't quite understand the concept of death. I think he refuses to acknowledge that Donny's not coming home."

Sawyer closed his notepad and drank his coffee in three sips. He took it black and barely any time had passed since she'd handed it to him. Surely it must have burned on the way down, though he gave no hint of being in pain. "We'll send someone out to the docks to check there."

"Thank you. I mean it."

"I think I have all I need from you right now. We'll keep you updated. Please keep your phone nearby at all times today. Make sure it's charged."

"Of course."

He handed her the empty mug and stared at something on the table. Something she'd managed to forget about.

Karl's leather-bound book lay inches away from Officer Sawyer. "What's this?" he asked.

"Nothing," Eric said, reaching out quickly and grabbing it.

In the process, a single slip of paper fell onto the table. It sounded like thunder in the silence.

One of the many drawings of sea snakes.

Sawyer looked at the image for a long time.

"Is this supposed to be Lea Bay?" he said, pointing to what looked like the city hall in the background of the picture.

Eric didn't answer.

"I drew it," Daphne blurted out, surprised at her own voice. "Just a hobby of mine for when I get a few moments to myself."

Sawyer's face did not change but she would've bet the rest of her coffee that he didn't buy her story.

He pushed the page across the table and Eric tucked it back in the book with the others.

"You know," Sawyer said, "my father used to tell me ghost stories about this town. We moved here when I was three. He grew up here but relocated before I was born. For his business, he used to say, but I never believed him. He said there are all sorts of urban legends here. Ghosts and monsters and all that good stuff. But the one that used to get under my skin, used to keep me up at night—well, it was about some serpent or snake or something. Stalking the bay and waiting for the right time to surface. He said the old timers and barflies would tell you all about it for a free beer." He turned to Daphne. "You must have heard the same story somewhere along the way."

She shrugged and suddenly her mug was much too heavy. She set it on the counter and placed her shaking hands into her pockets. "Must have," she said.

And some kernels were larger than others.

CHAPTER NINETEEN

Squad car ninety-two pulled up to the Jordan residence and stopped in the street, the engine continuing to run. As Brendan Sawyer casually strolled over, the smiley-faced driver lowered the tinted window.

"Hell of a busy night, Sawyer," the officer said. "Hell of a busy night."

Sawyer flashed him a weary smirk, all he could muster at this ungodly hour. The coffee had done some good, but not nearly enough, and the night would require no less than two more trips to Dunkin' just to keep his eyes open. "We're just getting started, Hawthorne."

"The mother give up anything useful?"

He thought about the book on the table left out for anyone to see, almost as if that were her intent. He recalled the picture Daphne had claimed *she* had sketched, which had been a total lie and he knew it from the second he'd laid eyes on it.

He shook his head. "No, nothing. She said her boy's been missing for going on three hours. Which means he could be literally anywhere by now."

"Well, not *literally* anywhere."

"You know what I mean, butthead." He tapped the hood of the cruiser. "It's just an expression."

"*Literally* the worst expression ever."

"Are you the real police or the grammar police?"

"Can I be both?"

"No, you can't."

Hawthorne chuckled. "Okay, so what are we looking at? The kid went outside for a midnight stroll, maybe because... I don't know, kids do that sometimes."

"Do they?"

"I did. Did that shit all the time. Tortured my parents."

"Well, you were a pretty troubled kid from what I remember."

"And Jake Jordan isn't?"

Sawyer considered the family tree and recent events, and smirked. "Fair point."

"So the kid walks outside to get his mind off things—I mean, he just lost his father whose body's gone missing from the morgue, there have been all sorts of strange rumors flying around town, people are getting spooked, seeing shit that isn't there, his mom's probably not in the greatest state of mind..."

"And?"

"And what? Some weirdo snatches him up. It's late as fuck. Only weirdos are out this late on a school night."

"Okay, so he's been abducted, obviously. You think it was a random grab and go?"

Hawthorne shrugged. "Mmmmmmaybe. Yeah, I guess that's what I'm saying."

"I don't know..."

"You know something I don't, Sawyer? Do tell."

Sawyer peeked over his shoulder, aiming his attention back at the house. The lights were still on. In the window, he caught a glimpse of Daphne Jordan crying, Eric Jordan offering his condolences in the form of a clumsy hug. In that moment, Eric glanced out the window, spotted Sawyer, and shot him a stern look, one that said, *Watch yourself, buddy. Tread ever-so lightly.*

Sawyer slapped his notepad against his open palm several times. "I don't know," he said, grimacing; turning back to Hawthorne; pinching his lower lip between his teeth. "Something doesn't exactly feel right, does it?"

Hawthorne jerked his shoulders again. "I dunno, dude. Does it?"

"No, it doesn't. I mean, Donny Jordan was a junkie, sure, everyone knew that. Hell, his death doesn't surprise damn near anyone. But the *way* he died..."

"Heard he was all chewed up in places. Like an animal attacked him."

"Then his body goes missing. The two men tasked with his autopsy are slaughtered. Now this..."

"That's not all, though."

"Oh no?"

"Nope. Report just came in that two more bodies were found. Murdered. Gunshot wounds. Professional job. Tasker and Philips said the killer used a silencer and everything. Didn't bother cleaning up the mess, though. Brains everywhere. I mean, *everywhere.*"

"What?" Sawyer couldn't believe it. Gooseflesh spread down his arms, and a crawling sensation brushed across his neck. In Lea Bay, more death and murder had taken place over the last week than the last two decades combined. "Where?"

"Cream Briar Apartments."

Junkie Haven, the locals called it. Cream Briar was the only affordable housing complex in Lea Bay, and priced just under six-hundred dollars a month for a single-bedroom apartment, they made for the perfect living situation for any low-life scum who sold smack or ran small-time scam jobs. Over seventy percent of the calls Sawyer and the rest of the squad received were about Cream Briar and the dealings that went on there. Discovering a dead body on site would normally come as no big surprise, but they usually stemmed from overdoses, not gunshot wounds. And not a professional job, at that. That was next-level weird, and with all the strange things that had happened in town over the last week, Sawyer shouldn't have been as surprised as he was.

"Christ, how long have they been dead for?"

"Day or two. Won't know until we get a replacement M.E. to open them up."

"Are the deceased anyone we know?"

Hawthorne took a bite of his cream cheese bagel. "Yeah, actually. Know them pretty darn well."

"Who?"

"Kevin Kane and Barry Dillinger."

Sawyer nodded. Kane and Dillinger were two thugs that had often been busted, mostly for petty crimes, sometimes scooped up on suspicion for larger infractions. They often worked in tandem, lifting merchandise from department stores so they could return the products for store credit and, in turn, sell the credit on the Internet for cold hard cash. They were also known to assist various underground betting rings. It was rumored they cooked the books for some bigger outfit based in Brooklyn, but that had never been confirmed. That wasn't his department's problem so Sawyer never got involved. He'd gone to high school with the two nitwits, graduated in the same year, and he found their deaths somewhat interesting because they'd often been seen hanging around Donny Jordan and Rick Lopez in the hallways between classes. The quartet had continued to run together long after graduation and was often suspected in almost every criminal activity that had taken place around town.

Now, Donny was dead. And Rick, wanted by Detective Striker for questioning in the Historical Society's treasure chest heist, was missing.

The pieces were starting to come together, but they weren't fitting.

"What'cha thinking about?" Hawthorne asked.

"Hm? Nothing. Just... a lot going on over the last week. Hard to wrap my brain around all of it."

"Yes, sir. A lot indeed. We got our work cut out for us."

"Holbrook still looking for the kid?"

"Dunno. He *was* helping Striker. They were tracking down Rick Lopez. Trying to, at least. They think he was the one who lifted the shipment of artifacts imported by the Historical Society."

"Yeah, that's what I wanted to know about."

Hawthorne, who continued to munch on his bagel, raised his brow. "What's that?"

"Well, it's weird. Lopez's known goon squad included Kane and Dillinger. Donny Jordan, too. Three of the four have turned up dead, and one of them is missing."

Well, two of them are missing, he wanted to say, *if you include Jordan's missing corpse.*

"Coincidence?"

Sawyer rolled his eyes and chewed his tongue. "Come on, Hawthorne. You were taught better than that. Weren't you? No such thing as coincidences in our line of work. Coincidence means connection."

"If it sings like a duck?"

"Quacks."

"Whatever. Yeah, I guess." Another bite and some bagel crumbs fell on his lap. "What do you think it all means? Best guess."

"I mean, it is strange how they're all turning up dead. I guess it has something to do with the chest they stole, assuming it was them who stole it."

Hawthorne nodded. "It was them. Who else would be dumb enough?"

"I don't know. What's more curious is *why* they stole it. Holbrook told me the chest looked like a movie prop from *Pirates of the Caribbean.*"

Hawthorne's eyes shot open. "Maybe it contains some sick pirate booty! Like real treasure, you know?"

"Not likely. That stuff is to sell books and movies. No such thing as real-life pirate treasures. Not in Lea Bay, anyway. Pirates never came this far north." That was a downright lie he'd convinced himself was true. Back in high school, he'd learned in American History that some pirates were known to travel as far north as Boston. Blackbeard himself was rumored to have visited the Jersey Shore on multiple occasions, and it was said he'd left a good portion of his plunder around the bays and coves, none of which was ever found. Sawyer knew he'd lied to Hawthorne, and the lie felt righteous and good to say aloud—*this has nothing to do with pirates. Nothing.*

Hawthorne smelled bullshit. "If it doesn't, then why'd they steal it? And if there weren't pirates in this area, why does the Historical Society host a big pirate festival every year? You know, the one where the whole town shuts down. Shit, man. I've seen flyers all over town. I believe it's next week. And wait—why does our high school call themselves The Raiders?"

Sawyer felt himself grow heated. "I don't know. To sell things.

Memorabilia and toys and stupid knickknacks to fill your office with. It's all garbage. All of it."

Hawthorne, his mouth full of bagel, put his hands up in surrender. "Geez, I was just asking, that's all. I mean, you might want to get your facts straight, though. In grade school, we had Pirate Week, remember? They made us dress up and present speeches on our favorite pirates. Shit, I just remembered that. Just now. Isn't it weird how talking about certain things can instantly bring back your childhood?"

Sawyer closed his eyes. "Yeah, it's real weird. A real riot."

"What's the matter? You're getting all *Emo* on me."

"Just tired."

"Pirate talk wearing you out?"

"Not a fan of pirates, that's all."

"I hear you. Kind of stupid. Kid's stuff, really."

"Yeah," he said, opening his eyes, glimpsing into his past and all the terrible things that hid there. "Kid's stuff. That's all it is."

CHAPTER TWENTY

Jared Edwards was far from an outdoorsman. He'd gone camping all of twice in his life and that was two times too many. Rubbing cream on mosquito bites and shitting in bushes was mostly what he remembered. He received no joy from being in mother nature's midst, which was why his wife was so shocked when he'd taken up jogging. Normally he'd settle for his treadmill in the den, but the place smelled of mold and dust and he'd nearly fainted each time he worked out. His gut had tripled its size these last few years and, per his doctor's orders, he'd been trying to lose weight ever since. Jodie claimed she liked him just the way he was but there were subtle hints to the contrary.

Was he *sure* he needed that second helping of mashed potatoes and did he *really* need to smother his meals with butter?

So he'd started jogging, losing a pound here and there, but since his den was quickly becoming hazardous, he'd taken to doing so outdoors.

Today he chose Lea Bay State Park. With its rich history and gasp-worthy water views, you'd expect the place to be crawling with tourists, but most of them were taking pictures near the entrance and the generic pirate statue before heading further toward the pier. On most days, this one included, Jared had the place to himself.

He smiled as he increased his pace. Two months ago, he already would've turned back. But today he was just getting started. He listened to a podcast through his earbuds, something about the glory days of pro wrestling, though he didn't pay too much attention to the words. The co-hosts served as background noise to the view.

And the view, to put it lightly, was fucking gorgeous.

The trail began with dense forest, but walk a mile and a half and you had yourself a small cliff and a view of the ocean for miles. He slowed his pace to take in the surroundings. The day was as beautiful as the weather forecast had promised. Not a cloud in the sky. Gulls cawing, flying in circles. In the distance, the lighthouse splintered the horizon. He was glad that Jodie hadn't convinced him to move south for cheaper houses and land. It was true, this place *was* a rip-off. Hard to argue with that, especially when property taxes were damn near five digits. But that view, the town's secret overlooks—it made the hefty mortgage and the mindless tourists all worth it.

He slowed to a stop, clearing layers of sweat from his brow with his shirt. He could've stayed here all day, admiring the Atlantic. Would have too if he hadn't heard the sound of footsteps.

Jared rolled his eyes and spun around, certain that someone had lost their way from downtown, but instead, saw two shapes in the distance, moving through the tight spaces between the trees.

A man and a boy.

Under normal circumstances, it wouldn't have raised suspicion. Fathers brought their sons here all the time for a crash course in nature, something Jared's own father had tried (and failed) on several occasions. But the word *normal* did not come to mind when he caught a glimpse of the man's skin.

In the sunlight that peeked through the branches, the man's pallor was gray. *Dark* gray, like he'd been sick for a long time. He was littered with what looked like deep cuts, long lacerations that surely should've been bleeding even though he saw no evidence. His face was the worst. Ruined and sunken and if Jared didn't know any better, he would've thought the guy was...

Dead.

He couldn't hear what they were saying but the thought of getting any closer sent ripples along his sweaty back. He ought to mind his business and head back. It was almost lunchtime. His stomach grumbled, yet food was the furthest thing from his mind. Further the longer he observed.

The boy was maybe six or seven, smiling as he spoke but also looking around as if someone might find them. Or, Jared suspected, perhaps looking for someone to rescue him.

The man's skin seemed to deteriorate in real time. Something wet and dark fell from his face, revealing what looked like an ivory-white cheekbone.

A Halloween costume. That was all. The boy had begged his father to dress up like a zombie and together they would play a game of manhunt in the woods. Father would count to ten while his son hid and then he'd stumble around, searching for *braaaiiins, braaaiiins.*

It was a solid theory, but Jared was almost certain it was false.

This was no game of hide-and-seek.

And that hunk of flesh on the ground was not department-store-quality latex.

He took one last look at the path and the ocean beyond before ducking and moving toward them.

He walked roughly ten yards before his knees locked up.

The man was speaking, though he sounded nothing like a man. His voice was hoarse, beyond deep, roughened from years of smoking too many cigarettes.

"Of the blood."

"You keep saying that," the boy replied. "But what does it mean?"

"It means, what runs through you, runs through me."

"I know that, Dad. Why wouldn't I know that? Why are you talking so weird anyway?" The boy kicked a rock. It flew through the bushes and landed dangerously close to Jared's feet. "Can we just go home now? Mom is probably worried about us both. She's gonna be happy to see you. Especially since everyone thinks you're dead."

Jared's heart skipped two beats, and in those horrible moments he was certain he'd drop dead himself. It didn't matter that he'd lost weight. He'd have a heart attack right here and, assuming these two strangers didn't happen upon him, his body would go undiscovered for days, maybe weeks. By the time the cops located him, some animal would feast on his carcass, pick his meat to the bone.

Then he'd look a lot like the man.

Dead.

He thought about the boy's choice of words and risked a glance.

This close, he could see a cloud of flies hovering over the man. There was something strangely familiar about him.

Everybody thinks you're dead.

No, it couldn't be.

No way in hell that could be Donny Jordan, right?

He'd gone to high school with Donny Jordan and his brother. While Eric had been an overachiever, Donny had skipped class every chance he got. He was a burnout from the time Jared had met him. Nice enough guy, though. They'd shared more than a few warm cans of PBR underneath the football bleachers, praying to catch a view up a skirt or five. And while they'd rarely succeeded in their efforts, Jared had appreciated the company. He looked back fondly on that memory now, but the mirage was shattered when he remembered where he was and what stood mere feet away.

He looked closely and decided that *was* Donny Jordan.

There was just one problem.

Donny Jordan had turned up half-chewed no more than two weeks ago. It was all over the papers, the Internet. Facebook. He couldn't scroll through his newsfeed without seeing one of his friends sharing an article from the local rag. It hadn't come as a shock exactly. Donny was headed for an overdose if rumors were to be believed. He'd probably bought a bad batch, shot up, and fallen into the bay. Drowned. Crabs had themselves a feast when he sunk to the bottom.

But despite the news, Jared was certain that the man standing before him, the man with the tattered flesh and dried blood caked to his arms and face, was Donny Jordan.

He couldn't make sense of the revelation, but he knew two things.

That boy was his son.

And he was here against his will.

"Why can't we go home?"

"Home? This is your home now. Now listen to what I've got to say. This vessel grows short on time."

Vessel?

What the hell was he talking about? And why was he talking like a...

...like a pirate?

Jared had no answers, but it didn't matter. The thing to do was head back on the path and call the cops. He backed away, wincing and holding his breath with each snap of a twig and crunch of a leaf. Eventually, he reached the path and stood. The boy and Donny—*dead* Donny—stayed where they were. It was perhaps a twenty-minute walk back to the park's entrance, where his cell service would be strong enough to make the call. He jogged quickly, made the trek in half his normal time, and dialed three digits. He wasn't sure what he'd tell them, wasn't sure of anything except that he wouldn't be sleeping tonight. Too busy recalling that gray flesh and those flies and, of course, that poor boy's words.

Everybody thinks you're dead.

CHAPTER TWENTY-ONE

Sally Jordan was hand-washing her dishes when a cold breeze swept through the kitchen. She glanced over her shoulder and saw the front door open, which she found odd since she'd shut and locked it an hour ago. After putting the bowl in the sink, she turned and headed for the entrance, chiding herself for not double-checking her work. Lea Bay had the reputation of being a relatively safe community—especially where she lived—but one could never be so sure, especially nowadays. Pushing the door shut and locking it for the second time that night, Sally felt another chill enter her home, this one cutting through *her*, an icy sensation that soaked into her flesh and claimed her bones. She moved away from the door and into the living room, examining the floral-patterned couches and the matching throw rug. Looking beyond the room, into the half-bath, she saw nothing. No one. It was exactly how she'd last left it.

She smiled, admonishing herself for being so silly. *Still...* the notion played with her, conjuring up thoughts of Karl and the haunting things he'd warned her about.

This is real...

All of it...

I'm not crazy, Sally. Honest...

Sally Jordan had never considered her husband a crazy person, an opinion not shared by everyone. He'd been well-known as Lea Bay's resident whackadoo, yes, and had his fair share of incidents, stuff worthy of front-page headlines. Like when he'd awoken naked on the front steps of city hall, with no account of the time between closing his eyes and the moment he awoke in his birthday suit on the stone patio. Like the *times* she'd caught him staring in the mirror—just staring—almost catatonically, as if something in his reflection had sucked out his brains, rendering him mentally deficient in almost every way. There was also the time he'd forgotten to pick up Donny and Eric from soccer practice, and when she had questioned him about it, demanding to know why he had abandoned his duty as their parent, as their *father*, he'd simply said, "I had important tasks that required my attention."

She never forgave him for that last part.

Karl Jordan hadn't been the greatest father, nor the greatest husband, but when he wasn't waking up naked in strange places or forgetting where he dropped off his children for the afternoon, he was actually an above average partner. He'd given her love over the years, support, worked three jobs just to put food on the table and keep the mortgage paid. He'd worked as an engineer at the local power plant as his regular nine-to-five (plus OT when they offered it), stocked shelves at the supermarket at night, and updated logs at the county library on weekends (his favorite of the three). After he'd retired from the plant and quit the supermarket, he worked at the library full-time, which meant he got to research local history full-time, which was really what had started him on this whole "Lords of the Deep" obsession.

Sally sighed as she went over and shut the kitchen window. She didn't remember opening that either.

The Lords of the Deep.

She shuddered at the name. Just thinking about them, the stories her husband had told her over dessert or when neither of them could fall asleep at night, made her blood freeze. She knew her husband wasn't the crackpot most of the town had made him out to be. He'd had his quirks, his issues, and when the drinking became a major part of his diet, that was when things truly went downhill. She blamed most of his paranoia and ill-thoughts on the bottle, not the local legends of Lea Bay.

It had become hard to ignore what was happening in town now, after everything from the tragic death of her second son to the reports of strange oceanic activity off the coast; Donny's missing body; the treasure chest that had been stolen in transit to the Historical Society; the sea serpent sightings that had been tucked in the back pages of the local newspapers. It was all happening, a lot like her late husband said it would.

The Lords of the Deep.

If she stayed still and silent long enough, she could almost hear Karl whispering their names: *Blackjack Philips, Edward Mars, Henry the Savage, Anne Slaughter, and, of course, their leader—Captain George "Graysoul" Godfrey III, though everyone simply called him "Gray" on the account of his eyes, as they held no discernible color. Demon's eyes, his. Said they, those who could stand more than three seconds' worth of a look.*

He'd recited the names so many times—often when he dreamed— that the roster had been engraved in her memories. She'd learned a lot about the Lords when he slept. About their vessel, *The Black Ambrosia*. About their history, how they'd come to be. About their time spent in Lea Bay, when the town was nothing more than a small village of fewer than three-hundred people. About the lost treasure and their ability to summon behemoths from the ocean's undiscovered depths, eldritch beasts under their control.

She remembered the poem he'd sometimes recite as he dozed off:

Welcome, welcome
The Lords of the Deep
Bring us new fortunes
and all ye seek

For there be no tomorrow
no light and no shine
the beasts of yesterday
hath eaten the hands of time

So welcome, welcome
The Lords of the Deep
Bring us new pleasures
from lands of foul sleep

She remembered those lines word for word like she had so many Catholic prayers. There was more to the poem, much more, but those first three stanzas were embedded in her thoughts, and on lonely nights such as this, they never strayed too far.

Shaking the memories away like cobwebs, she hustled back into the kitchen. It was strange how an open door and cool draft could poison the mind, make it return to the darkest corners of the past. She laughed it off as she returned to her chores; finishing up the dishes and then wiping down the counter. She couldn't wait to hit the sack and indulge in pleasant dreams, and not dwell on the nightmarish thoughts the wind had blown in.

Just then, she felt a presence behind her. She spun her entire body around and stared at the vacant kitchen.

Nothing.

No one.

Odd. She had definitely felt someone behind her. In fact, she was confident she'd seen a shadow move across the wall.

But there was no one. Nothing. Just her and the kitchen table with the little wire basket full of outgoing mail resting in the center of it. The countertops and the cabinets. The papered walls patterned with depictions of bowls overflowing with fruit. The sink full of dishes and a garbage bag that needed to be taken to the curb.

No shadows.

Nobody.

Nothing.

She was all alone, though, it didn't feel like it.

When she turned back to the sink, she caught the reflection of her intruder in the window. She pretended not to. She went about her business, scrubbing the dishes until they were spotless, hoping the apparition would leave, begging her Catholic God for it to vanish from her sight. She blinked several times, hoping that would do the trick.

It didn't work.

The figure stepped closer. Then she noticed the figure wasn't alone. Two more shadows filed into the room via the hallway. A fourth entered through the living-room wall.

The four ghosts stood behind her, closing the distance between them. She didn't dare turn around. The glare on the window, combined with a few greasy smudges on the glass, didn't allow Sally to see their faces clearly, all their distinct features, and for that she was thankful. As she closed her eyes and expected the worst, a chill closed around her throat like two hands ready to wring her neck.

The ghost whispered in her ear: *"Are ye scared, ye plump cow?"*

Sally wouldn't have answered even if her throat allowed her to.

Hot breath in her ear. As the moments passed, the faint fetid odor grew bold, an earthly combination of rotten fish and ocean salt. *"We've come for what belongs to us. We've come for what was taken from us."*

"I-I," Sally stammered, unable to complete a thought. She wished Karl were here now; he'd know what to do. He'd know how to make the apparitions go away, indefinitely. She thought about his journal, the one she'd kept in the attic, wondering if it would ever prove useful. Now, she thought, that day had come. And if she survived this, somehow made it through the night alive, she'd read the journal page by page, several times over, study the damned thing like a bible.

"We're looking for the one ye call Blackjack Philips," the ghost spoke in a West Country English accent. His dialect reminded her of the jolly bearded man who helped Harry and his friends in those popular wizard movies. *"Ye seen him?"*

Slowly, Sally wagged her head.

Something forced her around, making her face the dead pirate and all the horrors his appearance contained. She shrieked the second her eyes fixed on him. Thick white scars marred his face, skin that had been slashed away by sharp metal. A tricorn hat sat snug atop his head, long black curls of hair flowing out from under it. Her eyes fell on his clothing, his captain's coat, sporting buttons as big as her fist. The open jacket revealed the poet's blouse beneath, a collection of white frills that poked out beneath the pirate's bushy, colorless beard. Finally, her eyes settled on the apparition's gaze, beholding silvery eyes of the dead. They shone brightly like polished chrome.

Captain Graysoul.

Gray, the settlers of Lea Bay had called him.

The pirate's dry, cracked lips spread apart, and the stink of oceanic rot filled Sally's nostrils. *"Aye, call me Gray, ye cow, if it pleases ye."*

She wanted to respond, say something, but she couldn't find the strength to unhinge her jaw.

Run, her internal voice begged her. *Run. Get out of here.*

But she was pushing seventy years old and her sprinting days were past her. She hadn't kept in shape over the last five or so years, ditching her treadmill for reruns of *Maury.* How far would she get before these evil beings caught up to her, snatched her like a hawk would a field mouse? Not far, she mused. Probably not past the living-room threshold.

Graysoul's image flickered before her like a flame caught in a soft breeze. It disappeared for a brief second; in a blink his visage returned, keeping the gray and soulless presentation of his ghostly self.

She looked beyond the captain, her attention drawn to the rest of the pirate's crew. Their images wavered too, flickering on and off, blinking in and out of existence like an extravagant light show come Christmastime.

They're ghosts, she told herself. *That's all they are.*

In her mind, the fact that they *were* ghosts meant they couldn't touch her. Their flickering in and out proved that much. They weren't a solid mass; they were nothing at all. Energy of the purest form, maybe.

A part of her considered she was dreaming this scene, that once the specters advanced and gutted her like a fresh catch, she'd awake to sweaty bedsheets and the beams of first light filtering in through the shades.

The other part of her sensed that this was, indeed, really happening.

And that she needed to *run,* worn-out bones or not.

She pushed off the countertop and took off toward the front door. Maybe she could get to a neighbor's house and find safety there. Maybe the apparitions were confined to certain places, her kitchen chief among them.

As she headed for the door, one of the spirits stepped into her path. He wore a long bandana—gray, void of color like the rest of him—and a mask of lumpy scars. His facial disfigurements differed from Graysoul's in the sense that this pirate had taken fire to the right side of his head at some point during his glory days. The burn marks blanketed half of his face, reminding Sally of refrigerated pizza. He opened his mouth and yelled but unlike the captain, this ghost had no volume. He revealed a mouthful of black, rotted teeth. An acrid smell polluted the room, burning her nose hairs.

She charged forth, hurling herself through the silent specter. The pirate ghost didn't block her escape. As she suspected, their bodies were transparent and able to be trespassed.

Sally scrambled for the door but her foot slipped on the hardwood floor. She'd recently cleaned and waxed them, and she hadn't been wearing shoes. Socks and waxed floors were not a good combination, and gravity brought her down like a brick. Sally hit the floor with so much force she heard her hip crack, splinter under the weight of herself. Rolling over, she let loose a strangled howl, her cries echoing throughout the (almost) empty house.

Dreadful shadows crowded around her.

The ghost that bent over and sunk its hand into her chest, wrapped its fingers around her heart and pulled, was a woman pirate, the one history books often referenced as Anne Slaughter.

"Join me, lady," she said in a voice that was eerily pleasant and strangely welcoming. *"In death, we will sail the uncharted."*

The next thing Sally Jordan knew, she was a prisoner in her own body.

CHAPTER TWENTY-TWO

"This is crazy," Daphne said for the dozenth time.

Eric ignored her and watched through the windshield. They were parked outside the Lea Bay Historic Society building. Had been for the last three hours. "These guys in the suits are connected to everything. Donny and the murders and maybe even *this*." He held up *Lords of the Deep*. It felt too warm in his hands, like it was more than just a book. A window of some kind. And there were always two sides to every window. You could look out and something else could look *in*.

"I admit they're probably with the government but I hardly think they're going around murdering people."

"Who's to say they aren't? The government kills people on a daily basis."

She sighed. "Fair point. But what're we going to do, grab one and give them the shakedown?"

In truth, he hadn't thought that far ahead. All he knew was that *they* knew something. And he intended to find out. Whether this was a stakeout or pre-emptive strike would depend on a number of things.

"It's getting late," Daphne said, fidgeting in the passenger seat. She'd been checking her phone constantly and now she could see it was running low on battery. "You mind if we start the engine for a while, so I can charge this thing? Not to mention it's hot as hell out here."

"We've been here for a few hours. Don't you think that'll be a little conspicuous?"

"Look, I agreed to come here with you. I'm not sure why but I went willingly. If you're not going to let me charge my phone on a day like this, when a fucking call is going to change my life in one of two ways, then I'll march right up those front steps and tell them we're here." She reached across, grabbed the keys, and turned.

"We'll leave it running," he said. He needed to take it easy on her. She'd been through more in the last day than most people had in their entire lives. His time here hadn't exactly been a cake-walk but her son was missing. He couldn't imagine. Didn't have kids himself, but Anita always wanted them. She'd dropped hints on more than a few occasions. Talked about getting a house with four bedrooms. Just in case. He'd never been keen on the idea of babies screaming and the smell of shitty diapers but he'd also never been good at telling her *no*.

God, he missed her.

He couldn't wait until this whole ordeal was done. Drive back home.

Start over. Forget that Lea Bay ever existed.

But you can't forget. You've tried for years and look where that got you.

And besides, what's to say the town will let *you forget?*

He turned down the air conditioner.

"What's your theory on all this?" Daphne said.

"Huh?"

"I mean, you must have a theory if you're taking a risk like this. If those are government agents, and they catch wind of us keeping tabs, you think they're just going to give us a slap on the wrists and let us go home?"

"No, I guess they wouldn't."

"Exactly, so like I asked: what's your theory?"

He sighed and opened the book to a random page, an image of a massive snake-like thing surfacing from the water. The art was rendered in pen and ink, the details awe-inspiring and much too realistic for his taste. "It all comes down to money, doesn't it? Or in this case... *treasure.* This thing talks about treasure every chance it gets. My dad was onto something. I think the treasure is real and it's here in Lea Bay. I think whoever killed Donny wants it back. Donny probably got himself mixed up in it. Theft if I had to guess. And when they cornered him, he either tried to run or keep the goods for himself."

She sniffled. "I wish I could say he wasn't the kind of man that would do something like that."

"Yeah. Me too."

"Okay, so there's treasure at stake. *Expensive* treasure. That doesn't explain everything. We've had underwater earthquakes and things appearing in the harbor. Things that definitely aren't whales or stingrays."

He went quiet for a moment, watching the sky grow dim in the distance. It was late afternoon now. The day seemed short, night closer than it should be. "Maybe whoever wants that gold is a descendant or something. A descendant of the Lords. At least I hope they're a descendant. I hope it's just a crazy guy in a mask going around slashing people and once he finds what he wants, he gets the hell out of here, drives north until he hits the border."

"You don't sound so convinced."

"There's been a lot of strange shit happening if that's what you're getting at. I didn't say my theory was a good one. But it's a start."

Her phone vibrated and her hands fumbled. "Shit."

"False alarm?"

"It's my sister checking in for the thousandth time. Like I wouldn't call her the second I knew something."

"She's just worried."

"And I'm not?" She stared at him with bloodshot eyes and pale skin. The face of a woman so sleep deprived she looked ravenous.

"I'm sorry. I didn't mean anything by it."

She texted back and though he couldn't see the words, he was certain they weren't pretty. "Look, I don't like your theory, okay? It would be so much easier to blame this all on a guy in a mask, but in the end, it doesn't matter. My son is still missing."

"We're gonna find him," Eric said, finally taking his eyes away from the Historic Society. "I might not be the world's greatest uncle or brother-in-law but I'm not resting until we have some answers, okay?"

Across the street, the side door of the building opened. Two men in dark suits stepped outside. They looked cancerous against the Greek columns and three-hundred-year-old architecture. One of them spoke into a miniature microphone while the other stepped into a black Escalade and started the engine.

"Where do you suppose they're going?" Daphne said.

"Probably not on their lunch break, that's for sure."

"Do we follow them? Won't they notice?"

The Escalade backed away from the curb and started to head toward Main Street. He cut the engine when they turned out of sight.

"What're you doing?"

"We could follow them, keep a safe distance, but I've got a better idea."

He eyed the side door they'd exited from. The Historic Society was foreign to him. He'd never handed in his local history paper in high school, had skipped class the day of the field trip. But looking at it now, he had a distinct feeling it wasn't just an old building or a museum.

He opened the door. "Come on, let's go."

"Eric, this is crazy."

He ignored her and walked across the lawn. A banner hung along the wall, advertising the Lea Bay Pirate Festival. Eric had never attended and after what he'd been through, he'd keep it that way. The door was nondescript. You wouldn't have seen it if you weren't looking, or if two suspicious men hadn't just appeared from behind it. He tried the knob and, mercifully, it was unlocked. Inside was an equally nondescript hall, void of any charm or color scheme. He waved Daphne on and held a finger to his lips before she could protest.

From nearby he heard muffled voices. He walked down the hall, turned the corner, and spotted a set of elevators. The front desk lay in his periphery, the attendant speaking to someone on the phone about a guy she was seeing on the side. She giggled every so often, loud enough to mask the elevator's arrival.

"Where the hell are we going?"

He studied the buttons on the panel and chose the letter B.

"The basement? Are you nuts?"

"Probably. But if I were working for the government and I wanted to hide something, don't you think I'd do it out of sight?"

Before she could answer the doors opened and they were greeted with a dimly lit hall. Old water stains covered the walls and ceiling like ink blots and cobwebs the size of bowling balls hung in the corners. They stepped out and followed the hall as it rounded to the left and ended at another door. The wood was splintered, the knob rusted beyond return. He twisted it, wincing at the cool metal, and the door gave way to another elevator. Nothing like the antique above ground. It was less art deco and more akin to a mine shaft. He pressed the sole, unmarked button, no sign of any numbers or letters, and it arrived quickly.

"What if they're down there?" Daphne asked.

He didn't ask her who *they* were. She'd meant the suits of course but Eric found himself picturing someone else. Someone with rotten flesh and jet-black eyes. A soulless creature, grotesquely malformed.

The Lords.

The door closed and they descended for a long time. He had the feeling of falling, of never stopping. There was nothing down here but darkness.

He let out a seconds-long sigh when they reached the bottom and saw a room that could've been an office or a fallout shelter. Leather-bound books decorated wooden bookshelves. The place smelled of must but it wasn't entirely unpleasant. It reminded him of a library but libraries weren't usually this far beneath the surface. Not as damp.

They stepped out of the second elevator and he wondered how far down they were, wondered if anyone would hear them scream if the need arose.

A desk lay ahead, large and antiquated, like something you might find in the Oval Office. But he wasn't concerned with who used this space for work. Not when he saw the vault. Not when he saw what had been stashed inside.

The chest.

The treasure chest stood mere feet away and he suddenly knew his theory had not been that far from the truth. He didn't have time to feel victorious when the elevator doors closed and began to rise.

Again, he pictured a skull with thin, dead skin pulled tightly, two missing eyes, the cavities filled with writhing maggots.

"Shit." Daphne grabbed his wrist and pulled him into the vault, into the darkness. They found shelter behind the chest and moments later the elevator returned, bringing with it several visitors.

CHAPTER TWENTY-THREE

For Brendan Sawyer—and the rest of the Lea Bay Police Department for that matter—tonight had gone to hell and back. The second he ducked into his squad car and sank into the leather seat, dispatch was paging him, a three-ninety down at Pasquale's Pub, a little dive about two blocks from Captain's Cove.

Two blocks from the marina where Donny Jordan's body had washed up.

Two blocks from where this shit-show began.

Sawyer told dispatch he'd check it out, even though he was searching for a missing seven-year-old whose mother was one more slice of bad news away from slashing open her wrists. Dispatch, a local college student who Sawyer had a short fling with not-so-long ago, suddenly went silent. The quietude lingered long enough for Sawyer to figure out something wasn't right.

"Saw-yer?" the dispatcher said, her voice cracking between syllables.

Sawyer recognized her no-bullshit tone and he immediately stiffened in his seat. "Go for Sawyer."

"Can you switch over to *five?*"

Five. The only channel that wasn't being recorded.

"Sure thing," he said, and immediately switched over. "You there?"

"Yeah, I'm here."

Sawyer breathed deeply through his nose. "Look, Kendall, I know we've had our—"

"That's not what I wanted to discuss, thank you very much. That call from Pasquale's—it was the bartender." He pictured her face twisting with confusion as if he were sitting across from her. "He was really freaked out."

"I'm gonna need more details."

"It was Sally Jordan."

"Sally Jordan?" He wasn't surprised to hear a *Jordan* had been at the center of a three-ninety, but hearing the mother's name threw him. "You said *Sally* Jordan?"

"Yes, that's right."

"Well, what did she do?"

"About four o'clock and Pasquale's was about to close. Bartender said a few locals were still hanging around, finishing up their drinks, ready to pack it in."

"Does Pasquale's have a summer license? They allowed to be open until four?"

"Don't know offhand. Place is kind of a shithole. I can pull the paperwork."

"Don't bother."

"Anyway, they were closing up when in strolled Sally Jordan. Bartender claims she was already hammered. Bombed out of her *mind* hammered. Walking like she never learned how."

"Jesus. Honestly, I didn't even know Sally Jordan was still alive until a few days ago."

"Weird, right? I mean, throughout the years, she was the one who kept that whole family together."

Sawyer knew a thing or two about keeping a family together. "Everyone has their breaking point."

"Bartender said she was acting all sorts of weird. Speaking English that almost sounded foreign. Like Shakespeare or something."

Like a pirate, he almost said aloud but refrained from doing so. "What else she do?"

"She... um... she started asking about treasure. Sawyer, what the hell is going on in this town? People are starting to talk. People are getting freaked the *fuck out*. Murders, missing bodies. The other day a woman called in and said she thought she saw the Loch Ness Monster splashing around the lagoon."

"You know how it is. A few strange occurrences and everyone starts connecting their own dots, drawing conclusions. It's the human way. Has been since humans existed."

"Well, whatever it is, *I'm* getting freaked out." There was a brief pause and both of them spent it catching their breath. "I feel like I should move or something. Go to school in New York or Maine. California sounds nice too. Or Canada. Any place that's not Lea Bay."

"Might not be a bad idea."

"Really?"

"Sure. Why not?"

"What's keeping *you* here, Sawyer?"

He didn't have an answer for that, not a truthful one anyway. A thousand lies funneled through his brain but he couldn't bring himself to speak a single one.

"I better go check out the three-ninety," he said, turning the dial on his radio. "Goodnight, Kendall."

"Good—"

A click of the dial and she was gone. Silence swept through the squad car.

* * *

He reached Pasquale's a little after five and pulled into the dirt lot out front. The sun was beginning its ascent, peeking just over the horizon, spilling splashes of orange across the sky. The place looked worse than usual. The sign dangled awkwardly from one side. No one, not even the bar's owner, had bothered to fix it. Mold caked the left side of the building. Sawyer wondered what kind of health violations he'd find inside but the thought turned his stomach. So he focused on the task at hand.

Question the bartender, get the fuck out.

And then find Jake Jordan.

As he climbed out of the cruiser, he wondered what Daphne was doing in that precise moment. He wondered about that often.

In the summer between high school and college, when Daphne Jordan—Stillwell at the time—slipped away from him. He had a thing for her, a little crush, though it manifested into something much more, at a speed that surprised even him. He loved her, or so he thought. At eighteen, *love* is often illusionary, and thinking back to that summer, he still wasn't an expert on the subject. He'd been through his fair share of flings and one-night stands, but the long game was one he'd never played. He'd never met a woman worthy of giving up that single life. That freedom.

Until that summer.

Until Daphne Stillwell.

He'd had his chance with her. *Multiple* chances. They'd worked together at an ice cream shop on the boardwalk. He learned of love that summer but also what he wanted to do with the rest of his life—*not* working in that fucking ice cream shop was one of them. The other was to become a cop. The boardwalk had its fair share of police activity. During every shift Sawyer saw action, officers busting petty criminals and helping people in need. It seemed rewarding. And he hadn't been completely wrong. Even now, when law enforcement wasn't exactly a respected profession, he still felt a sense of pride. Fulfillment. An understanding that he was making a difference even if the world was going to shit.

As he pushed through the front door of Pasquale's, he thought back to Daphne. Her lips. How he almost kissed them once in the back room of the ice cream shop. After hours when no one else was there. Near the freezer. They'd been close. Inches from each other. Her lotion smelled of fruit and vanilla. And he *had* leaned in but something stopped him. She'd stared at him blankly, expectantly. No resistance on her part. Yet he couldn't follow through. He couldn't kiss her.

Why then? It was a question he'd come back to many times over the years.

Why then?

He often wondered how different his life would've turned out had he completed that kiss, if he could've saved her from marrying that douchebag Donny Jordan. He wondered if Jake would've been *his* son instead.

Jake.

Gotta find him.

No matter what.

"Took you long enough!" the bartender shouted, waving his hands over his head. Above many things, he looked flustered and tired and irritated by Sawyer's leisurely pace.

"Calm down, Pete," Sawyer barked. "I'm not in the mood. I've had a night and today's not looking much better."

"Allow me to apologize for the inconvenience."

Sawyer stared at him. "You done with the patronizing, or you want to keep dragging this out? How about we sit down and you tell me what Sally Jordan was doing in your bar at four o'clock this morning?"

Pete sighed, then took his seat. Sawyer plopped down across from him. "Where do I even begin?"

"My guess would be the beginning."

"You always were a smartass."

"Learned it from old, salty bartenders."

"I'm honored. Look, the crazy broad waltzed in here drunker than Johnny Depp in a winery and started spouting crazy shit. That about sums it up."

"What kind of crazy shit?"

"She was all *ye* this and *ye* that. To be honest, I didn't know if she was loaded up on PCP or rehearsing for the local production of *A Midsummer Night's Dream*."

"That's Shakespeare, right?"

Pete stared at him incredulously. "I can tell you graduated from Lea Bay's finest academic program."

"I'm a cop, not a librarian. Okay?"

"Everyone knows Shakespeare."

"If we're being honest, my eyes have seen enough of your ugly face and I'm coming off a twenty-six-hour shift. My feet and back and head feel like they've been through a meat grinder. And I'm hungry. So unless you start giving me something, I'm walking the fuck out of here."

Pete's eyes widened. Sawyer had his attention.

"Now," he said, leaning forward, "Jake Jordan, Sally's grandson, went missing around midnight. We think someone took him. And for some reason, I have a sneaking suspicion that a crazed Sally Jordan might have something to do with the case. Now, Pete, please tell me something useful."

Pete paused, studied his nails. "She asked about treasure."

"Okay," Sawyer said, getting out his notepad. "That's good. Anything else?"

Pete shook his head. "She was really freaky, man. Pale as a ghost, and that's not hyperbole. She was literally white. Like a blank sheet of paper."

"Got it." He jotted down *treasure* and *white* and realized he wasn't getting too far.

"She just... wasn't herself. Remember back when Karl Jordan was losing his shit? Well, she was sharp as a whip then. Kept the whole family from crumbling. The Sally Jordan that entered through those doors," he said, pointing to the front of the bar, "that was not the same woman. If I didn't know any better, perhaps if I were a spiritual man, I'd say she looked...possessed."

"Possessed?"

"By a demon or something."

"A demon that quotes Shakespeare."

Pete's whole body went slack. "I never said she quoted Shakespeare, asshole, I said she spoke like him."

Sawyer pumped his hand. "Calm down."

"She was fucking weird and she freaked me out. Everyone else in the bar, too."

"I'll need their names." He slid the pen and paper across the table. Pete scribbled down the handful of names and returned the paper to Sawyer. "Did she say anything about Jake? Did you see him? Did she drive here? Did you see a car?"

"No," Pete said as if the questions had insulted him. "Don't you think I would have mentioned something like that, genius?"

Sawyer gritted his teeth. "Did she mention where she was going?"

"No. She asked everyone in the bar about the treasure, then left. She was foaming at the mouth. Literally. Come to think of it, the bitch might have rabies. Can people get rabies?"

"I don't know but I'm sure she doesn't have it."

"Well, I'd check into that if I were you."

"Pete, as always you've been more than helpful." Sawyer pushed himself up from the table. He flipped his notepad closed and returned it to his pocket.

"Oh, Brendan," Pete said, sticking his right forefinger in the air. "She did mention a name. Didn't make any sense at the time—still fucking doesn't—but maybe it'll help."

"What name?"

"Blackjack Philips?"

For some odd reason, Sawyer winced.

"Yeah," Pete said. "I had the same reaction. Doesn't make a lick of sense. Been in Lea Bay my entire life and I'd goddamn know if there was someone walking around with a name like that." He shook his head and snorted with laughter. "Almost sounds like..."

"Like a pirate?" Sawyer asked as he chewed the inside of his mouth.

Pete snapped his fingers. "Like a fucking pirate."

Sawyer turned and headed for the door.

He walked out, headed for his cruiser and never looked back.

CHAPTER TWENTY-FOUR

Three of them in total. Two of those suits and one whose rosy cheeks screamed functioning alcoholic. Eric risked a closer glance as the men walked toward the desk. Was that Frazier Wilton? *The mayor?* What the hell was the mayor doing in an underground office?

"We counted them, sir," said Sunglasses. "The coins."

"Excellent." Frazier sat and leaned back in the chair. He loosened his tie and placed his feet on the desk. One of his shirt buttons had come undone, revealing a patch of his sizable gut. "What're we looking at?"

The suits eyed each other. Ear-Bud answered, "A couple. There's a couple missing."

Frazier opened a drawer and retrieved a cigar. He lit and puffed and considered. "That's a couple too many."

Neither suit answered, and to Eric, they almost looked... *scared.*

"You do know what that means, of course?" Frazier asked, eyeing them.

"Yes, sir," Ear Bud said.

"Yes, sir," Sunglasses said.

"Do we have any leads? Any names?"

"Unfortunately not." Sunglasses stared at his shoes. "It's entirely possible they were lost during the heist."

"Entirely *probable.*" Frazier Wilton scratched at his graying stubble. The collar of his shirt had yellowed from sweat and age, and his cigar smelled cheap even by a small-town politician's standard. Eric had never cared for the man. Their interactions had been limited but people talked. Talked about how he had his hands in things less than legal. Eric had assumed that meant drugs or guns—*not* pirate treasure. "But that's not good enough, boys. Sure, we can safely assume whoever took the coins has rendered it useless. Maybe one of Donny's buddies pawned them somewhere. Can't blame him. But if a coin were to, say, get into the wrong hands or be placed in the bay... well, I don't think I need to tell you what that would mean. But just in case either of you has forgotten, it would mean we're all royally fucked."

He stood, pointing at the two men. "And before the shit hits the fan, before those things come out of the water and turn this town to rubble, I'll make sure you have a front row seat for it all."

Silence for much too long. The men swallowed and fidgeted, and Eric's pulse quickened. To his left, Daphne was nearly hyperventilating. He was halfway there himself. Whatever they were getting at, it sounded a lot like his father's ramblings. Sounded *secretive*. Which meant these three men would not take kindly to strangers listening in on their conversation.

"We'll find the coins," Ear-Bud said. "You have our word."

Frazier smiled around the cigar, a bit of ash floating onto the deck. "Of course you will. That's your job. Maybe you ought to keep a closer eye on Daphne Jordan. She might know something. I'm sure you've heard about her son by now. Missing since late last night. I'm no detective but with Donny coming back and walking around town—well, maybe the kid went to be with his dad."

Daphne tensed, leaning too hard into the chest. From inside, one of the coins shifted. It was a small sound. Faint. But in the silence of the room, it went off like a gunshot.

All three sets of eyes peered toward them. Eric ducked and went rigid and stopped breathing. He held Daphne's hand, squeezed until the flesh ran bone white. Put simply, there was no escape if they were to be found. This conversation was classified and then some. And aside from the elevators, there was no foreseeable way out. Eric could maybe take on one, two at the most, but for how long? He hadn't been in a fight since eighth grade and even then, Donny had saved his ass at the last minute, just before Eric had needed dentures.

Don't fight unless you need to, he'd said.

You fight all the time.

Yeah and I need to. You got the brains. So use them.

"You hear something?" Wilton said.

Eric could feel them watching, practically sensed the suits reaching beneath their jackets and drawing their weapons.

He closed his eyes and awaited death's eager fingers. His brain had failed him once again.

Footsteps.

Coming closer toward the vault.

Closer.

A phone rang.

Wilton sighed and the steps froze as he picked up. "What is it now? Jesus, when? Okay. Yeah. Got it." He hung up. "Boys, you'll never believe who showed up dead at Pasquale's."

Neither suit answered.

"None other than sweet ol' Sally Jordan. Course she's not actually dead. Not in the classic sense. She came by, up and walking. Pasquale thought she was just drunk. Called the cops and everything. I don't know if Donny's trying to keep it all in the family or what, but we need to find that coin. Not later. Not next week. Not tomorrow. Right goddamn now."

He leered at them. "Do what you have to."

"Yes, sir," they said in unison. Their footsteps retreated toward the elevator, where Eric heard them press the sole button, heard the ding of the cart's arrival, listened as all three men got on and rode it to the basement, where this forsaken building should've ended in the first place.

Neither he nor Daphne spoke for a long time. When they were certain the elevator wasn't making a return trip, they helped each other up, ensured the office was empty, pressed the button themselves, and stood on either side when the cart descended and the doors opened. Empty, thankfully. They rode in silence and when they reached the first floor, they walked in silence.

They did not speak until they were back in the car and the Historic Society was in the rearview mirror, and even then it was only one word muttered under Daphne's breath.

"Fuck."

* * *

Jake had never been to a family reunion. He'd heard about them, seen cartoons and movies that spoke of them, but the idea seemed like such a strange concept. His family didn't get along that well to begin with. Those that had left, his mother had patiently explained, were never coming back. Families did that sometimes. A falling out, she called it. But mothers didn't know everything. Or maybe they did and they lied about things. Because she'd also told him his father was never coming back.

And from where Jake stood, on a small private beach a mile and a half from the pier, his father had most certainly come back.

Though it wasn't him anymore.

His grandmother had stumbled up the path an hour ago. *"I could feel you from a mile away, lad,"* she'd said. Whether she'd been talking to his father or Jake himself was still a mystery.

Grammy didn't welcome him with open arms, didn't even speak to him by name. Instead, like his dad, she spoke about being *of the blood*. Whatever that meant. Probably that they were related, shared the same DNA. Hence the family reunion.

"Can we go see Mom now?" Jake said, shivering in the wind. The moon was nearly full and reflected off the bay like a negative sun. He tugged on his dad's sleeve and recoiled. The flesh beneath was cold and dry like sandpaper.

Donny didn't answer. Instead, he kept going on and on about vessels and blood and pacts and other words his young mind couldn't comprehend.

Jake kicked up small arcs of sand, watching the waves come in and out before he remembered what rested within his pocket. He'd found it a few days back, in the bushes in the front yard. Near where that chest thing had been before the guys in dress clothes took it away.

The coin was large and round and reminded him of the gold-foiled chocolates he got in his basket last Easter. But this wasn't candy. This was *real treasure*. Maybe he could make a deal with his dad. A reverse allowance of sorts. He tugged on Donny's sleeve again and finally got his dad's attention. Grammy too. They stopped talking and watched him with their mouths open, foul breath spilling toward Jake. They smelled like seaweed and raw sewage.

"Daddy, if I give you this coin, can we please go see Mommy? I'm hungry and tired and she'll be worried about me because she thinks you're dead even though I told her you were coming back. You aren't like Skeletor, are you?"

Donny did not answer but he did smile and Jake couldn't help but take a step back. There was something wrong with his dad's face and it was getting worse. They needed to find a hospital. Same with Grammy. She looked worse than usual. He'd asked her how old she was but the number had been too high to count. Now she looked *ancient*. Like a mummy or something.

Donny reached out and took the coin, studied the texture in the light of the moon. *"How long have you had this, boy?"*

He shrugged. "A few days, I guess."

"A few days," Donny mimed.

"We waited hundreds of years," Grammy said.

"Aye. And we wait no more." His dad turned toward the bay and wound his arm back. Surely he wouldn't throw the coin into the water. It looked like it might be worth a lot of money. They could buy a new car and a house and be happy like his friends' families.

Donny let go and the coin soared through the air, splashing far in the distance.

Grammy shouted.

Daddy watched.

And Jake fell back when something came out of the water so quickly he would've missed it if he'd blinked. But his eyes were wide open, and he was certain he'd seen something long and large and not unlike a snake. What was it they called snakes that lived in the water? Serpents. That was it. *Serpents*. But this was bigger than most boats and it had to be a nightmare. Right? He'd wake up any moment and be back in his bed and Daddy would come home from the hospital, all healed, perfect as if nothing had happened to him at all.

He did not wake up.

But he did watch the water for a long time after, and though he didn't see anything else rise to the surface, he *felt* it out there. Like it could see him even if the opposite was true.

CHAPTER TWENTY-FIVE

Brendan Sawyer jerked awake and nearly fell out of his chair. He'd fallen asleep behind his desk sometime in the early morning. The station had been empty and quiet when he'd sat down, the entire force out attending to the needs of Lea Bay—and there had been many needs. Over the last twenty-four hours, the town had lost its shit, calling in ludicrous reports, things didn't make a lick of sense. By now, every available cop was out investigating monster sightings and missing persons.

He found himself staring up at the square-jawed face of Lieutenant Trent Jakobson, a lean man with a thin mustache more like a black pipe cleaner. His receding hairline had almost completely retreated, and despite his position on the force, he always neglected to follow dress code, opting to wear a cap sporting the Lea Bay Police Department's emblem.

"How long was I out?" Sawyer asked, yawning.

"Few hours," Jakobson replied, messing around with things on Sawyer's desk. It was a nervous tic, one Sawyer and the rest of the force had grown used to. Jakobson lined up the stapler, pen holder, and stacks of sticky notes in the right-hand corner of the desk, perfectly aligned with the edge. "Sorry," he said, realizing he was doing it again, rearranging other people's things.

"It's fine." Sawyer rubbed his still-heavy eyes. If he closed them again, he'd fall back asleep in seconds. "Where is everyone? Don't tell me they're all still running around town."

Jakobson breathed deeply as he glanced around the near-empty office. Sawyer followed his gaze and saw only a few cops rushing to finish their reports. Kendall sat behind her desk, hunched forward in her chair, taking call after call, the office phone lighting up with new problems every twenty seconds. Her counterpart, Peggy Robinson, was on vacation down in Mexico with her husband, Ed. If Sawyer were her, he'd be afraid to return.

"Whole town has gone apeshit," Jakobson finally said, "And it don't seem to be getting any saner." He scratched his neck. A small rash broke across his skin. "In my twenty-five years in this shit hole, I've never seen anything like it." His eyes narrowed. "Can you feel it? It's…almost *indescribable*. Like something big is happening. The prelude to a really bad storm."

"Yeah, I can feel it." Sawyer sensed something wrong as soon as Donny Jordan had been found mauled, mouthfuls of flesh missing from his dead body.

"Freaky, huh?"

"Yeah, freaky."

Jakobson fished a crumpled sheet of paper from his pocket, unfolded it, and slapped the flyer down on the desk. "Pirate Festival. This Saturday."

Sawyer checked the calendar on his desk.

Two days away.

"I forgot about that stupid festival," Sawyer said, and would have laughed had he the strength. "My father used to love the parade. Took us every year."

"Yeah, *everyone* loves a good parade." Jakobson shrugged as if the festival were something of a nuisance. "The mayor thinks it might be a good idea to have a strong police presence during the festival. Seems to think the turnout will be greater than usual."

"Since when does that douchebag care about people?"

"Since last night when he called me." The lieutenant placed his hands on his hips. "I was hoping I could count on you to head up the team. Tell whoever you can convince to work that overtime is not an issue. Frazier sure loves to waste money and he's sparing no expense."

"Lovely. I'll sleep when I'm dead I guess."

"You're single," Jakobson said. "Make money while you can, before you have a wife and kids. Soak up every second of OT while it's around. That's my advice."

"I appreciate you putting me in charge of something so prestigious. Means a lot."

"I'm blaming that on exhaustion and not you being an asshole. How we lookin' on that Jordan kid's case? Any news?"

Sawyer shook his head. "Trail's gone cold. No breaks. It's like he vanished into thin air."

"Well, keep on it. We got half the precinct looking for this little shit. He'd better turn up soon. You hear all those calls? Hate to be a pessimist but eventually something worse is gonna turn up and that boy's gonna leave the front page."

Before Sawyer could open his mouth, Kendall came trotting over, out of breath. Bending over, she put her hands on her knees and sucked wind.

"Kendall?" Sawyer asked, rising from his seat. "You okay?"

"Jesus, girl," Jakobson said, putting a gentle hand on her back, rubbing her between the shoulder blades, a creepy gesture that almost caused Sawyer to react. *Almost.* "You dying on us, sweetheart?"

"Just got a call. It was about Jake Jordan."

Sawyer stepped around his desk. "What is it?"

"Some jogger saw him in the woods, near the State Park."

"Shit," Sawyer said, sounding breathless himself. "Was he with anyone?"

Kendall's eyes bounced between the two men. "Yeah, they saw someone all right."

"Who?" Sawyer asked, stepping within a few inches of her. "Who did they see?"

She shuddered. "Guy said he saw Donny Jordan with him."

Jakobson snickered. "Donny Jordan's dead, sweetheart. No way this guy saw him. Must've been someone else, someone who looked—"

"This guy was very adamant. Said he saw Donny Jordan, only...." She trailed off and glanced down as if she'd dropped the words there on the floor.

Sawyer folded his arms across his chest and said, "Jakobson's right. The guy must be confused. Donny's dead. Someone lifted his body from the morgue. Remember?"

She nodded, her eyes darting back and forth. "Yeah, dead. That's what the guy said."

Sawyer winced as if someone were squeezing his intestines like a tube of toothpaste.

Something big is happening, Jakobson had said, and Sawyer couldn't agree more. "What do you mean?"

"I mean," she said, gulping, "the guy claims Donny Jordan *is* dead. Dead and walking around."

* * *

On the way to the State Park, Sawyer called Daphne. "Pick up, pick up, pick up," he said, taking his cruiser around the tight bend on Old Mills Road. He was ten minutes from the park but aimed to make it there in five. "Dammit," he said as her voicemail picked up. He listened to her recorded voice and then recorded one of his own after the beep: "Daph, it's Sawyer. I need you to call me back as soon as you get this. It's about Jake, and...Donny too."

He hit the gas, taking the turn a little too fast. *Slow down,* he heard his father's voice say. *Slow down and enjoy the ride.*

Pop's voice conjured up memories of his past, his childhood, and most importantly—the stupid pirate festival Lea Bay held annually. He could almost smell the cotton candy and sugar-coated zeppoles, the freshly-baked pizza slices coming from the many street vendors. If he closed his eyes and concentrated hard enough, he'd see the streamers hanging from the welcome banner that hung across the town line. He'd see the parade floats, all designed to look like wooden pirate ships, some more elaborate than others. He'd see the mayor on one of those floats, that shit-eating grin plastered to Frazier's face, waving to a crowd full of costumed pirates, adults and kids alike. He could see the *River Queen,* one of Lea Bay's year-round attractions, set sail from her dock, painted like an old buccaneer ship, crowded with college kids, chugging from red Solo cups. *The Booze Cruise,* they called it.

Sawyer wasn't sure why the town loved the parade so much, or the festival for that matter. If you've seen one pirate festival, you've seen them all. It was the same every year—face painters and henna tattoo artists, lectures on local pirate lore and street performers acting out fabled pieces—it was all much too silly for Sawyer to wrap his head around.

But his father had loved it. Had helped with the lectures. Horace Dweyer had given his pops his own room to hold a lecture on pirate lore, one being the infamous cast of The Lords of the Deep. It was during one of those lectures that he'd met Karl Jordan. The two hit it off. Started hanging together. Drinking rum together. Writing together. Spending way too much time away from their families together.

All of which led to John Sawyer going missing a year later. A few months prior, Karl had gone off the rails, waking up naked in public places with no memory of how he got there.

Sawyer's ringtone blared through the car speakers. He answered the call, hands-free.

"Daph," he said, trying to hide the anxiety in his voice.

"Sawyer," she answered, unable to hide the panic in hers.

"Someone spotted Jake in the woods near the State Park. I'm headed there now. I don't know if he's still there—doesn't sound like it—but it's a lead."

"I'll meet you there. I have a lot to tell you. We found out some stuff about—"

"We?"

Silence.

Great, he thought. *Here we go. Stupid, stupid, stupid. When are you going to learn to keep your mouth shut, idiot?*

Sawyer chewed on his tongue as the silence lingered. "Maybe you should come alone." He immediately regretted the words. "I mean, I was thinking that... um... it might be better for the...*investigation* if we were alone."

"Eric's here to help. And he's driving. I don't think I should get behind a wheel even if I wanted to."

He cleared his throat. "Couldn't agree more." With Eric around, there was no way he could tell Daphne how he felt about her, how he'd always felt about her.

Sawyer turned into the State Park's entrance. The long driveway was flanked by a stretch of lush forest. You had to be mindful of deer this time of year but Sawyer didn't slow once.

"I'm here, Daph. I'll be waiting."

"We'll be there soon." Before he could hang up, she said, "And Sawyer?"

His heart fluttered at the sound of his name. "Yes?"

"Thank you. Thank you for taking this seriously."

He felt his brow wrinkle. "Of course."

Then she hung up.

CHAPTER TWENTY-SIX

It was dawn by the time they arrived at the State Park.

Two cruisers were stationed at the entrance where a small crowd had gathered. Police tape had been strung between two towering pines, yellow plastic flapping in the wind.

"We're going to tell him everything," Daphne said, examining her eyes in the rearview mirror. They were covered in broken blood vessels, as if she'd been on a week-long bender instead of staying awake for nearly two days straight, worried sick about losing her son.

Not gone, just missing, she thought for the thousandth time.

"What? Are you kidding?"

She turned toward him. "Do I look like I'm kidding? And when we're done with the supernatural shit, we'll tell him about the mayor."

"Daph, he'll think we're nuts, lock us both up. Hell, he might even think we had something to do with it."

"I don't care what he thinks and besides—whoever called this in reported seeing Donny. You think the caller's nuts too? You think this entire town has lost their shit?"

"It would be a hell of a lot easier to accept."

She removed the book from her purse, running her fingers over the engraved text. *Lords of the Deep.* The name still conjured things she'd prefer not to think about. Things with decayed faces and shriveled skin, shrunken heads and sinister charms. Things that harnessed the power to conjure *other things* from the ocean's darkest depths.

Eric reached for it but she pulled back. "He needs to read this. It's our only chance at having him halfway believe what I'm about to tell him."

"Think about what you're saying. My dad wasn't exactly a gleaming face in the community. His memoir, or whatever the hell you want to call that thing, isn't going to help our case. Plus... Sawyer's family has a bit of history with mine."

She held the leather tightly. It felt like skin in her hands. Cold, dead skin. When this was all over, when Jake was in her arms again and the town was finished losing its shit, she'd make sure this book was destroyed. Burn it in her fireplace while she enjoyed a glass of wine, stoking the ashes with glee. It had brought her enough grief for several lifetimes, let alone one. "I'm doing it, Eric. It's non-negotiable."

He punched the glove compartment, rubbing his fist and shaking his head. "You're not the only one who's lost something here. My mother, she's out there on her own, too. She can barely walk up the stairs these days. I used to have this horrible dream. She'd be at the top of the stairs, calling to me, and she'd take her first step, lose her footing, and tumble down in slow motion. I'd scream but nothing would come out, of course. Dream logic. Finally, at the bottom, she'd lay on the floor in front of me, every bone in her body broken. I hope to Christ that dream doesn't come true."

She placed a hand on his shoulder. "Your mom's as tough as bricks. And so is Jake. You said so yourself. We're going to find them and we're going to end this."

He nodded and she handed him a tissue from her purse. He blew his nose and sighed for a long time. "Thanks, Daph. For everything. We'll show him the book and we'll tell him all of it."

"I'm going to take the longest vacation of my life when this is all over," she said, opening the door, planting one foot in the grass lot. Deep down, she wanted to leave Lea Bay for good. A *permanent* vacation. She had some distant relatives up north, somewhere in Maine. She hadn't seen them for a decade or more but she was inclined to call them. There was nothing left for her in this town.

Especially if you can't find Jake.

She stepped outside, willing her inner thoughts to shut their inner mouths.

The morning was cool by summer's standards and the crowd was growing. She and Eric walked past them and stepped underneath the police tape.

The officer guarding the entrance held up a hand. "This is a crime scene."

"I'm aware of that," she said. "I'm Daphne Jordan. The missing boy's mother."

"I'll need to see some identification."

She felt her pockets, rummaged around her purse, and suddenly remembered she'd left her wallet in her *other* purse, which was currently sitting on the dining room table.

"That won't be necessary," said another voice from nearby.

Brendan Sawyer stepped from a line of trees and waved the officer away. "They're with me."

The officer eyed them both for a long time before he nodded, let them pass, and told the crowd to get back. *This is still a crime scene, people.*

Daphne winced. A crime scene and the last place her boy had been spotted.

"Hope you brought your walking shoes," Sawyer said, waving them on. "It's about a mile out."

A mile. She thought about Jake walking this path with a stranger. A stranger who was definitely not Donny.

Who's to say? If something the size of a city bus can stick its head out of the bay, who's to say it wasn't really Donny? He's missing. Remember?

She shivered. This close to the water, the breeze had picked up exponentially. Her hair blew onto her face and into her mouth, and not for the first time she wished she'd cut it short despite Donny's pleas. *I like your hair,* he'd insisted. *Like the way it feels in my hands.*

That bastard.

Even after everything he'd done, everything he'd put their family through, she still missed him.

"What do you think of all this?" Eric asked Sawyer.

"You'll have to be more specific. I've got a town losing their collective minds."

"This. Jake going missing and being seen with someone who looks an awful lot like my brother."

"You insinuating Donny Jordan is still alive somehow?"

"I'm not insinuating anything. Just asking an innocent question."

Sawyer stopped, turned, and removed his hat. "Might I remind you that I'm the cop here? I'm supposed to ask the questions."

Eric gritted his teeth, stepped closer to Sawyer. "Then start asking."

They held each other's stare for a few long moments. Daphne groaned. Enough was enough. "Whenever you two are done measuring each other's dicks, I'd like to see the crime scene and then Eric and I have something we'd like to discuss with you, Sawyer. Isn't that right, Eric?"

Eric nodded slowly, putting his teeth away for the moment. "Yeah, that's right."

Sawyer turned around without answering and headed farther onto the path.

"This guy's starting to be a real asshole," Eric said under his breath.

"It's just a tough guy act," she whispered. "He's a gentle giant."

"You *know* him?"

"Used to." The words came out more somber than she had intended, that *oh-what-could-have-been* tone making her cringe.

Ten minutes later, the trees thinned out, revealing a view of the bay that reminded her why she'd stuck around all these years. The sun was just coming up in the distance, the sky a cascade of pinks and oranges and she wished she could take in the view under better, *normal* circumstances.

"This is it," Sawyer said from behind.

Part of her didn't want to look. Part of her wanted to watch the sunrise and pretend she was out on a scenic walk.

She turned anyway and saw more police tape, a few plastic markers on the ground.

"They were here?" she asked, walking closer, kneeling down.

Sawyer nodded. "Your son and his... *abductor* were last seen here by a local man, jogging through the trail yesterday morning."

"Yesterday morning?" Eric asked. "Why the hell wait so long to call it in?"

Sawyer shrugged. "Some people need time to process something bad. You'd be surprised how often people wait to call things in."

Daphne shivered.

"Not that anything bad has happened *here,*" Sawyer told her. "Just a turn of phrase."

"Where'd they go?" she asked.

Sawyer pointed down the trail. More evidence markers. More piss-yellow tape. "We spotted some footprints deeper into the park. We'll take a look once it gets brighter. Any minute now."

"Brendan, Eric and I have something to show you." She'd nearly forgotten about the book, still clasped in her hand. She held it out.

"Not exactly in a reading mood, Daph," he said.

"You will be." She handed it to him and his eyes widened as he studied the cover.

"*Lords of the Deep.* This the book I saw on your kitchen table?"

"The very one."

"Are you telling me this has something to do with your son's disappearance?"

"I think it just might. In fact, I think it has to do with most of what's going on in Lea Bay."

"Care to elaborate?"

"My old man wrote it," Eric said, fingers on the crown of his nose. Daphne could practically feel his headache and embarrassment from here. "And before you say anything about him, I know he was completely off his rocker. Hell, the whole town knows it."

"I knew Karl, all right." Sawyer rubbed his chin with the back of his hand. "Our fathers were friends, you know."

"Yeah. I've heard that story."

Sawyer nodded. "They used to get together and talk about all kinds of strange stuff. I think your old man rubbed off on him. Caught his crazy."

He's rubbing off on all of us, Daphne thought.

Sawyer turned the book over, opened it, and flipped through a few pages at random. "What do you want me to do with this?"

"I want you to read it," Daphne said. "I want you to read it and keep an open mind along the way. And when you're done, we'll talk. But in the meantime, I want you to find my boy." She was crying now, wasn't sure when the tears had appeared. "Eric and I—we had a little run-in with the mayor. And if you think we sound crazy, you should hear him. Sawyer, this town, well, there's something living here. Something rotten, something—"

Sawyer's radio hissed. "All officers, respond, over. Unknown incident at the local docks by Washington. Possible fatalities."

They eyed each other in the morning sun, neither one speaking, only breathing shallow breaths.

The docks.

Where Donny had met his end.

Where this whole thing had started. The docks meant water and the water meant—

"Repeat," the radio's voice said. "Possible fatalities."

CHAPTER TWENTY-SEVEN

Rick Lopez shivered beneath the bedcovers. For the last hour, he'd been running over his options. The first was obvious—keep running and never look back, get as far away from Lea Bay as possible. The second was what he'd been doing so far—hiding out in this cheap, filthy motel just outside the city, waiting for the whole situation to blow over. He didn't like the idea of heading home once the dust settled. Who knew what the cops had figured out, if his crew ratted?

Who knew if Donny's walking corpse had been discovered.

There was a lot wrong with option number two, so he glossed over to option number three—head back and fix whatever was wrong with Lea Bay. Whatever *he* was responsible for, whatever his actions let loose in his hometown. He, with the help of three desperate deviants, had stolen that treasure chest, brought death to Lea Bay. Death and something much, much worse.

Since he'd left town almost a week ago, he'd come down with night terrors. The dreams showed him all sorts of things, mostly Donny being alive when the deep wounds in his flesh and the dull-gray color of his skin suggested otherwise, not to mention the sea monsters that had risen from the depths of the ocean to attack a cruise ship he'd been on. Not any old cruise ship either, *The River Queen,* one of Lea Bay's most profitable tourist attractions. Whenever he closed his eyes, he found himself onboard with his friends, Kevin and Barry, getting hammered and acting like fools, drunk and celebrating something, what exactly the dream never revealed. Then the voiceover kicked in, *Donny's* voice, speaking the same words from when he'd come shambling into his apartment almost a week ago: *"The treasure. Where is it?"* Repeated over and over again, getting louder and louder until it sounded like the voice was his own.

Rick had seen the last of the treasure when he'd cast the gold coin into the ocean, when he'd seen a serpent as tall as any building in Downtown Lea Bay rise from black, midnight waters. He'd shed the treasure and the burden it carried, but, for some reason, he still felt weighed down by its power. As if the coins continued to line his pockets. Fill his shoes. As if he'd consumed them and they now sat at the bottom of his belly.

They were all gone. He'd made sure of it.

The fourth option, the one he'd given the most thought to, was to nestle his chin on the end of a shotgun barrel and pull the trigger. That'd surely stop the dreams, the haunted feeling that had followed him here.

But no matter how attractive oblivion seemed, he couldn't find the strength to go through with it. Lying beneath the covers, spread out on the mattress that felt more like a stone slab, he leaned toward redemption. He wanted a chance to make things right. Rick wasn't a bad man. He'd done some bad things, *stupid* things, had tarnished his reputation over the years. But deep down, he wasn't bad. Now he needed to prove himself. To Daphne. To the cops. To the people of Lea Bay, the people he'd known since he was a child.

He threw off the covers, put his shoes on, and dressed quickly. He left the week's rent on the bed and dropped a little extra for the maid. Then he was out the door, heading toward his Civic.

Heading back toward Lea Bay.

* * *

When he crossed the town line, an indescribable wave crashed into him, almost causing him to lose focus on the road. He felt heavier, an invisible weight pressing down on him. In the distance, he thought he heard change jingle as if in a pocket.

I'm losing my mind, Rick thought. *Losing my goddamn mind and it's all because of that goddamn treasure chest.*

If he'd known then, he'd have told their mysterious buyer to fuck off. Half a million or not, no price was worth this madness.

He drove with no clear destination in mind. The coast was his best bet. Captain Cove's Marina, the place where Donny had turned up dead. Rick stomped on the gas, ignoring the whispering, the constant stream of voices that heckled him.

I need to stop this before I lose my shit. For real.

Treasure. Where is it?

It took ten minutes to reach Captain's Cove. He put the Civic in park, left the engine running just in case. The sky looked ominous. Dark clouds assembled over the cove. The stillness of the water unsettled him, and the phrase *calm before the storm* never held more meaning.

Rick advanced toward the docks. He noticed the police had roped off several sections of the marina with caution tape. The area near the shoreline, where Donny was said to be found, caught his attention first but he didn't allow his gaze to linger there. Instead, he focused on the docks where the boats were being kept, despite the grim horrors that had taken place. He wondered if that was the police's doing or if the boat owners had simply left them out of convenience. Judging from the ample usage of caution tape, he went with the former.

Rick ducked under the tape and headed down the wharf. He surveyed the waters, and as he did so, the voices in the back of his head, that incessant chatter, amplified. He heard them more clearly, a thousand conversations at once. Men's voices, women's voices, children laughing and playing. He heard people praying, or what he *thought* were prayers. Behind it all, he heard Donny's voice—his raspy, dead voice—asking about the treasure.

Where is it?

Where is it?

The treasure, where is it?

Rick clapped his hands over his ears but it did nothing to drown out the sounds.

In the distance, near the horizon, he saw a faint slice of greenish light. It glowed near the edge of the cove where the water met the rest of Barnegat Bay.

And it was getting closer.

Rick strained to see. He used his hand as a visor, shielding himself against the ascent of the morning sun. It did nothing to help him see into the distance. He waited for the green glow to make its move.

Then there was a flash as if from a camera, a bright green explosion.

And the object that had been in the distance was suddenly closer. A ship with black sails, something that looked four-hundred years old. The emblem on the sails showed two crossed swords, white, forming an X, and curled around them was a drawing of a snake. The wooden structure sailed toward him, a hazy green aura outlining its massive frame. In big block letters, *The Black Ambrosia* had been painted across its hull.

He made to back away but his legs had gone numb. Fear had rendered his limbs useless.

Another green flash and the ship was closer, approaching the docks much faster than should have been possible for a ship that size.

His paralysis finally broke but when he turned, something flashed in his periphery. *Two* somethings. They flanked him. He turned to the left and saw a figure, a thin, nearly-transparent image of a person dressed like a pirate. His beard was tied in three separate braids. He set one hand on the top of his sword, ready to free the blade if need be. Rick opened his mouth but nothing came out. The pirate, face soiled with dirt and grime, arched his back and glowered at him. Rick felt something hot on his right ear and he knew someone was behind him, breathing. Heavy, labored breaths. The scent of his newfound friends invaded his nostrils, and he smelled rotten fish and something sour, perhaps the stink of a thousand dead sailors.

He wrestled with the invisible rope that tied itself around him. The ship's shadow had fallen over the wharf. The faded image of the pirate, the one standing near the edge of the pier, began to stroll toward him, boots clacking on the loose deck boards.

"What do you want from me?" Rick asked, finally locating his voice. "I'm sorry I did it. I'm sorry I took the treasure. I didn't know!"

Nose-to-nose, the pirate glared at him, deep into his eyes, into his soul. He sniffed Rick like a dog meeting a stranger's shoe. *"He is not of the blood."*

"What does—hey, what does that mean?"

Before Rick could receive a response, he felt his restraints untwist from his body and fade away, though he didn't have a chance to enjoy his freedom. An invisible force plowed into him, knocking him off his feet.

Water rushed all around him. He choked. Struggling to find the surface, he waved his arms in a panic, kicking his legs as if his life depended on it. And his life *did* depend on it. There was a presence in the water with him, he could sense it.

Finally, he broke through the surface, staring up at the baby-blue sky. The cove was aglow with the rise of the eastward sun.

The ship was gone. So were the pirates. Vanished as if they hadn't been there in the first place.

I am *crazy,* he thought. There was no other explanation. In the near distance, he still heard those voices. Maybe they were from his dreams, the ones where he was partying with his friends on the *River Queen.* Maybe that was what he'd heard.

And Donny, of course.

Where is it?

Rick swam toward the shore, doggy-paddling because he'd never been taught properly.

Something splashed behind him.

He corkscrewed around. Nothing there. Just displaced water, moving fluently on the surface, a bubbly white foam.

Something was out there with him, that dark presence he'd sensed underwater.

A shadow fell over him. He turned and expected to see the ghost ship, *The Black Ambrosia* towering over him, ready to crush every bone in his body and leave him floating amongst the cove.

But what he saw wasn't a ghost ship. Or any other ship for that matter.

It was a monster. The long-necked beast he'd seen when he ditched that last coin. The coin that had somehow climbed out of the chest and into the front seat of his Civic.

The sea serpent opened its maw, revealing endless rows of hacksaw teeth, ready to shear through skin and muscle. Rick got the impression that the sea serpent was smiling, if such a thing *could* smile, savoring these final moments.

He was a good thirty yards from the shore; he considered pleading with it. The thing was here because of the treasure, the coins. It was all connected.

"Please," Rick said, crying now, tears mixing with bay water. *"Please, I didn't mean to. Didn't mean to steal it."*

Slowly, the serpent lowered its triangle-shaped head, smoothly navigating through the air, cutting the distance between its prey in half.

"I can get it back," Rick promised. *"I can help. Please! Let me help you!"*

The monster opened its mouth, lashed through the air toward its target.

The last thing Rick heard before the lights went off was, "WHERE IS IT? WHERE IS THE TREASURE?"

CHAPTER TWENTY-EIGHT

When Jake saw the ship in the distance, he thought he was dreaming. Big and dark and old-looking, like something out of a movie. The sun was just coming up and Dad and Grandma were fixated on the thing. They watched without moving, spoke to each other in those voices that reminded him of ghosts, only... *worse.*

"Aye, she's here. She's finally here," Dad said, his dead eyes wide and staring.

"Never thought I'd see the day. The Black Ambrosia... she's back." Grandma held a hand to her chest as if touched by the sight. She didn't seem to notice as one of her fingernails fell to the ground. Her skin was getting worse. So was Dad's. They were both sick. Literally falling apart. Jake was certain now. He wasn't sure what kind of cold or flu could do that to a person, make their skin shrivel and turn the color of a rainy sky, but he knew it couldn't be good. Knew they needed to find a doctor soon before it was too late. But he also knew they wouldn't listen to him. He'd already asked a thousand times if he could go see his mother but was only met with riddles. Told he was *of the blood* and only the treasure would summon the rest of the Lords. Whatever that meant.

He cleared his throat and gave it one last shot. "Dad?"

No answer. His father still watched the bay as the ship, surrounded by a cloud of green smoke, drew closer. From far away, he saw shapes moving on the deck. They looked like his father, only worse. More bone than skin.

"Dad?"

Nothing.

Transfixed on the scene before him, he held a decaying hand over his decaying eyes to block the morning sun.

Jake knew it would be wrong to sneak away. His parents had always told him to stay where they could see him. Never wander off or else. There were strangers out there. Strangers that drove white vans and collected children. But if he was being honest, he'd rather try his luck with the vans than stay here a moment longer. He was tired and hungry and frightened beyond description. His father was supposed to protect him but safety was the last thing on Jake's mind. It was weird, watching Dad and Grandma as the ship approached the harbor. Weird because he was beginning to think they weren't the same Dad and Grandma they'd been last week. Like they were *something else* pretending to be his family. The thought had kept him up most of the night, while they'd slept within the woods on a bed of tick-infested grass. His scalp tingled. And not just from the possibility of parasites.

It's okay, he told himself. *They won't mind—if they're really your dad and grandma to begin with –if you just slip away for a while.*

He was fairly certain that if he followed the docks toward the street and kept walking straight, he'd reach downtown Lea Bay. Main Street. And from there he could either take his chances going home or try the police station. There were probably people looking for him now. Neighbors. Classmates. He'd been gone a long time.

He closed his eyes and gulped and tried to wash away the guilt.

"Dad," he said, much softer this time. "I'm going home."

Dad cheered, though Jake realized moments later it wasn't in response to what he'd said.

"They're hungry tonight."

"Hungrier with each day, they are," Grandma said, watching the tide.

In the distance, on the docks, a man fell into the water. He flailed around, swimming this way and that, and for a while it looked as though he'd make it back to shore.

Until something large broke through the surface and pulled him under.

The same something that had appeared when Jake had tossed the coin into the water.

A monster.

It hoisted the man into the air and though Jake couldn't hear the crack of his spine from this far out, he felt it. The man stopped moving after that. Stopped swimming. The thing pulled him under effortlessly.

If it wasn't before, the choice was clear now.

He backed away slowly, never taking his eyes away from Dad and Grandma, not until his feet touched pavement.

Not until the pirate ship vanished in the distance, behind the trees.

Not until he was certain he'd slipped away undetected and they weren't following him.

Then he turned around and ran and did not stop until—

* * *

"How're you holding up?" Eric asked.

"How do you think?" Daphne stretched and yawned and took two Excedrin, washed them down with lukewarm coffee. Earlier, she'd managed to drift off for a half hour or so, before waking up in a panic. What had she missed? Had the cops called? Had Sawyer discovered any leads? Since then, she'd called him twice but there was no news. She'd showered and eaten dry toast and decided that sitting around the house and biting her nails wasn't the best use of her time.

"What're those?" Eric pointed to the kitchen table where a stack of printer paper sat in the corner, next to the stapler.

"I'm making flyers."

He nodded. "Good idea. Mind if I help?"

"Suit yourself."

He sat across from her, sipping from his own mug. They worked in silence for a while, neither speaking until Daphne heard sniffling. Not her own this time. She looked up and saw Eric crying, holding his hands over his head, shoulders hitching.

"Hey," she said. "It's going to be okay."

"That's what I've been telling you all morning. Look where that got us."

"It's true."

He shook his head. "It's just something to say. Who the hell knows what's going to happen? I don't mean to sound pessimistic but I came here less than a week ago and now half my family's gone. And I didn't have much of one to begin with."

Daphne set down the flyer and slid over to him. It was her turn to be strong. "You have me. I'm your family and right now that's good enough. It has to be. We're going to find them, okay? You said so yourself and it doesn't matter if you were just trying to lighten the mood. We *will* find them. Your mother is tough as nails. *Tougher.* And Jake. Well, he's got his father's genes. The good ones, anyway. He's resourceful. Has been since he weighed ten pounds. You know we baby-proofed this entire place, Donny and I, but it made no difference. That boy found a way into every nook and cranny he wasn't supposed to. And I know he can find his way *out* of a bad place. I have to believe that right now. Okay?"

Eric nodded slowly. "Okay."

"Now help me finish these, will you?" She forced a smile, went back to her side of the table and tried to hide her worry. Deep down, she agreed with Eric. He wasn't being so much pessimistic as he was *realistic.* Her mother-in-law had been missing for twelve hours, her own son more than twice that. The odds were not in their favor. But she had to hold onto something. If not hope, then these flyers. They were pitiful, would probably catch no one's attention, but they were a start.

Her hands grew shakier with each completed flyer. She'd used a picture of Jake from last year, holding Skeletor in his circular clear fishbowl, and smiling his gap-toothed grin. It was a pleasant memory. Donny had been just out of frame, home for the afternoon. Such a rarity.

It was a happy memory but one seen through the lens of nostalgia. In reality, Jake had just finished crying two hours prior, watching his parents argue and not understanding that his dad was riding high on something. Skeletor had died a few months later.

She set the flyer down, guzzled the rest of her coffee.

"I'm going outside for a cigarette," she said.

Eric looked up from his work. He'd only finished two and a half. It was going to be a long day. "Since when do you smoke?"

"Since I was sixteen. I'm just good at keeping secrets."

She grabbed her pack from the junk drawer, hidden beneath a small pile of take-out menus. Neither Donny nor Jake had ever known. She usually only smoked late at night when the day's stress had weighed her down. But now there was plenty to be stressed about in broad daylight.

She stepped outside. The summer air was unusually chilly but the sun warmed her skin regardless. It was too bright to do anything but wince, so she lit up with a lighter that nearly failed her three times, and held a hand over her eyes.

"Mommy? I thought you said cigarettes were bad?"

Her mouth hung open at the sound of the voice, the cigarette sticking to her lip, still smoldering. She looked toward the street and saw no one, nearly chocked up the phantom voice to nerves. Until she looked to her right.

Standing next to his small junkyard of Tonka trunks was Jake Jordan, the last good thing in her life.

A mirage, she thought.

A hallucination.

A ghost.

"Mommy?"

The boy stepped forward, freckles and gap-toothed and all.

She flicked the cigarette, didn't even think about snuffing it out with her foot. "Eric! Eric, get out here quick!"

She ran.

Jake ran.

They met each other in the middle of the front walkway. She hugged him fiercely and in that moment she was certain she'd never let go. "Where were you? God, I thought we'd lost you."

"It was Dad," he said. "I was with Dad. And Grandma."

"Sshh, it's okay, sweetie." She rubbed the back of his hair, dirty and greasy. Poor thing. She'd run him a bath first thing when they got back inside.

From behind, the door screeched open. "Daph? What is it? Everything o—"

He skipped the steps and jogged toward them, kneeling down and making it a group hug. He sobbed and so did she and she asked once more where Jake had been.

"I told you. Dad tricked me. I went with him. He's not who he says he is. He's not really Dad and neither is Grandma. They're just pretending. I think they might be... pirates or something."

Daphne and Eric eyed each other.

"You're just exhausted is all," she said. "Not thinking straight."

"I'm thinking fine," he said confidently. "And you need to believe me because once they realize I'm gone, they're going to come here and find me. But they're not the only ones who are bad. There are other things."

"Other things?"

He nodded, looked around as if they were being watched.

"Things in the water."

CHAPTER TWENTY-NINE

"We have to get him somewhere safe," Daphne said, running her fingers through her son's hair. Exhausted, Jake had fallen asleep on the couch about twenty minutes after he'd told them the story of being abducted by his father. Daphne had felt her skin crawl as he relayed the information. *He's not really Dad and neither is Grandma. They're just pretending. I think they might be...pirates or something.* It couldn't have been the truth but she'd seen so much over the past week—mysterious shadows in the bay and a hidden book with tall tales of a pirate cult calling themselves The Lords of the Deep—that she couldn't immediately discount her son's claims. Part of her had believed every word. "Somewhere where they won't come for him. Where they can't *find* him."

Eric nodded. She was surprised to see her brother-in-law buying into Jake's story. No skepticism on his part whatsoever.

"You believe him? You believe your mother and brother are out there? Possessed?"

Eric rubbed his chin and paced back and forth. "My old man practically gave his life buying into this shit. He loved us, me and my brother. He loved his wife. He wouldn't have abandoned us if it weren't for the right cause."

She nodded at the small leather-bound book poking out of her purse. "What do you think your father intended to do with that?"

"I think he meant to stop whatever is happening in Lea Bay right now. And I think he did. Once. With the help of your boyfriend Sawyer's father. And, I think, a guy named Horace Dweyer. He's mentioned in there, too."

"That Historian guy?"

"Yes. I think, together, they helped stop this thing before."

"What does the mayor have to do with it then? Why is he hoarding the treasure? Is he protecting it?"

Eric shrugged. "Judging from what we overheard, I don't think he's protecting it."

Her eyes fell back on Jake, his still body. She watched his chest rise and fall. She wanted to hug him, hold him tight, but also wanted him to sleep for as long as he could. He'd need his rest for the coming days. *We all will*, she thought, and couldn't even imagine the hardships ahead. They would have to do what Karl Jordan had done thirty years ago. They would have to stop The Lords of the Deep from rising. "I don't understand. What's he want with it?"

"Well, according to my father's journal..." Eric plucked the book from Daphne's purse. He leafed through torn and tattered pages, stopping on the desired section, his finger running down the edge of the paper, locating the line and reciting it aloud: *"He who possesses the Lord's plunder, possesses the power of the sea."*

"Power of the sea?"

He turned the page and showed her the sketches.

"Oh..." she said, glancing at them. "Them. Those... *things.*"

The next page was filled with drawings of sea monsters, beasts from the aquatic deep. Tentacled behemoths and a serpent that resembled a fire-breathing dragon.

As he turned the book around and glanced down at the sketches, Eric cleared his throat. "I think our good mayor, Frazier Wilton, doesn't want to protect Lea Bay. I think he wants to destroy it."

"Why on Earth would he want to do that?"

Eric furrowed his brow. "I have no idea. The only person who does is probably Frazier himself. I doubt we'll get close enough to ask him."

Daphne sighed. All she wanted was a good nap, an eight-hour slumber to recharge her battery. She pictured herself next to Jake, the two of them sleeping for days. But she knew that wasn't possible, not now. Her dead ex-husband and ex-mother-in-law were out there somewhere looking for Jake, and it was best to not be here when they came looking. *Hunting*, she thought. *When they come hunting.*

"We need to meet back up with Sawyer. He can help us."

Eric rolled his eyes and turned.

"What is it?" Daphne asked, huffing. She stood up from the couch and crossed her arms. "You two have been at each other's throats since the moment you came home."

"I just don't like the guy." Eric placed the book back in Daphne's purse.

"He's just trying to help."

"Yeah, help himself to a piece of you," Eric said under his breath.

"What was that?"

"Nothing. Forget it."

"So he has a thing for me. So *what*? I don't see how that matters when we have a dead pirate cult on our hands."

"It's just..." He spun to her. "It's just you're my brother's wife. That's all. And I don't like how he looks at you. I mean, technically, you're still married."

She stood there, silent and still, for at least twenty seconds. "I'll let you in on a little secret, Eric. I've been *technically married* for a while now."

Eric scratched his scalp. "Yeah, I know. My brother had his problems. That still doesn't give Sawyer the right—"

"I was going to leave him."

That shut him up. Eric stopped mid-scratch and stared at his sister-in-law.

"I tried, Eric. I tried to fix what was broken so many damn times. But after six arrests and twenty rehab stints, I just couldn't anymore. I couldn't do that to Jake. I didn't want him to grow up knowing his father was a..."

"...was a what?" Eric asked, his upper lip twitching.

"That he was a fucking loser. A fucking *criminal.*"

Eric glared at her, the tension in his face tightening, and then, slowly, it all bled away and he nodded. "Yeah, okay. I get it. Just promise me you won't entertain that cop's googly eyes."

"I loved your brother," she continued, "and in a way, I still do. He was a troublemaker, but back then, he never *did* anything. He smoked pot with his buddies once in a while—I could deal with that. But the coke. The heroin. I mean, fuck, Eric, I caught him shooting up while Jake was *in the same room.*"

Eric put up his hands as if she were accusing *him* of something. "I said 'I get it,' Daph. I don't blame you for wanting out. I guess a part of me wants what's best for you and Jake. And what's best for you is not in Lea Bay. I got out and my life has been better ever since. I just thought you oughta do the same. Not shack up with some Lea Bay cop and spend the rest of your life in this shitty section of the world." He smiled. Genuinely, she thought. "But that's just me and my wishful thinking."

She nodded. "We can talk about this later. Right now, we have to get Jake out of here. If what he told us was true..."

"Then my brother and mother are on their way here."

"Exactly."

Eric sighed a heavy breath. She could sympathize. Her lungs were concrete, weighing down her entire body. "All right," he said, walking over to her. He kissed her forehead and suddenly he was the same Eric she'd always known. Surely he hadn't been acting...*strangely* during his time here. She was being unfair, complicating things that weren't meant to be complicated. They were family after all.

Weren't they?

"Let's go find your new boyfriend."

CHAPTER THIRTY

Sawyer hadn't had a chance to visit the docks since the call came in.

Possible fatalities, the dispatcher had said.

Possible, my ass, he thought as he surveyed the scene.

The place had been cordoned off just like the park. A crowd of curious onlookers stood behind the yellow caution tape. There were two other officers, Pike and Bradford, making sure the group didn't try to overstep their boundaries. They'd been partners for nearly a decade, were known as the class clowns of the force, but today they hadn't uttered a single joke. Instead, they eyed each other every now and then, perhaps thinking the same thing as Sawyer himself.

Something bad's coming.

Only... that wasn't right. Not after everything he'd seen these last few days.

Something bad *was already here.*

Evidence markers had been placed along the dock. He'd seen only a handful during his tenure. Today there were twenty-two.

A cool wind blew through the bay, whipping the first piece of evidence. A shredded flannel shirt that had become lodged on a stubborn nail. It had once been green. Now it was mostly red.

"Been a long time," said a voice behind him.

Sawyer shook his head and turned.

Hal Brooks, a borrowed county coroner, held out his hand. They shook. He hadn't seen the man in years, not since a drunk driver had wrapped his Volvo around a tree near the state highway a couple of years ago, when their now-deceased coroner was on vacation. That had been an easy prognosis. This, though—this was a bit more complicated.

"How've you been, Hal?"

"Just peachy. Doctor thinks my prostate's twice the size it should be and I'm up half the night pissing my brains out. Great otherwise, though."

"How're Jane and the kids?"

"I work long hours for a reason."

Sawyer nodded. Enough said. Hal had never been a family man, spent as much time away from his wife as legally possible. Whenever someone asked Hal why he bothered staying in the first place, he always cited her cooking as the culprit. Sawyer had thought it was a joke. Now he wasn't so sure.

"What about you?" Hal asked. "You manage to settle down yet?"

"Afraid not." He thought of Daphne again. He always thought of her.

"Maybe someday. Now, how about we talk about life's mysteries later and get down to business. Otherwise, I'm gonna have to piss off this dock in front of an audience, and that probably won't look too great."

Sawyer forced a smile. "What're we dealing with?"

Hal nodded toward the torn shirt. "I see you've already found exhibit A."

"Looks like the guy took a knife two dozen times."

"No way in hell that was a knife."

"How do you mean?"

Hal bent down, both knees creaking, and pointed toward the largest laceration with a latex-gloved hand. "See the way these rips aren't even?"

"Sure."

"A knife would've gone flush in but this... this is something different."

"Different," Sawyer said, testing the word aloud. He was beginning to form a theory. "Body must be in awful shape."

"Must be," Hal said, "though we haven't found it just yet."

"What?"

Hal groaned. "Sounds like Pike and Bradford forgot to fill you in on one important detail. There *aren't* any bodies. Not a single one. Only evidence of a struggle topside. My best guess is they were killed before they ever hit the water."

"Jesus. How many?"

"Hard to say. We've got two more shirts, a bathing suit, a mismatched pair of flip-flops, some glasses."

"How the hell did this happen without notice?"

"That's a great question. Whatever did this was in a rush." He began to walk further down the docks, toward the marina. "Come on. Something else I wanna show you."

Sawyer wasn't sure he *wanted* to see more. He *wanted* to go back to the station and punch out. He *wanted* to drink that six-pack in the fridge he'd been neglecting.

He *wanted* to call Daphne and tell her everything.

"You got a handkerchief?" Hal asked, stopping halfway down the dock, obscuring whatever piece of evidence he examined.

"Yeah, sure," he said, pulling the strip of fabric from his pocket. "Here."

"Not for me," Hal said, stepping aside.

A pile of innards lay in a heap on the splintered wood, dried out from their time in the heat. The flesh attracted a tornado of flies. Hundreds of them. Hal waved them away. Sawyer covered his mouth and nose, the acrid stench all too much for his senses to handle. "What am I looking at?"

"Hard to say. My best guess is intestines. A whole bunch of them. See, whatever did this, well, it must've been awfully big and, like I said, in a hurry. There are countless marks that match those on the fabric. So what I'm saying, Brendan, is that this whole situation is fucked. We won't know for sure until we drag the bodies up but I think you're looking at a massacre."

*"What*ever?"

"Not the response I expected, but okay."

"Just now you said 'whatever' and not 'whoever.' Twice now. And that gets my imagination working."

For the first time in all the years he'd known the man, Hal Brooks looked worried. His eyes narrowed. "Call it a slip of the tongue."

"Yeah," Sawyer said. "Slip of the tongue."

The two men stood in silence for a few moments, each staring into the ocean. The waves were picking up with the breeze and the water was a deep blue. Add the sun and the cloudless sky to the mix and it was hard to believe anything bad had happened here. Surely murder wasn't possible on a day like this.

Sawyer was growing lightheaded from the handkerchief and back at the station, a mountain of paperwork called his name. He thanked Hal for his help, asked him to call the moment they found those bodies. The two shook, firmer this time, and Sawyer made his way back down the docks. Past Pike and Bradford, who simply nodded as he stepped through the crowd.

A trio of reporters asked him standard questions he didn't exactly have answers for. How many dead? Foul play? Was there any cause for alarm?

More than you know, he thought as he stepped toward his cruiser and ignored the press.

Three more individuals stood near the hood of the car. At first, he took them for more journalists but the closer he got, he saw they were quite the opposite.

Daphne, hair blowing in the breeze. Eric, face contorted in annoyance. And—

"Jake?" Sawyer said, questioning his eyes. He was jogging now. *"Jake?"*

He knelt down, eye to eye with the boy. "What happened? Are you okay?" They'd only met in passing but now he felt a primal urge to protect the kid. He had to remind himself that Daphne was not his wife and he was childless.

"Don't bother," Eric said. "He's going to tell you his dad and grandmother kidnapped him, brought him to the beach, and summoned something out of the water. Oh, and there's a pirate ship somewhere out there too. We must sound crazier than before."

"You got that right," Sawyer said, thinking of the ripped shirt and torn flesh. "But after what I've seen today, I think you just might be on to something."

"It's the truth," Jake said. "I promise."

"I believe you, buddy." Sawyer ruffled the boy's hair. "Should he really be down here, Daph? You're feet away from a crime scene."

"If you think for one moment I'm going to let him out of my sight, then you must be the crazy one."

He knew then. Knew why he loved her so damned much. It was her maternal instinct. That survival gene that ran bone deep. Her family may not have been nuclear but she'd defend it to the death. And he hoped it would never come to that. Daphne Jordan was everything he'd ever dreamed of. Everything he didn't deserve.

He smiled. "Don't know what I was thinking."

"Look, there's more we need to tell you," Daphne said, her hands clutched onto Jake's shoulders, not letting him step away an inch.

"Why don't you come down to the station? I'm sure there'll be more questions than you can count now that your boy's back."

"We don't have time for that," Eric said. "In fact, I don't think we have much time left at all."

Sawyer eyed Daphne. "What's he talking about?"

"We'll tell you on the way."

"On the way? We going somewhere?"

"Yeah," Eric said, opening the cruiser's passenger door. "City Hall."

CHAPTER THIRTY-ONE

They'd lost the kid. *Their blood.* The last piece of this enigma. He'd been there one second, gone the next. As if he'd disappeared. Like a...

Ghost.

Like me, thought the thing that had assumed control of Donny Jordan's body.

Sally Jordan's mouth opened and growled a single name: *"Blackjack?"* Only it wasn't Sally Jordan who'd said it. The spirit living inside her flesh worked her mouth like a sock puppet. The one who called herself Anne Slaughter.

Blackjack *(Donny)* turned away from the bay just as the serpent—that dragon of the deep sea—dipped below the surface, just as *The Black Ambrosia* faded into the cracked light of down. The horizon was aglow with a warm, golden haze. Without any true enthusiasm, Blackjack said, *"Aye, my lady?"*

"You've lost the boy. The blood."

Blackjack nodded. *"Aye, we've lost him."*

"No, you *have."* Her lips writhed with disgust. She spoke with venom on her tongue, a deep rasp that poisoned Blackjack's spirit. He hadn't enjoyed it when she'd spoken to him like that in the *before times,* and liked it even less now. *"The Captain will be none too pleased with your carelessness. Graysoul won't like that you've failed him. Especially given your history of betrayal and such."*

Blackjack didn't respond. He focused on the calm waters of the bay, listening to the world around him. The sights were amazing. Since he'd returned from the void, that perpetual state of nothingness, he hadn't seen anything so beautiful. His journey back to the land of the living had been chaotic from the start. From the second he'd returned from the black abyss, the moment he'd crawled out of those eternal pits of suffering, he'd been tasked with missions that were not his own.

Now, with still so much ahead of him, he took a moment to appreciate his surroundings. The world that no longer belonged to him, to men of his time. He'd seen many changes since his resurrection, most of which he did not fully comprehend. Ships (for the lack of a better term) that sped across gravel and glowing devices of the devilish sort, magic machines and odd clothing. His mind had almost gone insane trying to figure out how those things were possible. Probably would have if he hadn't had access to Donny Jordan's memories. It was difficult to see *exactly* what the dead man saw, but he was able to see enough to keep him from wondering, to keep his mind from walking the plank and plunging into an ocean of insanity.

"Are you listening to me?" Anne asked, her voice grating. Blackjack Philips wished he had come back alone, *without* the rest of the Lords. But that wasn't the deal. That wasn't how the resurrection worked.

I gave up that life, he thought to himself. *I left the Lords.*

But the Lords of the Deep hadn't given up on him. A convert never left. Unless Captain Graysoul sent them off to Davey Jones' Locker with a sword in their chest, buried to the hilt.

Blackjack knew this because *he had tried.* More than once. He'd escaped, commandeered his own ship, and assembled a crew, but wherever he'd ended up, Graysoul and his crew of the damned were there to follow. There was no escaping the Lords like there was no escaping Hell.

And if the Lords *were* Hell, Graysoul was the Devil.

O Satan, Blackjack thought, looking out across the water. Even though his body was deteriorating, the majority of his flesh eaten away with rot, he found dawn on the bay soothing. It cured what ailed him, and what ailed him was being thrown into the twenty-first century, forced to do the bidding of men—*alive* men—men who wanted nothing more than control of the new seas.

His master had a name.

And that name was *Frazier Wilton.*

The rat bastard currently held all the chips, or in Blackjack Philips's case, all the gold tokens that had once been looted from the lost city of Babylon. A chest that was said to have once sat next to the throne of a god. And not just any god.

Tiamat.

A goddess of the ocean.

Mother of many sea monsters.

Blackjack sighed.

"Are ye listening?" Anne asked, her patience clearly diminishing. *"Ye know what we must do, yet, here thou remains? What ails ye? Speak thou troubles, my old flame."*

"Life," Blackjack said through his teeth. He faced Anne, looking upon her dark features. Dawn cast deep lines in her aged skin. Despite her fragile appearance, her host was still alive and she looked much better than he. It wouldn't be long before the body she occupied gave out, succumbed to the possession. It too would die, but if the body was healthy, if its owner had taken proper care of the vessel over the course of time, then perhaps the owner had a shot at seeing this through to the end.

"Life ails me," Blackjack said. *"Death too."*

"You're a bloody failure. We've been summoned. You know what that means, don'tcha? We do this, we can achieve what no one else has. Not even Graysoul."

Blackjack hung his head. So much death and chaos. Since his resurrection, he'd killed and done the will of others. He longed for the days when he was free, able to come and go as he pleased. *If the situation favors me,* he thought, *I'll earn my freedom once again.*

He knew what he needed to do. Betray the man who called himself Frazier Wilton. Betray Graysoul.

Betray the Lords of the Deep.

Kill them all, a voice spoke within himself, and he wondered if it belonged to the body.

But the soul within that encasement had perished, its thoughts along with it.

No, the voice within was his own. And it was correct—he needed to betray them, kill them all.

All of Tiamat's children, too. Those ancient water beasts.

It was a hefty task. It would require help.

"The master is summoning us to the center of town," Anne told him. He felt the pull, a tug on his invisible leash. *"You know the place?"*

"Aye. I know it well."

"Many ceremonies were held there. It's a special place. A place where Tiamat lives. A place where she breathes."

"I can feel her there."

"You seem less inclined than ye ought to be."

Fact was, he wanted to stay clear from the center of town, where Wilton held hostage a trunk full of Babylonian gold.

"Thou won't betray us again, will ye, Blackjack?" Anne's eyes seemed hopeful. *"Will ye?"*

"No," he said too quickly. *"I am with the Lords, until the last wave breaks and carries me off."*

"Are ye the pirate, Blackjack Philips, the savage warrior who dispatched an entire village of innocents in the name of your god, Tiamat? Are you that very same pirate?"

He swallowed. His gaze lifted toward the heavens. It felt good to close his eyes, and for a moment he felt as if he'd never open them again. *"So I am."*

She was closer now. Close enough to smell her. Not her carrier, but the woman who'd once gone by the name of Anne Slaughter, the most feared woman in the entire Atlantic, from the New World to the Old one. She smelled like fresh blood and ocean air, and when he drew in a deep breath he swore he heard the screams of every man, woman, and child who'd met the sharpness of her sword.

"Good," she said, snarling. *"Good. Graysoul will be proud. You'll prove your worth to him, to our master. To our god—to Tiamat."*

So many captains and masters and gods. Blackjack only cared about one thing—his freedom.

"Take my hand, my sweet," Anne said, extending her arm. *"We must do our master's bidding. We must raise Tiamat's children. It is the final piece. We will achieve enlightenment."*

"Aye," he said, bowing his head. *"Enlightenment."*

He grasped her hand and the two souls, misplaced in time, headed toward the center of Lea Bay, a place they hadn't been in over three-hundred years.

CHAPTER THIRTY-TWO

The man with the sunglasses, sitting across from Frazier, had not moved for quite some time. Though he didn't show it, he was scared. Frazier knew fear. Instilled it whenever he had the chance, which was often. He prided himself on that. "Mr. Wilton," the man said, "with all due respect, we should move the target to another location."

Frazier sat back, placed his feet atop the three-thousand dollar oak slab. "Son, those things have remained there for over three hundred years and they'll remain there much longer."

"It's dangerous."

"It's the way it is." He reached into the bottom right drawer and removed a cigar box. Took one for himself, cut the end, lit it. "Want one?"

"This is a no-smoking zone."

"I know," Frazier said. "I signed that bill." He puffed and blew rings of smoke out of his mouth. The doctor had been on his ass about quitting, cutting down on precious things like booze and red meat. No way in hell. He carried with him a deep burden, one that would drive a man of less intellect out of his mind. This town, these people, had no idea the amount of pressure he was under nearly every waking moment of his life. They didn't know about pirates and ancient promises, of priceless treasure and curses. And most of all, they didn't know how fragile their pathetic lives were. Everything could end faster than it took Frazier to puff his cigar or pop the cork off a nice deep red. So if he wanted to indulge himself every now and then—or every *day*—then his doctor could take a hike.

"Mr. Wilton," Sunglasses said, "if you don't mind me asking, what do you plan to do?"

"How do you mean?"

"There have been several sightings in the last day alone. We can't keep this a secret forever."

"We've done okay so far. What's another three hundred years?"

Sunglasses sighed, scratched at his sweaty forehead. It was a game of sorts. Frazier had admired the man's ability to keep his cool throughout this whole thing but now, under immense pressure, he was finally cracking. It was almost funny when you thought about it. This man was hired by powers much higher than Frazier, yet Frazier was the mayor and this was his jurisdiction. He was, effectively, the boss. And he'd put good old Sunglasses through the ringer recently. "What's your real name anyway?"

Sunglasses fidgeted. "I'm sorry, sir?"

"Your name. I don't think I ever caught it."

"I'm not at liberty."

"What about a code name? Anything like that?"

"Sir..."

"Because I've been calling you Sunglasses in my head. Doesn't really roll off the tongue, though, does it? Do you ever take those damn things off?"

"Mr. Wilton, I'd like to get back to the matter of the treasure."

"Sure, talk away. Talk until you're blue in the face for all I care but let me remind you who's in charge. I'm the mayor of Lea Bay, a town whose history gives me certain...*liberties*. So you can keep giving me that speech all you want but it's not going to get you very far." He pointed toward the vault. "That thing's staying shut from here on out and that chest isn't going anywhere."

He thought for a moment that Sunglasses had finally cracked. The veins in his neck strained like worms working toward the surface. His face turned dark crimson and beads of sweat dripped down his cheeks in teeny tiny rivers. He was going to speak up. Sunglasses was going to grow a set and lose his job in the process. Then, when he was relieved of his duty, Ear-Bud would be made first in command of the operatives. And Frazier would start work on cracking him too. Yes, life in this town was stressful, but levity existed in many places. You need only look.

The man said nothing, his jaw grinding back and forth. Frazier could practically hear the teeth chipping. "Nothing else on the matter? Good. Now, I'd like to talk about something else. As I'm sure you're aware, the pirate festival is taking place tomorrow. In light of recent events, we'll need to make sure there's triple the normal security. We've got thousands of assholes traveling to the Bay to take a picture with a pirate mime and get some shitty fried dough. The most trouble we've run into during the last decade is public intoxication and indecent exposure. Let's hope it stays that way. If need be, we can cut things short. Hell, my speech is pretty much the same as every other year."

"I'm not sure you understand, sir. Increased police presence isn't going to help matters."

"Those things don't seem to like the sunlight very much."

"I'm afraid you're wrong about that."

Frazier's mouth froze on the cigar. "You wanna repeat that, son?"

Before Sunglasses could utter another *Sir* or *but the coins, Mr. Wilton*, the elevator buzzed.

The red letters on the screen above counted down.

Two.

"You expecting company?" Frazier said, another cloud of smoke poured from his mouth.

Sunglasses watched the doors and though Frazier couldn't see his eyes, he sensed they were wide with fear. "No, sir."

One.

Sunglasses retrieved his walkie-talkie from his pocket but when he pressed the sole red button there was only static and white noise and what sounded like screaming. Surely a trick of the ears.

B.

Only one floor left. *This* floor. Frazier's office of twenty years. Not the place he shook hands and kissed ass and pretended to care about the citizens of Lea Bay, but his *real* office. The place where his true work was done. He'd created laws within these walls. Ordered deaths, too.

The light stopped moving.

The doors opened.

Green mist poured into the room. It smelled ancient, like rotting timber, like something left in the shadows for mold spores to blossom on.

Frazier spat his cigar into the trash and covered his mouth. He wiped at the mist but it did no good.

Sunglasses stood quickly, his chair toppling over. He backed away and for a moment he was inches from Frazier, hand on his pistol and preparing to draw, but then the mist covered everything. There was nothing in the world but a deep, dark shade of green.

And the sound of footsteps.

Several footsteps.

"Who's there?" Frazier said, feeling instantly foolish.

"Where is it?" said a voice, dry and raspy, as if it was speaking for the first time in hundreds of years.

"Where's what?" Frazier asked the unseen thing. His lips trembled and the cigar fell to the floor. He backed away, assessing how far away the elevator stood, but the mist made him dizzy.

"The coins. Where be the coins?" A different voice this time. Just as gravelly yet distinctly female.

"I don't know what you're talking about. This is a restricted area. I'm calling the police."

One of the individuals, though he couldn't tell which, began to laugh.

All laughs sounded the same in the dark.

"Sunglasses?" Frazier said. "Sunglasses, where the hell are you?"

No answer. The bastard had abandoned him, had probably managed to sneak away toward the elevator. Maybe he'd gone for help but it was doubtful. The way Frazier had put the boy through the ringer, he almost couldn't blame him for jumping ship. But if he survived this kidnapping or terrorist attack or whatever the hell it was, Frazier would make certain there was more than just a slap on the wrist heading his way.

In the mist, mere feet away, something rolled toward him, colliding against his feet.

He made to kick it away when he looked down and saw a milky white eye staring upward.

It was the first time he'd seen Sunglasses *without* his sunglasses.

His head had been severed, strings of red, ruined skin hanging from what had once been his neck. Though the room was small and he surely would've heard the struggle, the boy's mouth lay open in a silent scream.

From the mist: another giggle.

"Now, we ask again. Where be the coins, yer picaroon?"

"I don't know what you're talking about." He covered his mouth to keep his teeth from chattering. Could his pursuers see him? The feeling of cold, devilish eyes upon him prickled the hair on his arms. He backed away until the far wall touched his legs.

"We don't take kindly to liars and scallawags."

The mist cleared then. Not entirely but enough to give him a glimpse of the shapes standing before him. There were more of them than he'd thought. At least five. They blocked his exit and didn't seem to be in any rush.

The closest one stepped forward. His skin was mostly gone. His eyes were black craters surrounded by grey bone. Clothes tattered beyond return.

"Ye look surprised."

Frazier shook his head. "No way in hell. You're not real. This... this isn't real."

"But we are. We're as real as the sea itself. As real as the bay. As real as this." He presented a large curved sword and placed the tip against Frazier's neck. *"I ask once more, heathen."*

Surely Frazier Wilton, a man of the utmost character, couldn't betray his hometown at such a vulnerable moment.

But when the blade was pushed closer against his throat, he found his reputation was the last thing on his mind. He pointed toward the vault.

The shapes walked toward the opening and soon he heard the sound of the chest being dragged.

Then he heard the sword coming up and down and then he heard nothing.

He woke sometime later, wondering if he'd been dreaming or if he was indeed dead but he felt the cold wind on his skin. The world rocked back and forth, back and forth, and he realized he lay on a ship.

"He's awake," said the voice from earlier.

Frazier was lifted to his feet by a pair of skeletal hands. Here, on the deck, there were dozens of them. "Who are you?" he asked, though he'd known the answer all along.

"We're the Lords of the Deep and we thank you for yer service."

Among them he saw the chest and then he saw the sky as he was pushed backward, off the ship and into the water and just when he thought this was the worst of it, he felt something large latch onto his foot. It pulled him down and down and down until he could no longer see the surface. He sensed other forms surrounding him. Monstrous designs the size of city buses. His thoughts were confirmed when something sharp dug first into his shoulders, then his neck, and finally his abdomen.

He recalled the cigar back in his office, how wonderful it had tasted, how they always seemed to calm him on the most stressful of days.

He wished for one now.

But all he received was pain.

CHAPTER THIRTY-THREE

The unmarked SUV pulled up to City Hall under a twilight sky. There were no signs of life coming from within the government building. No lights on, not even a soft glow coming from the windows between the massive white pillars. Outside, the stars and a low-hanging crescent moon provided little luminance.

Sawyer hopped out of the vehicle first, wrapping his gun belt around his waist. He nodded toward Daphne, who was already climbing out of the backseat. "Where do you think you're going, lady?"

Her eyes narrowed as she froze in place. "Inside. With you. With all of you. And call me lady again, see what happens."

He ignored the latter half of her response. "Oh no you're not."

"We stay together, Sawyer. That's the plan."

Eric cleared his throat. "She's a big girl, man. She can make her own decisions."

Sawyer faced his slouched passenger, wishing they'd dropped him off at the nearest train station, saw him off back to Pennsylvania. "I don't remember asking you. It might be dangerous in there. I don't want to take any chances. Daph—you and Jake stay here, *right here,* and lock yourselves in. If you see a hint of trouble or we're not back in ten minutes, you drive on outta here. Head straight for the police station, find Jakobson. He's my lieutenant. You tell him everything. Understand? *Everything.*"

Crossing her arms, she mulled it over. "Fine. But seriously, call me *lady* again and you'll have more to worry about than pirates."

"Wouldn't dream of it. Now, Eric," he said, turning to the man who hadn't moved from his seat. "You're with me."

"Do I have to?" Eric asked, grabbing his stomach. "Not feeling well. I'd rather—"

"Get your ass out of that seat before I make you."

Eric Jordan hesitated. About ten seconds later he popped open the door and got out.

Sawyer waved Daphne into the front seat. "Come on. Let's go. It's best to get this over with as quickly as possible. I don't want to hang out here any longer than we need to."

Daphne planted herself behind the driver's wheel. Sawyer tried to put a hand on her shoulder, but she brushed it away.

"Hey," he said, returning his hand to his pocket. "I'm only trying to keep you and Jake safe."

She didn't respond, continued staring at the dark, abandoned road ahead.

Sawyer closed the door. He headed up the walkway that led to the steps of City Hall. Dark shadows waited for him at the top.

Dragging himself along, Eric followed. "So what's the plan?"

"Plan?"

"Yeah, what are you thinking?"

He reached the top step and turned to Eric. "You were the one who suggested we come here. I should be asking *you* about the plan."

"Well, in my Dad's book he mentioned City Hall a lot. And Frazier Wilton. Said he didn't trust him. That he was hiding something. Daphne and I saw Wilton down in the basement. He *was* hiding something. The Lord's treasure."

"And how's that connected to all of this?"

"According to Pop's journal, it's how they raise the Lords of the Deep. The monsters of the sea. Tiamat's children."

"Tia-what?"

Eric chuckled. "*Tiamat.* Babylonian sea goddess. Mother of the monsters. The Lords of the Deep, the pirate cult who had arrived at Lea Bay some three-hundred-odd years ago, they worshipped her. They thought they could control her sea monsters through a series of incantations and human sacrifices. And, of course, they needed the Babylonian gold believed to belong to Tiamat herself."

"How do you know all this?" Sawyer asked.

"Father's journal," Eric said, a bit too quickly if you asked Sawyer.

Daphne had shown him Karl Jordan's notebook and Sawyer didn't remember it being that detailed. There were drawings and newspaper clippings, a few articles written by Karl himself, but nothing that elaborated on the history of the Lords to that extent. Nothing that mentioned Tiamat, the Babylonian Sea Goddess.

"Do you know what happened to my dad?" Sawyer asked as he put his hand on the front door's knob. "Do you know what happened to John Sawyer?"

Eric only stared at him. Swallowing hard, he shook his head. "No. No, I don't."

"Are you sure? Your father never mentioned anything to you?"

Eric wagged his head. "I'm sorry, I wish he did."

Sawyer nodded, then tried the front door and was surprised to find it unlocked. The lockset loosened as he turned the knob and fell out when he forced open the door. The entire mechanism fell to the floor in several broken pieces. "Looks like someone beat us here."

The two men entered City Hall, but it was Eric who took the lead.

His stomach ache seemed to have vanished.

"The basement," Eric said, sounding worried now. A few minutes ago, he'd been acting like he couldn't care less. Now, he was panicked. "We need to head down to the basement."

"Hold on, chief. I should take the lead." But it was too late. Eric had already reached the stairwell.

Sawyer jogged to keep up with him. *What's wrong with this guy?* Sawyer thought, watching him disappear behind the industrial fire door. The more time he'd spent with Eric, the more off he'd seemed. Now, as Eric raced toward the basement without an ounce of regard for his own safety, he seemed more than *off.*

Manic was the first word that came to Sawyer's mind. The way he'd reacted to the question of John Sawyer's mysterious disappearance didn't sit well with him. Call it a cop's hunch, but he believed Eric Jordan knew a lot more than he was letting on.

He knows something, Sawyer assured himself. *Goddammit, he knows something.*

"Wait up!" he called down the stairs. But again, Sawyer was too late. He peered over the railing, down the stairwell, and saw nothing but the concrete that formed the stairs.

Eric Jordan had already reached the bottom.

Determined little bastard, thought Sawyer, his hand reaching for his gun belt.

Before he could set off after him, a familiar jingle sounded. He looked down at his phone and saw Kendall's smiling face, her Facebook profile picture staring up at him.

He almost tapped IGNORE but something about her calling— especially at this hour of the night—seemed urgent. He swiped ANSWER.

"Hey, Kendall," he said, hustling to the bottom of the stairs. "What's up?"

She sounded breathless. "Where are you?"

"I'm... um... out."

"Where?"

"I'm working. Why are you calling me this late?"

"Is Daphne Jordan with you?"

He didn't answer, not right away. "Why?"

"Is Eric Jordan with *her*?"

Sawyer's heart thumped. "What's this all about, Kendall?"

"Jakobson just received a call from some precinct in Pennsylvania."

"Okay... and?"

"It's Eric Jordan's fiancé, Anita Esporrin."

"What about her?"

A broad silence lingered, and Sawyer wondered if the call had been dropped.

"She's dead, Sawyer."

"Jesus," he whispered, making his way down the final flight of stairs.

"Yeah. They said she was murdered."

He stopped. "Murdered?"

"It gets weirder."

Sawyer looked through the small window on the door leading to the basement. He didn't see any movement—just an empty room full of dark shadows.

"She was found with her throat cut and all of these tiny symbols carved into her flesh. All over her body. They sent pictures over and I snuck a peek when Jakobson wasn't looking, and... it was *gross*. Her body was placed in the center of this white circle. The report said the murderer outlined her corpse *with salt.*"

"Sounds like witchcraft or something."

"Yeah, and also..."

"It gets worse?"

"They only discovered her body a few hours ago, after a neighbor reported a smell coming from their apartment. Sawyer..." She paused as if she'd run out of breath, "...you may want to sit down for this part."

"Just give it to me straight, Kendall."

"Okay," she said, flooding his ear with static. "They said it happened over a week ago. *Just before* Eric came back to Lea Bay."

Sawyer's voice-box seized, but he managed to croak out the words, *"Holy shit."*

"Look, Jakobson is about to issue a BOLO for Eric and Daphne. I wanted you to know first, in case, you know, you were with them. Might be a good idea to call Jakobson and keep him in the loop with...whatever it is you're doing."

Sawyer opened his mouth, but no words found their way out.

"Are you okay, Sawyer?"

He searched for the right response, but the best he could come up with was, "I'm not sure."

"I can meet you. You know, if you want some company."

"I don't think that's necessary." He hung up the phone and before pressing on, before throwing himself through the door, he took a moment to recapture his breath.

He killed her, he thought, *holy shit, he killed her.*

Not just killed her.

Sacrificed her.

Didn't he just say the Lords needed a human sacrifice? Was Anita Esporrin that sacrifice?

Sawyer cursed himself for not seeing it sooner. For not recognizing the signs. He'd left the son of a bitch alone with Daphne. He'd put her in danger.

And now, he'd left her alone in the car.

What if he's on his way back to the car right no—

Something struck him from behind. White, flaring pain spread through his skull. He stumbled to the floor. Something cold covered his scalp, crawling across his flesh like a tidal wave. He rolled onto his back and looked up.

"I'm sorry. Really, I am." Eric Jordan said, raising a fireplace poker over his head. "But I can't risk Daphne finding out. She can't know about my commitment to the Lords. They've already stolen back what belongs to them, Tiamat's treasure. The wheels are in motion, spinning their fate. Come tomorrow, during the Lea Bay's celebration, Mother's children will be released. Our Goddess will return us to the old world. There will be destruction. It will start here. But it will spread across the lands. It will cover the entire Earth. Then we will rebuild."

"You're... nuts..."

Eric didn't deny it. "There will be so many magnificent sights. So many *treasures*."

Sawyer went for his gun but Eric was too quick. By the time Sawyer brought his gun up, leveled off his shot, Eric was halfway up the stairs, bounding several steps at a time. Sawyer squeezed off several shots, none of which found their target. The bullets clanked against the stairwell, shooting sparks airborne on impact.

Sawyer used the wall to pick himself up. He could barely stand. There was no way he'd reach Daphne in time.

Quickly, he took out his phone and dialed.

Knocking his fist against the wall, he said, "Come on, Daph. For the love of God, pick up the damn phone."

It went to voicemail.

* * *

Something crashed against the SUV's window. Daphne screamed. Jake sprawled out on the backseat, kicking his feet wildly in the air as if whatever was outside had suddenly broken through the glass and went looking to grab him. But whatever caused the loud noise wasn't breaking in. It remained outside in the dark, lurking about the shadows.

Daphne's jaw dropped open. "No..."

"Hey, Daph," said a voice, and because of his position, Jake couldn't see who was there. He peeled himself off the seat and pressed his face against the window, looking to see who'd startled them.

It was Mr. Rick.

"Rick?" Daphne asked, voice shaking. His mother had never held a high opinion of Mr. Rick. She'd blamed him for his father's "missteps." In fact, now that Jake thought about it, she'd done a good job keeping his father's best friend out of his life. He couldn't recall the last time he'd seen him. Maybe his fifth birthday party?

"Daph!" Rick said, sounding out of breath. "Look, you're in trouble! There's no time to explain! They tried to kill me," Rick surveyed the area as if making sure he wasn't being watched. "But I escaped. God, it was close. You wouldn't believe what I've seen. Wouldn't believe me if I told you."

"You'd be surprised what I'd believe."

Jake leaned forward, sticking his head between the two front seats. "Mommy? What's Mr. Rick doing here?"

"Ssh," she said, kissing his cheek. "Relax. It's okay." She turned back to Rick, whose face took up most of the window. "Rick, what the hell are you doing here?"

"I tried to run. I *did* run. But there were people after me. And Donny..."

"You saw Dad, too?"

"I think they need him. For what, I have no idea." He hung his head. "I'm sorry I ran. I should have stayed, helped protect you guys. That's what Donny would have wanted."

"Never mind that now." She looked at the clock. "Look, why don't you get in and we'll talk about it, okay?"

Something zipped through the dark, landing on the back of Rick's head. His face smashed against the window, and Daphne looked surprised when the glass *didn't* break. Blood trickled out of his nose, leaving a small red trail on the window as his unconscious face sunk out of view. Jake heard his body connect with the pavement, and a new figure emerged in his place.

It was Uncle Eric.

And he was smiling.

"Eric!" Daphne went to open the door, but Eric slammed it shut. "No, you don't understand! He's on our side!"

Eric tilted his head to the side. "Stay still, Daphne. Things will go a lot less hostile if you just stay still."

"What?" She looked around the empty parking lot, back up the steps of City Hall. "Where's Sawyer?"

"Oh, he's around."

"Eric, tell me what happened. What is wrong with you?"

"Just keep your mouth shut. I don't want to hurt you. You may not be blood, *of* the blood, but you're family and I respect that. So, please, just don't try to stop me."

"Stop you from doing *what?*"

His whole body rotated and his eyes settled on Jake.

"No," Daphne huffed.

"Never trust a three-hundred-year-old-dead-pirate to do a twenty-first-century-man's job." He reached for the back door handle.

Daphne engaged the locks.

He snapped his head toward her, fury reddening his face.

She cranked the engine, but before she could put the SUV in gear, Eric was bringing something metallic against the window, shattering glass everywhere. Jake screamed and the SUV rocked and when she looked back her son was being dragged by his collar.

"No!" Daphne screamed, throwing open the car door. She hurried after him but stopped when she noticed the knife that had been applied to her son's throat.

"Don't take another step," Eric warned. "I don't exactly need him alive, Daphne. But like I said—we're all family and goddammit—I respect that."

"I trusted you," she said, and to Jake's ear, his mother sounded like a lioness growling at her prey.

"And I appreciate that. But I have to finish what my father started. I have to resurrect the beasts, the Lords of the Deep. It's the only way. Don't you get it? I'll be seated at the right hand of Tiamat. I'll be her warrior prince and she'll be my queen." Tears stained his eyes.

Jake didn't know what his uncle was blathering about but it sounded like lunacy, even to the ears of a seven-year-old. He dared not move because the cold metal started to dig into his flesh, and he felt something wet dribble down his throat. He clenched up, refusing to move a single muscle.

"Eric!" a voice called, and everyone turned their attention to the top of City Hall's stairs. Their eyes fell on Sawyer. He leaned on the pillar closest to the front door. "Drop the knife, step away from the kid. Backup is on the way. You won't get a hundred yards before they find you."

Eric called back, "You drop your gun, Sawyer! Or little Jake will journey into the Great Golgotha, where your father's soul awaits! *The Black Ambrosia* will arrange your transport! I'll see to it!"

"I'm warning you, Jordan! Drop the fucking knife!"

Eric only smiled. He started to back away, toward the forest that led through Lea Bay, down a path that would eventually lead to the cove. "Tomorrow is a big day for Lea Bay. I really do hope you attend the festivities. It's going to be quite the celebration!"

Jake quivered in his uncle's arms.

Eric bent over and whispered in his ear: *"Come now, child. Your father is waiting for you. Don't want to disappoint your family, do you, son?"*

And with that, Eric Jordan dragged his nephew into the darkness. Soon, his toothy grin faded into the shadowy veil of night.

Somewhere in the distance, black sails whipped in the south winds, signaling the world was ready to give birth to a new day.

A new epoch.

An epoch of minions and monsters.

An epoch of perpetual evil.

CHAPTER THIRTY-FOUR

9 HOURS LATER

THE PIRATE FESTIVAL

Saturday.

The weekend brought with it over a thousand tourists. The festival was Sawyer's least favorite event of the year. There had been talk of canceling the thing for years. Pirates weren't exactly the kind of thing to be celebrated. After all, they raped and pillaged and, after what he'd witnessed this past week, some harbored unhealthy obsessions with the black arts.

After last night, he'd brought Daphne back to his place, the very definition of a *bachelor pad*. A split ranch with one bedroom and an office the size of a port-a-potty. The walls were sparsely decorated, a photo of his sister, his five-year certificate of excellence from the police department, and a few tacky watercolors he'd bought at a knick-knack shop downtown.

"You should stay here," he told Daphne. "Although I wouldn't blame you if you didn't."

He expected her to protest but she remained quiet, walking through the living room and kitchen. "Nice place," she said, voice barely a whisper. Her face sparkled with fresh tears.

"Thanks." He made coffee, handed her a cup. She took it without meeting his stare. Her eyes were vacant, staring at something miles away. Staring, he supposed, at the memory of her son. Abducted for the second time in three days.

"Everything's going to be okay," he said, a promise he wasn't sure he could keep.

"You said that before."

He sighed. "It still holds true."

She sipped her coffee, black and piping hot, and if it burned her mouth, she gave no signs of pain. What she'd been through, the loss and the pain and the not knowing—it had numbed her. He wondered if, after all this was resolved, she'd ever truly be the same again. It was hard to recall how she'd looked with a smile on her face.

"I was wrong," he said.

"What do you mean?"

"I shouldn't have told you to stay in the car. You should've come

155

with me. Hell, you can take care of yourself. I see that now. I just…I don't know how else to say it but the thought of something happening to you, the thought of losing you—even if I don't have you in the first place—it's enough to keep me up at night. I've told every officer to keep an eye out for Jake and I'm meeting up with the search team right now. We're going to find him and I know I said this before but you have my word."

She studied her coffee as if it held some great secret. "Do you think you can ever know someone? I mean *truly*. Because I'm starting to think otherwise. All my life, I've thought I knew the people around me, but everyone has another side, don't they? Everyone wears a mask."

She was losing it, he thought. Any more trauma and she'd grow catatonic. It broke his heart yet he knew it to be true. "I'm not wearing a mask. Never have."

"But you *are* hiding something, aren't you?"

He looked at her for a long time, recalled all the daydreams and fantasies. Him and Daphne, walking down a beach, their toes sinking into the warm sand, holding hands and telling stories. He was pathetic. "Not very well."

She met his glance then, if only for a moment, and that faraway look was replaced with something else. Something he couldn't quite define. Something that put his mind at ease. But just as quick as the feeling had struck him, it began to fade. "I have to go," he said.

She nodded. "I know."

"I have something for you."

"Now's hardly the time for gifts."

"I beg to differ." He stepped into his bedroom. Clothes were strewn about and the place smelled musty. He hadn't opened the window in a long time, slept on the couch most nights. He opened the top drawer of his bureau, pushed aside a pile of boxers and socks, and revealed a nine-millimeter. He checked that it was loaded. It always was.

Back in the kitchen he set the pistol on the table. "Know how to use one of those?"

She nodded. "Been a while. My dad used to bring me to the firing range when I was a girl." She flipped the safety off. "It's coming back to me."

"Good. Use it if you have to. If anyone comes here that isn't a cop, hell, that isn't *me*, you point that thing in their direction and you pull the trigger."

They looked outside, facing the rising sun, studying the cloudless sky. It was hard to believe something so horrid could happen on a day like this. He thought back to Eric's words last night. *The Lords of the*

Deep. Tiamat's treasure. Mother of Monsters. "I don't know what's gonna happen today," he said. "It would be so much easier if we were just dealing with a nut job. If Eric was just out of his mind. But we both know that's not the case."

"If only."

He wanted to tell her much more, about how he felt and how he'd never thought Donny was good for her, but that hardly mattered now. His feelings wouldn't bring back Jake. He nodded at her once more, placed his hat on his head, and headed outside into the sun and the warmth and whatever lay beyond.

He did not look back, wondering, as he stepped into the cruiser, if she watched him leave. He liked to think she did.

* * *

After a huddle at the station, Sawyer headed toward the pier where the crowd was already starting to gather. Several food vendors were frying up sausages and peppers and the smell made his stomach rumble. He couldn't remember the last time he'd eaten. Yet the thought of pausing, even for sustenance, seemed wrong somehow. He passed the carts, passed the fried dough and cotton candy, the balloon animals and squirt guns, the tarot card readers, until he came to the water. He stared that way, waiting for a call to come in, though he knew it wouldn't be that easy. No leads since Eric took Jake last night. Going on twelve hours. They could've been past state lines by now but it was clear they weren't leaving Lea Bay. Not in the traditional sense at least.

He watched the crowd grow from a few hundred to nearly a thousand in less than an hour. Boys and girls, in full pirate getups, chased after one another, cheering. A group of college kids carried a cooler that probably wasn't housing lemonade. Somewhere nearby, a baby cried.

The podium near the edge of the street, surrounded by two poorly sculpted pirate statues, stood empty. The mayor would be giving his speech within the hour, yet there hadn't been any sign of him. He radioed officers Pike and Bradford, asked what the hold-up was.

"No idea," Pike said. "Not exactly high on my priorities right now. I'd much rather find Daph's boy than listen to Wilton talk out of his fat ass."

"I'm with Pike," Bradford said. "Guy probably had himself too much to drink last night. He'll show up five minutes late and slur his words and talk about good ol' Lea Bay for ten minutes before the fun starts."

"Yeah," Sawyer said, staring at the empty podium. "I guess you're right."

Something didn't sit well with him. Frazier Wilton may have been a full-of-himself, self-centered prick, but he was punctual to a tee. He'd once read Sawyer the riot act for showing up thirty seconds late to a town hall meeting. And not a particularly important one either. Bottom line was he should've been here by now. This wasn't just some fly-by-night carnival. This was the pirate festival, the source of about a third of Lea Bay's summer economy. He'd showed up early for the speech for as long as Sawyer had been on the force.

He shook his head, turned back toward the water. It didn't matter either way. What mattered was getting out there and finding Jake. Again. But that wasn't exactly right. It'd been Jake himself who made his way back home the first time. Sawyer hadn't been of much help then. He hoped that wasn't the case this time around.

Okay, he thought, breathing in the breeze and trying to slow his pulse, *if you were a freak show like Eric, on the trail of dead pirates and ancient deities, where would you go?* Somewhere out of sight. How many cave systems were there in Lea Bay? He could think of several off the top of his head. Kids got themselves in trouble plenty in Sting Ray Cove and that wasn't even the farthest cave. He figured that was as good a spot as any.

He lifted his radio to call back Pike and Bradford but his finger froze on the button.

A few miles out to sea, to the left of the lighthouse, a storm cloud was moving in quickly. He'd checked the weather that morning. No sign of rain or wind. No sign of anything but clear skies.

And besides, this wasn't a mere thunderhead.

Because it wasn't grey or blue or even black.

It was green.

It was green and it swirled in odd patterns like smoke. Making phantom shapes. A sunken face here, a deformed claw there. Sawyer blamed it on his nerves, told himself smoke couldn't do something like that.

The crowd went eerily quiet. All the cheers and the laughter were cut off as they collectively watched the mist roll in. Sawyer held his hands up as curious onlookers moved toward the edge of the pier. "Everyone stay back," he said. "There's no need for alarm."

The mother of three to his right seemed to disagree.

She screamed and pointed and he followed her line of sight as her children sobbed in unison.

There was something in the green. It was not just a trick of the eye.

Something like a ship.

A large, ancient ship with a black sail that fluttered in the sudden breeze. Even from here he could see the splintered wood and the suggestions of shapes huddled atop its hull. Too many shapes to count.

Impossible. All the boats should've been waiting in the southern side of the harbor, preparing for the dory races that afternoon. And besides, this was three times the size of any ship that should've been sailing so close to the shore. More akin to a cruise ship than a fishing vessel.

Sawyer's insides churned. It was all connected, he suddenly realized. Whatever this thing was, it wasn't a friendly Pirate enthusiast.

The Lords of the Deep, an inner voice screamed.

They're real and they're here in Lea Bay. Here to make their final sacrifice.

Jake. The plunder, those shiny gold tokens.

It all made a horrible sort of sense and he couldn't waste another moment. He made to use his radio but was met with only static.

"Pike? Bradford? You seeing this? Over."

White noise, harsh in his ears, and in the background was something that sounded like screaming.

"Guys, you there? We have an emergency at the festival. I repeat: *emergency*."

Again: nothing but distorted signals.

Before he could contact dispatch, he dropped the radio onto the ground as the first of the tremors shook the earth beneath him. The sidewalk split and cracked. Screams ripped across the crowd. Hundreds of them, and then a rush of quiet whispers.

The mist had almost reached the shore and the ship was moving much too quickly, those shapes growing closer by the second.

Surrounding the vessel, he swore he saw *other* shapes. Large, serpentine shapes. Something surfaced to his right, something with dark, smooth skin and a mouth filled with knife-sharp teeth. He only caught a glimpse of its eyes, its crimson eyes, but that was enough to weaken his legs. Enough to spike his adrenaline.

He told the crowd to get back once more but his voice was cut off when something propelled itself from the water and latched onto the mother with the screaming children. Its flesh was a patchwork of rough scales as it wrapped around her body and squeezed, twisting until red smeared through the crack. She managed to turn toward Sawyer, managed to reach out a hand, fingers frozen into a claw. She said something, though the words were lost in the screams.

He moved forward, trying to ignore the crowd and the serpent or snake or whatever it might have been. He got within inches of her, reached out with his own shaking hand.

Then it retracted back into the bay and she was gone altogether.

The crowd got the hint after that. They began to move back toward the street but they'd waited too long. The ship had docked and he saw those forms clearly now. Though he'd seen them once before, in that wretched book Karl Jordan had penned. The Lords of the Deep had made their return.

It didn't matter how far they fell back now.

Escape was no longer an option.

CHAPTER THIRTY-FIVE

(Fifteen Minutes Ago)

Under the darkening sky, *The River Queen* rocked against the fast waves the bay had thrown at her. The *Queen's* captain, Nathan Hayward, steered the tour boat toward the end of the bay, near the point of turning around, where he'd spin the old gal back to shore. He'd made the run so many times he could've closed his eyes and guided her back safely, but with the onset of the turbulent waters he figured it was best to pay close attention. As he stroked his whitish-gray mustache, the one his grandson always pointed to and called a *caterpillar*, Nathan scanned the skies, noticing how quickly the storm had assembled. In the distance, the horizon cracked with streaks of lightning, boldly defining the silvery shapes of slow-moving clouds.

Unexpected bad weather had come to Lea Bay and on the busiest tourist day of the year.

The goddamn Pirate Festival.

Nathan wasn't exactly a fan of Pirate Day. For one, he'd been the one to work the long Saturday, a day he preferred to spend with his wife, kids, and grandchildren. They had always attended the fair too, and right now they were probably uptown at Ruddy Park, where the town decorated the playground like a giant pirate ship. Or they were at the theater downtown, watching the local high school's rendition of *Treasure Island.* Or they were walking the boardwalk, soaking up the hot summer day, sharing pizza slices bigger than their heads or splitting a funnel cake. Whatever they were doing, they were doing it without Nathan.

Instead of enjoying the festival, he was forced to navigate a small cruise ship that was almost as old as he was. He had to entertain the fifty or so passengers, all of whom were drunk and couldn't give two shits about the bay's history, the coves, or the pirates that landed here over three-hundred years ago.

"And over there," Nathan said, pointing to a section of the bay that had been an infamous spot for pirate activity, *"was where Captain Graysoul himself led the infamous pirate cult, The Lords of the Deep, up to shore to meet the townsfolk of Lea Bay. It was a cordial meeting of sorts. Graysoul sought refuge from the Royal Navy, and in return, he was to give them treasures beyond their wildest dreams. I'm sure most of you are familiar with the legends and the rumors of the Lords. I'm here to tell you that it's mostly all hogwash. The treasures they promised the*

townsfolk were utterly worthless. You don't believe me?" He snickered, a phony reaction to the scripted story. He'd done so a thousand times before, would probably do it another thousand before he retired. *"Check out the display down at the old historical society."* And now a new portion of the script, added by town historian, Horace Dweyer, the man who'd gone missing over the past week. *"They've got on display the very same treasure from the Lords themselves!"*

Not a single one of his passengers seemed to care. They were too busy drinking their beers, talking amongst themselves, laughing at jokes Nathan hadn't heard over the cacophony of conversations taking place behind him. He almost stopped the story right there. Almost gave up. No one would have noticed. But then again, he was getting paid overtime.

Might as well finish it, he thought, holding the radio near his lips.

Before he opened his mouth, something moved beneath the water in front of him, near the buoys that warned him of going too far, the beginning of the Atlantic. Something big had passed into the bay. An enormous shadow. He swore it looked like a...

Nathan rubbed his eyes.

Did I just see that?

He followed the direction of the shadow and spotted it cruising toward the shore.

What the hell is that?

He turned back and saw another massive shadow taking shape, forming underneath the buoys like an oil spill, dark and sprawling.

Nathan began to panic. He hadn't realized he'd been holding down the button on the radio, filling the Intercom with static and his unintelligible mumbling. The passengers had taken notice, and most of them were facing him.

"You okay, Captain?" one of the passengers asked. The man, early twenties, sipped from his Miller Lite, a goofy smile playing on his lips. He scratched his scalp through his backwards Mets cap. "You look like you've seen a ghost."

No, Nathan thought. *Worse. I've seen a monster.*

Two monsters, he reminded himself.

The second shadow lingered near the mouth of the bay, and a fog began to roll in off the Atlantic. The encroaching clouds, thick and impenetrable, tumbled forth, bringing with it a shadow that rode atop the water.

Another ship. Torn black sails. An emblem of a serpent proudly raised. A crew of dead men, forty strong, crowding the deck. Behind the ghost ship, lightning crackled in the black roiling clouds. Faint outlines of skeletons belonging to long-lost behemoths were quickly shown in the bright flashes, quick glimpses into an alternate reality where beasts ruled the high seas.

Nathan felt the strength in his legs give out. He fell back against the cabin door.

Most of the passengers, after seeing their captain lose his balance, rushed over to him. They too looked out across the bay, saw the clouds and the phantom ship forming near the end of the inlet. Their jaws dropped in unison, and their jokes and laughter and good-natured conversations died and gave way to whispers of concern and disbelief.

Out of the water, a single tentacle stretched, climbing the sky slowly, whipping back and forth like an unmanned fire hose. Then another rose, sprouting from the bay like the blooming stem of a flower set in fast motion. Then another. Soon, several tentacles were reaching for the heavens, moving around, feeling their way through the air as if they had never done so before, getting a lay of the dry elements and the strong winds that had suddenly gusted.

As the tentacled beast rose from its deep sleep and stretched its limbs, Nathan put his trembling hand on the accelerator and began backing *The River Queen* away from the madness that loomed before him. He swore to himself that if he guided them safely ashore, he'd never set foot on the *Queen* again. Hell, he'd never dip his toes in the bay again. Retirement was the only thing on his mind now, and as the boat turned, facing the beach, he was confident that he could do it, reach land without disturbing the monster below. Whatever horrors had entered the bay would keep their distance. The terror he'd witnessed was not real. Illusions could not touch him.

He almost believed it.

From somewhere near the *Queen's* stern, someone screamed.

Nathan turned and saw one of the tentacles slither over the side of the boat and make its way across the deck. Another tentacle entered from the opposite side, crawling over the railing and squirming across the boards like a slug. Its pace was slow, almost relaxed, and if Nathan didn't know better, he'd say the beast was in no hurry.

Nathan grabbed the radio, and in the calmest voice he could muster, said, *"Everyone stay calm. Do not spook it."*

Nearby, a man shouted, "Abandon ship!"

As if the tentacled beast had heard him, it began its assault. One tentacle wrapped around the man who'd shouted and carried him off into the dark fog above. His screams faded as he traveled upward, beyond sight.

The *Queen* was quickly thrown into panic. People rushed the deck, searching for the first opportunity to hurl themselves overboard. Nathan tried shouting at them, telling them that that was the dumbest thing they could do.

"There are enough life preservers downstairs! Everyone grab one! We'll need to stay afloat!"

No one listened. Most of them were too intoxicated. One man climbed the roof and launched himself, but the beast snatched him out of the air before he hit the water. The tentacle hugged him tightly, coiling around his throat, cutting off his cries for help.

Nathan followed the man and watched him soar through the foggy atmosphere, the victim's movements becoming more sluggish as the thick purple cord squeezed him lifeless. Nathan followed his trajectory to the bay, and his mouth fell open when he saw a giant eye had risen to the surface. It blinked once and then opened like a mouth, revealing an entire bunker of teeth. It was larger than the *Queen* itself.

My god, Nathan thought.

It reminded him of a lamprey's mouth, the circular pattern of sharp points. When the tentacle brought the meal near the opening, it let go. The man dropped into the toothy cavity and disappeared when the Kraken sealed shut its massive opening.

It chewed. Then fed itself another passenger. Then another. One by one, the cruise's staff and guests were plucked from where they stood or swam, hoisted into the air, and delivered to the eager mouth of the sea beast. All this while the Kraken continued to break apart *The River Queen.* Nathan watched more tentacles board his ship. They constricted around the deck, snapping the boards as if they were chopsticks. The cracking sounds of splintering wood hit Nathan's ears and he imagined they were his own bones breaking.

Please let me get through this, Nathan thought. *Let me see my family one more time.*

He was hurled forward as the beast applied most of its weight to the center of the *Queen,* busting it apart with ease. The bow and the stern were launched into the air like an empty end of a seesaw. Before he could react, Nathan felt the cold rush of the bay all around him.

Clouds of white foam swirled around him, masking his underwater vision. The bay water was murky, even out here, away from the shore. A piece of flotsam bumped into him, and he grabbed onto what felt like a broken deck board. He rode the splinter to the surface and when he felt a cool breeze burn his face, he sucked in as much air as his lungs allowed.

But the scene ahead left him breathless again. Nathan counted eight tentacles, purple and thick as tree trunks. Each held in its grasp a survivor and was guiding them toward their deaths. *The River Queen* floated across the bay in ruin, the open water nothing more than a small junkyard of scrapped timber. That awful mouth harboring endless daggers continued to eat. Survivors from the *Queen* swam toward the shore, but Nathan was almost certain none of them would make it back alive, not with the quickness the beast had taken to its meals. It was in rhythm now. It had a system. If Nathan hadn't been so sure that he was next on the menu, he might have been impressed with its grace.

He paddled toward the horizon where dark clouds converged, hiding the entrance to the ocean in a shadowy veil. He could barely make out the two obsidian cliffs that partially closed off the bay from the ocean. Between the bluffs, the ghost ship sailed onward. *The Black Ambrosia* had set its course for Lea Bay. A faint green light glowed from the deck's hanging lanterns. Even in the distance, Nathan could make out the crew, those damned souls who'd sailed to hell and back. Who'd summoned eldritch beasts from the bottom of the ocean. Who'd pillaged and plundered and invoked Babylonian gods, leaving behind a legacy of death.

They're real, Nathan thought, floating amongst the wreckage. *The Lords are real and they've come back.*

Just before he felt something slither around his abdomen and squeeze his innards like a tube of toothpaste, Nathan Hayward locked eyes with the ship's captain.

Graysoul.

The man smiled and pointed and the beast below followed orders.

As the mouth of the beast claimed him, he swore he witnessed that old ghost smile.

CHAPTER THIRTY-SIX

For a long time, Daphne walked through Sawyer's home with no destination in mind. With *nothing* in mind. She picked up photographs and the occasional rare knick-knack, studying them without really *seeing* them. In fact, she didn't see anything. Not her reflection in the television's black mirror. Not the mug of coffee that had gone cold a half hour prior.

Not even the face peering in through the window.

Not at first.

She wanted badly to give up if she was being honest. She'd lost the one person in her life that hadn't had an ulterior motive. Jake was pure, the gift of childhood before the world soils you. He didn't care about her past, didn't care about her flaws. To him he was Mom and nothing more.

Leaning on the kitchen doorway, she pictured him. Not as he must look now, scared and crying and surrounded by *them*. She imagined him from a couple of years ago when they'd still been somewhat of a family. It was a special occasion, one where Donny wasn't drunk or high for a change. A Saturday morning if she recalled correctly. They'd gotten up early to surprise the boy for his birthday. First she'd made his favorite: pancakes with rainbow sprinkles and whipped cream, more dessert than breakfast but she hadn't once protested, not even when he'd asked for seconds and thirds. Then they'd gone for a walk through the park. Donny held her hand tightly, as if protecting her from something. As if part of him knew what was to come. She'd all but forgotten that detail. Small but crucial. He had loved her, her husband, though it didn't much matter now. After a lunch of burgers and fries on the boardwalk, she and Donny had taken their boy to the pet store to pick out his real gift.

"A puppy?" he'd asked, practically screaming upon entering.

"How about we start small, kiddo?" Donny patted him on the head. "How about a fish?"

Jake's smile wavered but only for a moment. Soon he'd forgotten all about the disappointment and he was pointing at tanks, saying *that one, that one*.

Twenty minutes later they'd come home with a new member of the family.

A goldfish named Skeletor.

Daphne sipped her coffee, surprised when the tears did not come. Perhaps there were none left. Perhaps she was done crying for good. She needed to stop standing around Sawyer's house. She was a stranger here, of no help to anyone.

But it seemed useless to search for Jake again. Surely she wouldn't be given a second chance at finding him. Surely he was gone now.

Surely—

Something caught her eye in the television screen. She'd flipped through the channels earlier, a western here, a talk show there. Caught the beginning of the local pirate festival coverage before shutting it off. Nothing but background noise and right now she needed to be alone with her thoughts. No matter how dark they grew. The day had clouded over but she could still see her reflection staring back, as well as the face inches behind her.

She spun around, and fell to the carpet.

Sally Jordan pressed a hand to the glass as if asking nicely to be let in.

She wasn't the same mother-in-law Daphne had known. She'd never quite gotten along with the woman. She was born out of time, fifty years too late. Her traditional values no longer fitted in the modern world and even though she wouldn't admit it, she was terribly disappointed with her son. The two had never argued. Not outwardly at least. But the tension was there, in her body language, in her cold stares and colder words. *You don't need college*, she'd said on more than one occasion. *A woman needs nothing but her man and children.*

But that had been a different woman.

This woman had undergone the same change as her son. Death and then some. Her skin, already aged beyond her years, was much too thin, now the color of ash. Bones peeked through in countless places. Her arms and face were littered with lacerations, yet Daphne saw no blood. No sign that she might have been alive.

Outside, behind the dead woman, Daphne could just make out the harbor.

The place was crawling with tourists but they didn't seem to be enjoying themselves as they had on television. Something had changed. Something bad. Many ran for cover while others stared in awe at the water.

Or, more specifically, at the remains of *The River Queen,* the tacky tour boat that Daphne had long despised, though there wasn't much left of it now. Bits of wood and metal bobbed on the surface while survivors clung for survival. Something else waded through the water. Something with large appendages.

We're too late.

Sally pressed her hand against the glass again. Harder this time. *"He wants you to watch. Wants you to see it all come to an end."* Her voice was a thousand knives being sharpened.

"Who does? *Donny*?"

"He wants you to watch."

"Where's Jake? Where's my *son*?"

Sally formed a fist and pounded the glass once more. A small crack appeared. It wouldn't hold for long. Her breath did not fog the glass, for no air lived within her lungs. *"He's one of us now. He's of the blood."*

Daphne dropped her mug, spilling her cool coffee. A dark stain soaked into the rug. She had to convince herself it wasn't blood. Not yet at least. She ran for the kitchen to find a weapon before she remembered Sawyer's gun. She'd left it on the counter, next to the half and half, but now it seemed blocks away because Sally Jordan wasn't the only unannounced guest.

The back door stood open.

And another corpse stood next to the table.

This one seemed much older and much more brittle. It was hard to imagine it had ever been alive to begin with. The cheeks were sunken beyond return and its eyes had long since dried to tiny husks. If it weren't for the thin, wispy beard, its gender would've been a mystery.

It tilted its head and studied her.

It blocked her way to the gun.

A cool breeze filtered in from outside, bringing with it a green fog that smelled strangely of faraway places she couldn't even begin to comprehend. Not a normal fog. No, the weather had mentioned nothing but sunshine.

The two watched each other for a long time while Sally Jordan bashed the window repeatedly. Daphne thought she heard the sound of splintering glass.

She could take this thing on, she told herself. She could defend herself against this centuries-old creature.

No, not just a creature. *A Lord.*

One of many and if she didn't get out of here quickly she'd never make it down to the harbor. If Jake was with them, then it was her only chance at getting him back—*again*.

She thought of Donny and Sally, both corpses now, thought of Eric and how he'd betrayed her during her hour of need, thought of all the screams and pleas that drifted in with the wind.

But most of all, she thought of all the sleepless nights, all the times she'd let life kill her one sigh at a time.

"You like coins, right?"

The thing responded by removing a silver sword from a sheath on its waist. The blade appeared freshly sharpened, glimmering in the kitchen light. Its bones may be brittle but the weapon wasn't.

"I've got some coins for you." She reached into her pocket, grabbed a handful of quarters, and tossed them across the kitchen.

The thing was not stupid. It knew these weren't its precious treasure, for those coins were with its brethren. However, the weak attempt to fool the thing bought her just over two seconds to reach forward, grab the gun, and aim.

It looked at the barrel and from its mouth came something like a laugh.

A horrible, deep-throated laugh that she would never forget.

She pulled the trigger.

The recoil came as a shock. It had been years since she'd gone shooting with her father and her aim was off. The bullet ricocheted off the blade and she ducked, narrowly missing the spent shell.

She shot a second round, this time just missing the Lord and hitting the fridge instead.

Steady your hand, her father said from somewhere distant. *Keep it steady and take a deep breath because there's nothing but you and the gun and whatever you're shooting at.*

Except those had been cardboard targets, not undead pirates.

But the advice still held true and if she didn't calm her nerves in the next few moments, she'd never see her son again.

Hands steady.

Deep breath.

Pull the trigger.

This time, the shot made contact with the thing's skull, blowing out the back and through the rear window. It went down quick but she wasn't convinced it was out of commission. After all, it'd already been dead before she fired.

She stepped forward, lifted her foot, brought it down on the Lord's skull, though *Lord* seemed too sophisticated of a word for this creature, this skeletal thing that should not have existed. She stomped on it three times, ensuring it would not get back up before she kneeled down and lifted the sword. Heavier than expected but she'd grow used to it. You could adapt to nearly anything, she'd learned these last few days.

In the living room the window was vacant again, though the glass had shattered.

No sign of Sally Jordan.

Daphne stepped forward carefully, the gun in her left hand, the sword in her right, but she didn't notice the television floating until it was hurled toward her. Her shoulders took most of the damage and she tumbled onto the floor, pistol sliding across the way.

Sally came at her quickly.

"I was wrong. It don't matter if you watch. Either way, you're already dead."

"So are you," Daphne said.

She raised the blade just as her mother-in-law dove.

Sally landed chest-first onto the sword, the tip sinking in with ease.

Daphne felt ribs crush like hard candy, felt the skin on the other side rip like wrapping paper but didn't let go until she stood back up and turned the blade, round and round, not until the thing that used to be a grumpy old woman stopped moving altogether. Then she pulled the sword free, lifted the gun, and stepped outside into a world gone green.

In the distance, she thought she saw a ship. Not *The River Queen* but something much larger and much older.

CHAPTER THIRTY-SEVEN

There was only green.

The mist hadn't just drifted in, it had unfolded like a cosmic blanket. Everything vanished from Sawyer's view. The boardwalk, the shops, the makeshift pirate statues—everything was gone. He could sense things happening nearby. Horrible things. Stay on the force long enough and you learned to use your senses differently. Just because you couldn't see something around the corner, say a dealer or a thief, didn't mean they weren't inches away, waiting to shove a knife in the side of your neck. Even in a small town like Lea Bay, a *quiet* town at one time, you always needed your wits. Things could turn sour on a dime.

But sour was an understatement for what had transpired here today.

All around him: screams. Pleas. Begging for the pain to end.

He moved forward, gun held high as if it would make any difference. The ground was slippery, though it hadn't rained for the last two days. The Bay was knee deep in a drought that had charred countless front lawns. He retrieved his mag light, shined it toward his shoes. Red. The ground was a dark shade of red that, combined with the mist, made him think of Christmas. Which in turn made him think of his father. He hadn't been the kindest man, hadn't always seen eye to eye with his son, but he'd been a provider. Someone you could, at the very least, respect. Now, though, Sawyer understood why his old man had spent so much time with his buddy Karl. Perhaps some part of him had believed he could prevent it. Hell, to even believe a fraction of what that damn book said, you'd have to be out of your mind.

Until you saw it come true of course.

But his father's involvement didn't matter anymore. Neither did Christmas or anything else.

Because the ground was soaked with blood.

Because something reached out and grabbed his ankle. He tensed, aimed his pistol, but it wasn't a pirate or a corpse. It was a teenage girl, her skin just as crimson as the ground on which she crawled. He bent down and pulled her forward, told her everything was okay. Help would be here soon.

She didn't respond, aside from a gurgle in the back of her throat. Even with the fog, he could see her eyes rolling back and when he pulled her closer, he smelled something metallic, something foul.

Her legs were gone, torn away, leaving only ribbons of hamstring meat in their wake.

"It's okay," he said as calmly as he could manage. "You're okay."

She lifted her other arm, mouth still moving in a silent plea, when something pulled her away.

She managed to scream after that.

Giggles in response to her dying breath. Giggles and the sound of flesh being torn from the bone.

He saw their shadows, the Lords, and he aimed, steadied his hand, fired.

He heard the bullet snag something, probably bone, but the silhouettes remained standing.

How could you kill something that was already dead?

He tried to call for back-up again, the tenth time in as many minutes, but was met with only static. No voice of any kind. It didn't sit right. One moment, he'd been talking to the dispatcher, Janine, her nasally voice cutting through him even during the massacre, and the next her words had cut *out*. Had the Lords managed to take out the cell tower? Surely that was beyond their means. How many were there? Too many questions, not even one answer.

But it wasn't just skeletons he needed to worry about.

He turned, walking slowly away from the water. Bodies lined the way, most of them still or in the midst of their final spasms. He wondered how many civilians had escaped before the shit hit the proverbial fan. Judging by the remnants, not nearly enough.

He tried to ignore the casualties, some of which he recognized. A postal worker here, a bus driver there. Good people. Sons and daughters, mothers and fathers, all of them dead because of something that shouldn't have been possible. He'd heard horror stories of first responders arriving to the scene of a mass murder or terrorist attack. They always noted the strange calm that took over, like the world stopped on its axis for just a moment, trying to cope along with you. Each time he'd heard such a story, his mind found it impossible to process.

Until now.

But the calm, they said, always led to a storm. And the storm wasn't just approaching. It was already here.

From the harbor he heard splashing, waves spilling water onto land. The wind was non-existent. It wasn't the breeze causing those sounds. It was those *things*. Serpents and something with tentacles. A giant squid or worse.

A kraken, he thought. *That thing you saw take out a ship with ease is a kraken. Doesn't matter how bat-shit crazy it sounds in that little head of yours. It's real and it's still out there. And if that's the case, who knows what's next. Godzilla doesn't seem so fictional anymore.*

He couldn't think on it too long, lest he lose what little sanity remained. What he needed to do was keep walking, keep stepping over limbs and heads until he came to Main Street. The force would be on lockdown. He could find a way inside and reassess the situation. Maybe their radios hadn't shit the bed. Maybe they could contact nearby precincts. If not, they'd send a party across the town limits. As long as they stayed away from the water, they'd be safe.

Right?

But what if there were other survivors, mere yards away, trying to stay hidden and silent and hoping to be saved? His efforts might be better served here but he was only one man, a flawed, tired, scared man.

From across the street, something moved within the gloom.

Though he couldn't see the shops, he could picture in his mind the butchery and the arcade, the diner that only opened when Gene, the head chef, felt like it. But Sawyer had a sneaking suspicion it wasn't that old curmudgeon coming toward him.

He held up his pistol again. His arms were weak and cramped, skin soaked with sweat and blood, the latter not his own.

"Don't come any closer," he said, feeling scared and foolish. If it was one of the Lords, he'd just given away his location.

The shape drew closer.

"I said hold it right there."

Closer.

"I'll shoot."

Closer.

"I will too," the shape said before the mist parted enough so that he could see her face.

In that moment, Daphne was as beautiful as ever. It didn't matter that her cheeks were bruised and smudged or that she looked as though she hadn't eaten a proper meal in days. Didn't matter that he was pining over someone who'd probably never love him back. What mattered was that she was here, alive, and together they would find Jake,

She held the pistol he'd given her and something told him she'd been forced to use it.

"We've got to get out of here," he said. "It's a bloodbath. Literally."

"No. Even though I can't see it, the harbor's right there. And that means so is Jake."

"What makes you so sure?"

"He might be dead. I know that. I'm not stupid. Not that pathetic. But if I were them, if I were a sadistic undead pirate who lived, so to speak, for pain and suffering, I'd hold on to him. Keep him alive."

"Why?"

She stared past him, into the wall of green. "Why else? To draw us to them."

The earth shook with something like thunder but the longer it lasted, he suspected it didn't come from the sky.

A roar. An inhuman roar that tore through the morning.

In response, the mist parted, pushed off to either side of them so that downtown and the State Park were still engulfed in green but they now had a view of the pier and the water and everything that inhabited the space.

He heard Daphne gasp from behind.

He didn't blame her.

In the water floated the remnant of the River Queen but there was another ship in its place. The Lords' main vessel. A flag flapped in the non-existent breeze. The logo was not of a skull and crossbones but the shape of some hideous thing with tentacles and teeth. Long, sharp teeth.

The ship had pulled up to the pier and docked. Shapes moved about, hurrying, preparing to step off the deck and onto land.

Two of the shapes were intact. No sign of bone or torn flesh.

The first was Eric, a grin spread across his face.

The second, struggling to escape his grip, was Jake.

Behind the ship, at least three snake-like forms lifted from the water. Large mouths opened, bits of skin stuck between the teeth, red foam dripping into the harbor.

Several survivors clung to shards of the River Queen but none of them made it very far.

Purple tentacles broke through the surface. From this angle they reminded him, oddly, of cotton candy. And something about the analogy seemed so preternaturally wrong. Cotton candy was for carnivals, for safe, fun places. But this place—this place was hell on earth.

The tendrils grabbed the hangers on with ease, lifting them into the air and snapping spines effortlessly. When they released the bodies, dropped them back to the wreckage, the serpents moved in, helping themselves. A vicious cycle with no end in sight. Not until everyone in the Bay was gone. And then they'd move on to the next town.

Daphne stepped forward, whispered into his ear. "I have an idea."

"It better be a good one," he said, watching the Lords shuffle onto the dock, reuniting with their other members.

CHAPTER THIRTY-EIGHT

Through the green, smoky veil, Rick spied on Eric and Jake. The kid was terrified, shaking uncontrollably. And with good reason: he'd just cruised around the bay on a fucking *ghost ship*. His uncle was holding his wrist tightly, causing the flesh around his grip to blanch.

Rick hung over the side of the ship, his feet dangling above the gun deck. It was surprisingly sturdy for something that wasn't truly there, a mirage in contrast to the real world. But it *was* there, and he could touch it, feel it, *climb* it. So he had, and the spectral ship hadn't vanished beneath him like he'd expected.

This shit is real.

He'd watched Eric and Jake make their way down the makeshift ramp, a messy assemblage of half-rotted planks and twine, and onto the dock. Rick's plan was to come around the back, sneak up behind Eric, and bash him over the head with a beer bottle he'd found floating in the bay amongst the *River Queen's* wreckage. He hoped the bottle would break, rendering the empty glass a jagged weapon. On the plus side, Rick had recovered quickly from his head. A killer headache continued to pulse on, but a few over-the-counter pills had taken care of the pain, and after several cups of black coffee, he'd been ready to go again.

Ready to help put an end to this madness, this chaos that he'd helped perpetuate. Rick clambered onto the deck. He started across the ship, swirling clouds of emerald moving out of his way like the lost remnants of ancient specters. Rick readied the bottle, picturing the way it'd break on the back of Eric Jordan's head. He imagined blood sluicing from the gash, pictured the violence so vividly he almost lost sight of the task at hand.

Something shiny flashed across his vision, missing his eyes by inches. The object hit the closest deck board, making a loud *thwacking* noise that shook Rick from his position. He backed away, glancing to his right to see where the attack had come from. At the end of the long metal blade, the semi-transparent shape of an arm reached out of the fog and grabbed the grip of the sword, which bounced back and forth with the same force it had been thrown. The pirate ghost, the unnamed member of the Lords, stepped out of the shadows and into the slab of dwindling daylight, grabbing the sword and wrenching it free. It turned and, all in one motion, swung the sword at Rick's head.

Rick ducked. The metal whooshed through the air and missed giving Rick a haircut by about three inches. He recovered, planting his feet evenly apart, and flung the bottle at the ghost's head, half-expecting it to sail through the figure as if the apparition were built like a hologram. But the bottle broke on contact, opening a scarlet line across the ghost's forehead.

The pirate scowled as a low, guttural growl emanated from the bowels of its throat. Feral, blood-orange eyes widened with rage. The pirate took the sword's handle in both hands and made a move, slashing through the air again. Rick backed away but not fast enough. The tip of the sword snagged his skin, ripping open his flesh. It hadn't hurt at first, but as he dodged another advance, the almost-numb sensation blossomed into full-blown agony. He looked down to find a stream of red leaving his body.

Then something stabbed him in the chest. He turned his eyes, saw the rusty metal protruding from the soft flesh above his heart. The smell of something rancid seized his nose, and he wasn't surprised to see the dead pirate had moved within an arm's length. The stink of a thousand gutted fish overcame the salty smell of the distant sea.

Rick dropped to his knees.

Goddammit.

Retracting the blade, the dead pirate abandoned its scowl and Rick watched the corners of its mouth curl. Satisfied with his work, the ghost examined the layers of blood that dribbled down over the sword's hilt.

I'm sorry, Donny, he thought as the pirate licked the blade clean. When it was done, the ghost slathered the lower half of its face with red—a beard of blood. A proud display of his victim's gore. *I'm sorry, Daphne. Sawyer.*

Jake.

I failed you all.

Rick wanted one more opportunity to undo his fuck-ups. But he'd lost his strength, his balance, and now he was struggling just to keep his eyes open. The ghost's shadow fell over him, blanketing him in darkness and fear. He watched the wretched thing draw its sword back, a slugger readying his bat for an easy grand slam.

Rick gulped.

In his last moments, he prayed to whatever god would allow this to happen, to whatever god would unleash these creatures upon their creation, prayed that they'd keep his best friend's son safe. Rick had done a fine job preventing Donny from becoming the father he'd needed to become. A bang-up job of getting him in trouble with the law. With his wife. With rivals looking to score the same jobs.

Watching the blade cut through the air, he thought about these things and more. Every mistake. Every wrong decision. Every broken promise.

Then the metal connected with his neck, embedding itself in the trunk of muscle and bone. Arcs of blood exploded from the wound. The blade stuck through his stubborn neck meat.

Before eternal darkness conquered his vision, Rick witnessed the nameless Lord finish the job as the apparition slowly hacked through the last remaining threads of pink tissue.

CHAPTER THIRTY-NINE

When Jake stepped off *The Black Ambrosia,* absolute fear crippled him. Ignoring the pain his uncle had applied to his wrist, he allowed new sensations enter him, a crawling numbness that spread from his chest and sunk to his toes. He hadn't recognized these new responses as apprehension and panic, not until he set his watery eyes on the small congregation before him. At least forty dead mariners, all of them expired centuries ago, sporting tattered coats and rotted gray flesh, collected at the base of the ghost ship, swaying back and forth on wobbly legs.

Uncle Eric finally let go of him. The man he'd never really known glanced down at him, hunched over, and whispered in his ear, "If a single fiber in your body moves, I'll hunt your mother down and fillet her like a fine piece of tuna." Jake could see from the look in his eyes that he was serious.

When his uncle stood and straightened his posture, he addressed the gathering.

"Lords," he said, changing the inflection of his voice. He spoke like a coach, leading his team into victory. "Lords, we have gathered here on this special day for an unprecedented event. It's no coincidence that the pirate festival of Lea Bay is held today. For it is a day filled with history. It is the day our savior, Tiamat, was summoned from the depths of the ocean, as were her beautiful beasts, her enslaved destructors, for all the world to see. But there were settlers in Lea Bay who stood against us. Fought us. Pushed Tiamat and her lovely creatures back into the void, abolishing them from our earthly plane. The treasures of Babylon were hidden from us for centuries, separated and distributed to different ends of the Earth. My father, rest his soul, sought these treasures, with the intent of bringing them back here, reuniting them with this town's history. He was a good man, mislabeled a fool and a kook."

Grandpa, Jake thought. *He's talking about Grandpa.* He'd heard plenty of stories about Karl Jordan—the bullies in school made damn sure he'd never forget. The naked walks the old man had taken, the crazy things that had come from his mouth, talk of gods and sea monsters, abominations of biblical proportions that rose from the deepest waters to feast on the townspeople of Lea Bay—sort of like what was happening right now. Maybe he hadn't been such a crazy person after all.

Either way, he was blood. And that scared Jake almost as much as anything he'd seen today.

"My father wanted to make sure this town's history was *never* forgotten." Eric pointed a finger toward the crowd. "And he wanted you, Lords of the Deep, to have your revenge on the people of Lea Bay, and to allow our god, our Tiamat, to rise to her position of power, her rightful place on the throne of existence." A knowing grin stretched his lips. "I've spent years in the backdrop, traveling the world, tracking down every piece of treasure, every goddamn token, collecting each one and putting it back inside that chest. Then I shipped it back to Lea Bay and paid some local criminals to steal it for me. One of them was my brother. He of the blood. The same blood that runs through you ran through his. Runs through *me*." He looked down at Jake. "And my nephew. We are of the blood, and together we will usher in the new epoch—one filled with the beasts of old."

One of the Lords stepped forth. In his right hand he held a sword, the blade long and curved. His beard had been tied into three separate braids. His frayed long coat flapped in the breeze, the storm that was nearly upon them. The captain's boots stamped the deck, leaving behind muddy prints.

"Ah," Eric said, settling his eyes on the pirate. "Captain Graysoul. It is an honor, sir." He bowed. When Jake didn't follow his lead, he pushed the kid's head forward until he understood what was being demanded of him. Jake arched forward the rest of the way on his own.

"Rise, ye sacks of flesh and blood."

Eric and Jake did as they were asked.

"For far too long have we sailed the waters between worlds. Now, thanks to ye devilish plots, we have once again found ourselves here, in Lea Bay, ready to do thy God's bidding. Ready to spread her knowledge and love over the lands, the seas, this earthly dominion."

"We are at your service, my captain," Eric said, closing his eyes.

Jake watched on in horror as a monster rose from the bay behind them. The sea serpent stretched out of the water, its massive neck extending above the ship. Bay water rained off its skin and slapped against the wharf in buckets. In its mouth, a lifeless human body dangled. When it reached peak height, it began to chew on flesh and bones. Blood spurted from its meal, drizzling over the Lords like a biblical plague come to life. Jake shielded his eyes, managing to block the crimson rain. But he wasn't able to block his ears from the victim's screams.

After the serpent threw its head back and allowed the crumpled body to disappear down its gullet, Jake turned toward the bay. It was full of frantic people swimming toward the shore. Behind them, the waters bubbled and whirled, creating pockets of tornado-like formations. And in those aquatic craters he spotted tentacles, alive and hungry.

The grabbing arms of the Kraken reached out and began picking off the swimmers one by one, dragging them toward their watery tombs. Their screams died instantly as they were dragged under the surface.

Jake squeaked with instant dread. *Am I next? Will those monsters get me too?* Then he started thinking about his mother, where she was and if she was okay. His head spun with dismal thoughts, a future without her. Tears spilled down his cheeks, unnoticed by his company. He pulled the collar of his shirt up to his eyes, hoping to hide his emotions behind the fabric.

The pirates, the Lords of the Deep, watched with admiration as their beasts—the serpent, the Kraken, and a third monster that looked like a three-headed version of Jake's favorite plastic plesiosaur—fed on the citizens of Lea Bay and the town's vacationers. The impending storm didn't seem to bother them. If Jake didn't know better, he'd say they welcomed it with open arms. Off in the distance, the tar-black clouds mingled with one another, forming a shape all-too-familiar to him.

It was a woman.

Jake heard the jingle of a belt buckle beside him. From the corner of his eye, he spotted Captain Graysoul, who towered over him.

"My queen," he said, his voice gruff and barely articulate. *"I give you, your Lords."*

The captain bent down on one knee, then hung his head. He rested his sword over his heart. The entire faction followed his lead, even Uncle Eric.

The enormous apparition taking shape over the bay wasn't just a woman.

It was a God.

"Tiamat," Captain Graysoul said with awe.

CHAPTER FORTY

"Where the hell are we going?" asked Sawyer, but Daphne kept walking away from the water. His voice was lost in the cacophony of screams and growls and waves and now, something else. He turned back, saw the clouds swirling like a tower-sized cyclone, saw them part and allow something to drop down from the sky. Even after what he'd seen, dead pirates, Krakens, snakes larger than boats, his jaw still hung open at the feminine form. He did not know who or what she was, but he did know one thing.

Every creature combined, every Lord put together, was nothing compared to her.

Her eyes watched him from afar, followed his every move, and he could sense them probing. Learning what he feared, warning without words that his days were numbered. As if he needed a reminder.

He jogged toward Daphne, just a silhouette in the fog, badly out of breath. He hadn't gotten this much exercise in years. Half the squad was morbidly obese. There was a time when this town saw no action. Now it was a war zone.

When he caught up to Daphne, holding a muscle cramp in his stomach, she was peering through the front windows of the hardware shop. The interior was covered with shadows, every light turned off. Most businesses had closed to attend the pirate festival. Not for the first time, he wondered how many people had been slaughtered already. Half the town's population? More?

"You want to tell me what we're doing?"

In response, she tried the door. Locked. A note was taped to the glass: *Will Re-Open Tomorrow, Maties.* "Cute," she said, bending down and picking something up. "Real fucking cute." Her hands curled around a rock. She told him to get back just before she hurled it, aiming at the piece of paper. The glass shattered and they covered their faces. She fished her hand through the new opening and unlocked the door.

The mist poured inside like something living, breathing, wanting to gain access to every nook and cranny of Lea Bay until it enveloped the entire landscape.

"Hope you don't plan on arresting me," she said, disappearing down an aisle.

"I'm afraid we have bigger problems to deal with." Back in the direction of the bay, things grew eerily quiet. The screams were still there but they'd lessened. Either everyone had already fallen victim or they stared in awe, just as he had, at their new visitor. Even now he could feel her, that thing from the sky, as if she were in the store with him. The thought of going back there, in the midst of such pure chaos, made his bladder shrink. But there was nowhere else *to* go. If they didn't try Daphne's plan, whatever the hell it was, this nightmare would only spread. Lea Bay was just the beginning. There was pressure on his lower abdomen and he wondered if this place had a bathroom. If he was going to die, he didn't want to do so pissing his pants.

He wandered the aisles until he found her in the back corner.

She'd already raided the landscaping section, held two axes and a machete to boot. He wasn't sure they'd be of much help, but it was better than nothing. He had one extra clip in his belt and something told him it wouldn't last long. She held the blades but her interest lay elsewhere. She looked at the display before her eyes and he saw for the first time how primal she'd become. In the face of danger, of potentially losing everything, she was no longer Daphne Jordan. She was something else. A feral being not unlike a Lord herself. Except she wasn't out for blood. Not human blood anyway. If anyone could get them out of this, it was her. Not him, an officer of the law with ten years on the force. When it came down to brass tacks, love was infinitely more dangerous than guns.

She examined the row of blowtorches carefully.

"Daph, I realize we don't have a whole lot of time but could you please, for the love of my sanity, tell me what you're thinking?"

She picked up the first one, miniature, no bigger than a bottle of water, but she didn't seem satisfied. She moved down the line until she found one more akin to a flame thrower. She lifted it, turned it in the air.

"This'll do," she said.

He stepped closer, inches from her face, from her bloodshot eyes that scared him almost as much as the bay. "I can't help if you won't talk to me. So talk."

She turned finally, looking him in the eyes for the first time since she'd arrived. "There's something I didn't tell you. Something I did without thinking and for a while there, I thought it was a grave mistake. But it might just be our only fighting chance. And it's a hell of a long shot."

She pulled something from her pocket.

"Back in Frazier's office, when Eric and I—that fucking bastard— were hiding out, I got to thinking. Stupid of me to think in the first place because we could've easily died in there, in that underground bunker with those... goddamn *things*. But fear does that. Makes you think ridiculous things. And it made me wonder if something like the Lords could ever truly fear anything. And the answer was painfully simple."

She held up her hands, and opened her palms.

And revealed four small gold coins.

"I reached my hand inside, Sawyer, when he wasn't looking. At the time, it was probably just a reflex, a way for my mind to take some sort of action. Call it fight or flight. I'm leaning toward fight."

Sawyer shook his head. "You shouldn't have done that."

"Maybe not, but I did. I slid my hand into that chest, grabbed four of them, and put them into my pocket. Don't you see? It's our only chance at having some sort of upper hand on them. These coins, their gold—it's everything to them. Their entire *existence*. Half the reason they came back in the first place. It's these coins that summoned those sea snakes, that brought forth a fucking Kraken. And they'll do anything for their gold. *Anything*."

"So, what, you're just going to make an even trade? Four coins for Jake? You really think they'll listen to you? You can't reason with the devil."

"No," she said, "but you can grab him where it hurts."

She raised the blowtorch with her other hand. "If they care about their precious treasure, then they sure as shit won't want to watch it melt before their dead eyes."

Sawyer covered his face. The quiet from earlier was turning back into screams of mercy. Whatever had come from the sky, that woman that made him want to piss his pants, was having herself a grand old time. "You really think this'll work?"

"It's the only idea I've got and you don't seem to be offering up any alternatives."

He sighed, scratching his stubble. "You know how to use that thing?"

"I'm a quick learner." She returned the coins to her pocket, set the torch back down, handed him the machete and one of the axes and started to walk away.

He placed a hand on her shoulder. "Daph, there's something I want to tell you."

"No time for talking."

He wanted to tell her how he felt, that he'd loved her for twenty long years. That it should've been him she married instead of a junkie. That Jake should've been *his* son. But none of that mattered now and quite frankly, it wouldn't have mattered even if they *had* wound up together. Because Daphne Jordan was a force to be reckoned with. Sawyer didn't deserve her. No one did.

He watched her head for the exit, then he followed.

The mist shrouded the store now, the shelves and aisles and counter

vanishing. There was only the fog and what lay outside.
He followed her toward the busted front door.

CHAPTER FORTY-ONE

The smoky statue of an ancient god lumbered toward the shore. Behind the gargantuan shape, bolts of lightning cracked the sky, stabbing the dark horizon. Walking across the water, Tiamat's massive form strode with confidence. Jake couldn't comprehend everything but he knew this: the smoke monster, this cloudy outline that oddly resembled his mother, had come to Lea Bay to destroy and conquer.

The closer Tiamat got to the docks, the smaller her stature became. What had started as a bonafide giant had now dwarfed into the height of a giraffe. Jake could hardly believe his eyes. When she was twenty paces from the wharf, she was the height of his neighborhood basketball hoop. The clouds that had formed her figure, contoured her face and accentuated her womanly features, had been lost during her travels and gave way to another form—a human-like appearance. His limbs shook, his knees barely enough to support him.

When the clouds cleared, Tiamat was naked. Her long brown hair draped over her shoulders, covering both breasts. Jake quickly scanned her body, noting her bronze skin and the ancient hieroglyphics that had been tattooed on her smooth flesh, then looked away out of respect. He knew he shouldn't be looking at a woman without clothes on, and the fact that she'd materialized from the sky complicated matters. Even though she was a woman, she was also something more.

She's a god, his uncle had told him.

"It's okay, Jake," Eric said proudly, bouncing on his heels with excitement. "Tiamat is a benevolent god. Do you know what that means?"

Jake hadn't the slightest.

"Means she knows mercy and will treat her servants kindly. Bow to her. Go ahead, son. Bow to her and grant her the respect she deserves."

The Lords of the Deep followed Eric's lead and bent at the hip. Some took a knee and lowered their heads. Tiamat's cold, dark lips stretched into a smile. Jake glanced up from the docks and took in the god's image. She didn't look *benevolent.* She looked scary. Like a witch. A hooked nose that held an awkward bend. Scraggly hair that fell down her back. Her teeth were outlined in black, the beginning stages of advanced rot. And her eyes. God, her eyes were practically on fire. He could see Hell within them.

Witch, he thought.

A naked witch.

Tiamat caught him staring, and Jake shifted his gaze toward the darkened sky.

"It's okay, child," Tiamat told him, those demonic eyes drilling through him. *"Behold your savior."*

"Tiamat, my Queen," Eric interrupted, continuing to focus on his feet. "It is an honor."

"Are you the one responsible for my resurrection?"

"Aye, my Queen. It is I who brought you back. Brought all of the Lords back. So that we can finish what you started eons ago."

Her twisted smile remained stapled to her face. She floated across the dock. She was thin, but not like his mother. Thin like... she was only an illusion, hardly a member of the physical world. Her body flickered as she approached, a light bulb threatening to fail. She had a dim radiance about her. One second, her body glowed, shimmered like the golden tokens Jake's uncle had unearthed from the farthest corners of Earth. Another second and her body went dark, cold and deathly.

It was an enigma Jake couldn't seem to wrap his brain around. Instead, he looked around for a way out. Away from her. If such a place would ever exist again.

The Lords occupied much of the space behind him. Even if Jake had the speed, he wouldn't get very far. His uncle had kept him close as if he were *expecting* the kid to run for it, sprint back to mommy.

Mom, where are you?

His eyes fell on the coastal town, much of it ruins now. People lay dead in the street, reduced to pieces and parts. Garbage tumbled down the sidewalks, the approaching storm whipping plastic plates and napkins into the air. Trees bent in the gales. Storefront windows had been smashed by residents seeking quick refuge. Overhead, dark clouds moved in, spilling shadows over Main Street. The Kraken slithered ashore, wrapping around streetlights and abandoned vehicles.

Everything around him was falling apart like one of those disaster movies where the main characters tried to survive a terrible global event. Jake wasn't sure if the event *was* global, but it sure felt that way.

Something cold touched his face.

He looked up and saw the goddess caressing his cheek, running her knuckles gently down his skin. The smile on her face seemed out of place, crooked. She was beautiful, yet she was broken too, the shell of a human being. Empty inside. A piece of her gone. As she touched him, he could almost envision her desires. Like in those brief moments, he'd become a part of her.

She wanted chaos, yes. She wanted her beasties to lay waste to Lea Bay before moving on to bigger and better things. She wanted this world

186

as her own. But most of all...

She wanted to be human. She craved the warmth of blood as it pumped through her, spreading life and joy. She wanted to know what it felt like to be alive. She wanted freedom from eternal damnation.

She wanted to be like *him.*

Jake's fear squirted down his right leg, dampening his jeans.

"No need to be afraid, child. Of all the elements of the physical world, fear is most easily conquered. Give yourself to me."

Without effort, he fell to his knees.

Uncle Eric said, "I have found you a physical body, Tiamat, my Queen. She's not of the blood. But she will work, I promise. My father believed, while the Lords needed to be bound to their hosts by way of blood lineage, yours does not. Your vessel—her name is Daphne. She is a worthy candidate. Strong-willed. Good heart. She's motherly, more so than any human I've ever met. She'll be willing to trade herself in exchange for the safety of *her blood.*" Eric glanced over at Jake. "She'll be willing to die for him."

Tiamat's face contorted with something like a smile. She grabbed Jake by his chin, and he felt her power course through his veins with an almost indescribable current.

Behind him, he heard loose change clink together. Tiamat turned her focus on the treasure chest that the Lords had dropped on the dock. The tokens glowed with a brilliant shine despite the crawling shadows born from the dreary sky.

Tiamat let go of his face and drifted toward the treasure. She babbled something in Babylonian, though to him, they sounded like random syllables strung together. Golden light flooded her face as she knelt down before it and thrust her hands into the sea of shimmering tokens. At first, she seemed excited with her gift, smiling and grunting in pleasure. But as she felt around the chest, digging up the tokens from the bottom, she seemed to notice something was wrong with her offering. Her smile fell off, one second at a time. Soon, her face was filled with concern. Then rage.

She screamed.

Her voice was a razor blade and it scraped the inside of Jake's skull. Loud and sharp, and after it was over, the shrill sound continued to echo inside his skull.

Tiamat spun toward Uncle Eric. *"The treasure. It's not here."*

Eric lifted his gaze. "My Queen. You must be mistaken. I've counted every—"

"You fool!" She marched over to him and gripped his face, much like she had done to Jake, only with more force. Eric screamed as his

flesh sizzled beneath her touch. Wisps of smoke curled into the atmosphere and Jake smelled his uncle's skin, an awful, acrid stench he wished to never smell again for the rest of his life. *"Four tokens are missing! Gone!"*

Eric struggled to move from under her grip, but Tiamat only applied more pressure. Layers of skin melted away, revealing raw, pink muscle underneath. Finally, she let go. Eric surveyed the damage with his own fingers, careful as the ruined flesh was tender to the touch. He glanced up at her, his eyes watering with alarm.

"The woman." Tiamat sniffed the air like a hound on the trail of something savory. *"She has them. She stole them from you. You fool. She must be stopped."*

"I'll stop her. I'll stop her for you." His voice trembled. "You have my word."

"She hasn't gotten far." Tiamat addressed her crew of the damned. *"Lords! Tear this city apart!"* Behind the goddess, her sea creatures stirred in the waters just off the shore. They seemed anxious, ready to come to land, wreak havoc there as they had the bay. The Kraken's tentacles retreated, shrinking back into the calm waters. *"My lovelies are limited without the treasure's unity. They'll be unable to come ashore without them. So find them. Marry them once again."*

The Lords spread out.

Uncle Eric shivered. Jake had never seen an adult so scared.

"You. Peasant. Help them." Tiamat's face *thinned*, her human features faltering, revealing the true nature behind the mask of skin and bones. Hideous, like a monster from Jake's wildest nightmares, her flesh charred and dimpled, her teeth long and sharp. *"Or I swear by Hell, I shall rip you apart for the rest of your eternity."*

CHAPTER FORTY-TWO

"Something's happening," Sawyer said, pushing the curtain aside and staring through the window.

He and Daphne stood in a bed and breakfast, just across the street from what had once been the pirate festival, now replaced with blood and bones. A massacre in progress. She followed his line of sight, thinking he was probably just scared. Under the circumstances, she couldn't blame him, but he was a cop. Shouldn't his survival instincts have kicked into gear by now? It seemed to her that the more shit hit the fan, the more his voice cracked and his hands shook. She'd need him calm and collected for what came next. Otherwise, they were, to put it lightly, fucked.

He was right about one thing, though. Something *was* happening. They watched as the Lords broke from their group, holding ancient swords toward the sky, chanting something she didn't quite catch. Five of them remained in place to guard the ship and the naked woman that had come from the sky.

Listen to yourself. You sound out of your mind.

But all things considered, it was the sanest thing to happen in the last twenty-four hours. A woman with the body of a goddess had descended from the heavens and now stood in front of the treasure chest. She did not blink or breathe or move. If you stared long enough, you could almost convince yourself she was a statue. But Daphne felt those probing eyes even if they remained static. Felt them searching for her and Sawyer.

"She's calling the shots now," Daphne said.

"But who *is* she?"

"We'll find out soon enough." She stepped away from the window as the Lords scattered further away from the pier.

"What're they doing?" Sawyer's voice was cracking again, on the verge of hysteria.

"Looking for *us*."

"They won't have to look far." He backed away and let the curtain fall back into place, cutting off what dim light was left of the day. Or was it night? The sun was nowhere to be found, shrouded in green mist. She closed her eyes and imagined a bright, sunny day but it was difficult to recall such a thing. Difficult to imagine the mist would ever clear.

The interior of the bed and breakfast was dark but she didn't want to risk turning on any lights. In the front foyer, on the floor, lay the remains of some poor woman, head cracked like an egg, brains oozing like a spent yoke. Had she been the proprietor of this place or simply someone who sought shelter from the end of the world?

The front desk was in disarray. Papers scattered and torn. Guestbook open to a blood-smudged page. The phone had been ripped from the wall, though she was certain there wouldn't have been a dial tone either way. Behind the desk, on the wall: a row of hooks, mostly empty, though a few held keys. She'd always wanted to stay here for a weekend, play tourist in her own town. But Donny had reminded her it was less than a mile from their house and would cost them half a month's rent. Unrealistic, sure, but alluring all the same. Like she could pretend she'd never been to the Bay. Pretend she wasn't married to someone who was sure to kill himself. But now, in a strange sort of way, she *was* a tourist. This wasn't the same bay she'd been born into.

A shadow appeared on the floor.

Something at the window.

She fell back against the wall, taking Sawyer with her. She held a finger to her mouth, mentally telling him to keep his jaw closed and eyes peeled.

They'd locked the door on the way in but it wouldn't keep the Lords out for long. She'd briefly considered finding something to barricade the entrance but then decided against the plan. She didn't plan on staying in here for long. That decrepit ship had docked and if Jake was anywhere, he'd surely be on board. Not for the first time she imagined what she'd do to Eric. Somehow, he was worse than all the ghost pirates and abominations the underworld had to offer. She'd been chased by things—super*natural* things—yet the most evil creature had been in her midst for weeks now. If only she'd had the intuition to sense it. Surely there'd been warning signs.

The doorknob jiggled.

The shadow moved.

Daphne and Sawyer were huddled just around the corner, just out of sight of the front windows. Another inch and they'd be spotted. She grasped his forearm, nudged him to follow her deeper into the hotel, but stopped short at the sound of breaking glass.

Followed by the click of a lock.

The door opened.

Warm, fetid air drifted inside, bringing with it the scent of saltwater and rot. It smelled like war.

She could hear them now, the collective drone of the Lords and the harbor swimming with behemoths.

The shadow grew.

Two shadows, she realized.

One tall, one short, both walking closer.

The blowtorch was several feet away, the coins still in her pocket, but she gripped the machete until her fingers turned white. A sweaty grip but strong. She wouldn't hesitate.

She caught Sawyer's eyes. He nodded, forehead dripping with perspiration. Hands wrapped around the ax. His pistol was holstered. They only had so much ammo and it wouldn't do much against an army.

She breathed deep, slowed her pulse as much as humanly possible. Which wasn't much.

You can do this. You can kill two of them with a blade meant to clear brush. You can use every remaining ounce of strength to find your son for the second time. And then, if you can't kill the rest of them, you can run. It doesn't matter how far. You can find shelter somewhere. A cave or a skyscraper. You can do this.

The shadows were huge now, moving past the floor and projecting on the key rack behind the front desk. They glided over the remains of the woman.

She raised the machete, blade catching the reflection of her reddened eyes. She looked like she'd been up for months. She looked like a madwoman.

She looked like Donny.

Just as she lifted herself to her feet, the shadows spoke.

"When are we going home?"

She covered her mouth to hide the gasp. Sawyer stood too, nodding at the same realization.

"Never," Eric said, stepping up to the desk. Stepping into view.

Beside him, just as red-eyed and scared as Daphne, stood Jake.

CHAPTER FORTY-THREE

"I can hear you, Daphne," Eric said, and Sawyer didn't need to see his face to tell the bastard was grinning. Sawyer's hands hugged the ax's handle, knuckles blanching against the rubber grip. "And so can Tiamat."

"Mommy?" Jake called.

"I know you have the tokens. I'm willing to offer a trade. Tiamat is a forgiving god. Very benevolent. She will forgive you for your transgressions against her throne. *I* will forgive you. Even Donny might when he sees you again inside the Golgatha. The Great Beyond."

Sawyer peeked over the check-in counter, past the computer monitor. Behind Eric, in the open doorway, appeared a wall of heavy green smoke. It moved like something alive, wispy arms curling toward the ceiling of the Bed N' Breakfast. In the tumbling fog Sawyer made out the silhouettes of the Lords.

He tucked his nose into the crook of his arm. The stench was awful. As the smoke poured into the lobby, Sawyer was reminded of sour milk.

"Give us the tokens, Daphne," Eric said. Jake tried walking around his uncle, but Eric stuck out his arm and snatched him. He looked ready to wrench off the kid's head if his mother didn't comply. "I have no patience these days. Please don't push me. My god might show benevolence, but me... well, sometimes my anger gets the best of me."

Daphne made to stand up but Sawyer stopped her. She shot him a death-stare, one he understood as *just-what-the-hell-do-you-think-you're-doing?* But he didn't care. She wasn't going to confront her brother-in-law. That was his job. Hers was to get Jake safely out of there. Away from this place. Away from the madness outside.

How many dead bodies? Too many to count. The dead lined the city's gutters. Parts had been strewn across the Gilford Park. Innocent people had been strung up and hung from the columns over City Hall, the hanging dead blocking the entryway.

He wouldn't let Daphne and her boy end up like *them.*

"Follow my lead," Sawyer said, and then stood up.

Eric's eyes widened at the sight of him. "Well, if it isn't the big ol' hero cop."

"Gig's up, nutjob." Sawyer eased his way around the counter and stood in the center of the lobby.

Eric tilted his nephew's head back, making the veins in the boy's neck bulge. "I wouldn't do anything rash, Sawyer. I'd hate to do something *bad* to him."

"Is that what you did to your wife, Jordan? Snapped her neck? Did you get angry? Couldn't control yourself? Then..." Sawyer snapped his fingers in the air, the loud pop echoing down the long hall behind him.

Eric's face reddened, a deep burgundy shade. "She tried standing in my way."

Daphne inched her way around the counter. "She figured you out, didn't she? You had this planned all along. She found out about your scheme, all the horrible things you were about to do, and... and she tried to stop you."

A proud grin split his face. "Yes. But she couldn't stop me. No one could. I was... determined. More so than my father had been. He could have done something great. He could have raised Tiamat from her watery grave. But he was insane. And worse, he was in *love*. He let my mother control him. Let her stand in his way..."

"But not you," Sawyer said, pointing the ax at him.

Green smoke tumbled through the doorway, faster now. "I asked her to join me, you know. But she refused. My lovely wife, she just didn't... *understand.*"

"Well, I don't blame her. Hard to understand the mind of a madman."

Eric chuckled. "It's easy to call someone you don't understand crazy. There are things in this world I don't agree with, things I'll never quite *get*. Politics. Policies. People who put mustard on their hot dogs."

Sawyer started to circle the room, hoping to close the gap. The plan was to keep the lunatic talking. Using his eyes, Sawyer told Daphne to circle the room in the opposite direction.

Doing so made Eric nervous. He stepped backward, allowing the green smoke to shroud his appearance. Jake's too.

"I always liked mustard." Sawyer was no psychiatrist, but if he had to guess, Eric had already launched himself into the deep end and was now quickly drowning. He needed to keep him talking so they could get close. Save Jake. Bring the town back from the brink of total destruction. "Always had a thing for it. Used to put it on everything. Hot dogs. Hamburgers. Even chicken wings. You ever dip chicken wings in mustard?"

Not fooled by their ploy, Eric glanced over his shoulder and caught Daphne sneaking around behind him. His reaction was to back up farther into the green haze.

While Eric focused on Daphne, Sawyer knew his moment had finally come.

"Step back!" Eric shouted, squeezing Jake's head. A small, shrill noise escaped the boy's mouth.

Sawyer lunged forward, swinging the ax. He let go of the handle and watched the tool spin through the air like a boomerang, only, this weapon wasn't coming back to him. He threw it just right, and the sharp end caught Eric underneath the shoulder blades, ripping away his shirt and drawing a scarlet line across his back. After hitting him, the ax spun a few more times, off its axis, and then hit the floor. It tumbled across the carpet and then landed, a small red trail of Eric's blood following in its wake.

Eric felt the ax's painful gift with one hand. The other he kept under Jake's chin, pinning the top of the boy's head against his chest.

"Now!" Sawyer shouted.

Together they rushed forward, sandwiching Eric and Jake.

Sawyer was able to get his arm under Eric's chin just enough to rip him back. Meanwhile, Daphne pried Eric's fingers off her son's face. Together they worked Jake free as the green fog began to cover them, that dead-sea smell polluting their lungs.

In the fog, they heard metal clanking together. Then, what sounded like a thousand blades being unsheathed from their scabbards filled the air.

Laughing, Eric said, "You forgot about my friends."

Sawyer hurled Eric aside and turned. The Lords appeared in the fog, packing the entrance and most of the lobby. Their eyes glowed in the haze, filled with hatred and the thirst for blood.

Eric threw his head back and howled with excitement.

Sawyer unholstered his gun and pointed, keeping Daphne and Jake behind him.

Eric Jordan, with his hands on his hips, clucked his tongue. "Naughty, naughty. Doesn't look like you have enough bullets for all the Lords. Not even half."

Sawyer shrugged. "I have at least one for you."

Before Eric could react, Sawyer pulled the trigger. A loud bang followed by deafening silence. The Lords hadn't moved, not a single limb. Their shrouded figures stood like ghostly statues, staring, awaiting direction from their master.

But instructions wouldn't come. At least, not from Eric Jordan's mouth.

A red dot appeared in the center of his head. Eric's jaw moved as if he were saying something but couldn't. He glanced up, looking at the ceiling or his new orifice. Sawyer placed bets on the latter.

As a small bubble of blood dribbled down the contour of his nose, Eric collapsed to the ground.

Before the Lords could react on his behalf, Sawyer turned to Daphne and Jake. Beads of sweat poured out of him, face glistening in the green glow of the crowded room. "Run!"

He followed them toward the emergency exit opposite of where the Lords had gathered, but not before he scooped up the blowtorch off the lobby floor.

CHAPTER FORTY-FOUR

For a while, there was only green.

The fog had grown so dense, the world was directionless. Daphne held onto Jake's hand too hard. He yelped several times, begged for her to lessen her grip, but if anything she clenched harder. Second chances were rare. Third chances? Damn near non-existent.

"Where are we going?" he asked, crying now.

Daphne and Sawyer told him to keep quiet in unison, though the kid had a good point.

Where *were* they going?

The rear exit of the bed and breakfast faced Main Street and further inland after that, though she couldn't tell if they were heading in that direction. By her estimation, they'd only walked straight, hadn't taken any turns, but it was impossible to know for sure. The fog played tricks, made things seem farther or closer than they truly were. Twice she'd walked into the side of a house, tripped over something on the ground. Something she'd told herself was a discarded traffic cone and not a severed arm.

And they were not alone.

Shadows flittered in and out of her periphery. There one moment, gone the next. It was *them*. The Lords. Playing tricks. They could see through the mist. She was certain of it. And because of this, she was doomed. They could walk for a hundred miles and still never be rid of them.

In her pocket, the coins, their only true defense, clinked together.

"What's our plan?" Daphne said.

"I'm all out of ideas." Sawyer kept his voice down. She suspected it wasn't just because they were being hunted but also because she held a boy whose mind was close to unraveling. He'd seen things no adult could comprehend, let alone a child. He was destined for a therapist, a few hours a week in a chair talking about the time some undead pirates rose from the deep to kill his family.

A therapist.

If we live to see one, she thought.

"You're the one who took the coins and the blowtorch."

"What good are they if we can't see more than a foot in front of us?" she asked.

"We're heading back into town. I'm sure of it. The post office is just up here, then the high school. Hell, if we keep up this way, we'll hit the highway in an hour, tops."

"How sure are you?"

But he never answered.

They froze as the fog began to spin around them. If moving had been disorienting, this was hallucinatory. Like being in the midst of a tornado's eye.

"Mommy? What's happening?"

She knelt down, eye to eye with her son. "It's just a storm. That's all. And this is the eye. Do you know what that means?"

He shook his head and cried harder.

She rubbed his bangs from his eyes, wishing she could do more to comfort him. But she herself was close to losing her composure. She couldn't be the mother he deserved. Not right now. But she made a promise to herself that she would make this up to him. She wasn't sure how but she'd figure something out. "The eye of the storm means we're in the middle of it. It means things are going to get bad again but that it's half over."

"I don't want more bad things," he said. "I can't take more bad things."

Me neither, she thought.

And then the fog cleared.

"Daph?" Sawyer said. "Daph, you'd better look at this."

She stood up, dizzy but not just from circulation.

Sawyer had been wrong. They hadn't been heading into town. The highway was just as far as it had been. The school and post office were nowhere in sight.

The pier.

They were back at the pier and they were surrounded.

At first, she took in the ground. It was littered with the remains of today's pirate festival. Littered with residents of Lea Bay. No one had survived. The concrete was red, and inches from her feet lay bones and skin and things too badly injured to classify.

Not a single traffic cone in sight.

Next she looked up and wished she hadn't. The Lords were everywhere. They shuffled together, forming a circle around them. They smiled with dead jaws, and those that didn't *have* jaws managed to convey their happiness with a twinkle in their dead eyes. The last remaining survivors had walked right into their clutches.

Among the crowd of skeletal figures stood one so immediately familiar Daphne thought she'd die then and there. If it hadn't been for Jake's firm grip, she would've given up. She'd fought so hard but what good had it done?

Donny.

Donny stood no more than ten feet away. His skin had gone grey and his wounds a dark brown. He smiled like the rest of them and within his dead eyes, she wondered if he recognized her. If he remembered their life together. The bad and the good, though the latter had been rare these last few years. Wondered if when he saw their son standing against her knees, he saw part of himself. Saw the hospital room that had been so humid. Saw the doctors telling him to step back as their baby was about to see the world for the first time.

She thought maybe he did. Maybe some inner chamber of his heart did see these things but that part was hidden beneath layers upon layers of rot. That chamber was sealed forever.

Behind him, in the ocean, dozens of creatures moved about. At least five sea snakes but they were only the beginning. Tentacles and teeth and appendages. Krakens. Things that, until last month, she'd thought were meant only for adventure novels and Hollywood blockbusters.

But none of this, not the Lords or Donny or even the creatures of the sea, made her insides shrivel more than the presence before her. The woman she'd watched materialize through the hardware store's windows. A being so beautiful and hideous, Daphne could actually feel her sanity fleeing with the breeze.

What was it Eric had called her, just before he got what he deserved?

"Tiamat," she said.

The woman nodded.

"You're a god."

"Goddess," she corrected. *"And you have something of mine."*

With one hand, Daphne shoved her fingers into her pocket, grasping the coins. With the other, she pushed Jake back, standing him behind her to shield him.

"You cannot hide the boy. We've already found him twice. Our reach, I must admit, is endless. He is of the blood and he will be with us. But you can spare your own lives. You and the man who loves you so boldly. Give us the coins, Daphne. Give us the coins and we will grant you immunity." A smile cracked through her bronze face. *"Of course, soon there will be no shelter to take. You'll be the last of your kind in a world filled with my little lovelies."* She tilted her body toward the water and the things that dwelled within.

Jake continued to cry.

Daphne winced at the sound. Every mother's most feared tone.

"Do they frighten you?" Tiamat asked. She snapped a finger and from the bay rose a sea snake larger than the rest. One so big, Daphne needed to crane her neck just to see its full profile. It bowed its ugly head

in tribute and Tiamat hovered above the ground. Higher and higher until she was seated at the base of the snake's head. Her new throne made of flesh.

"Give us the boy and the coins and you will live another day."

There was a commotion amongst the Lords. They grew impatient.

Sawyer stepped toward Daphne, leaning close to her ear. "Slip me the coins."

She shook her head. "No."

"Do it. I'll create a diversion and you take Jake. I'll burn those things until they're soup."

"No," she said again. It had to be her. These things had taken so much, had stolen pieces of her she'd never get back. They'd torn her apart in more ways than one and, if she did indeed live another day, it would be a very long path to recovery.

She held out an empty hand. "Give me the torch."

"Daph, please."

She snarled. "Just because you love me doesn't mean you get to call the shots. Give me the torch. Take Jake and run as fast as you can."

"Mommy?" asked Jake, his voice uneven. Despite the heat, his teeth chattered.

"Do it," Daph said.

Sawyer's face contorted and she thought for a moment he'd cry. He was a good man even if he had his faults. Everyone did, she'd learned. He opened his mouth to say something, then shut it just as quickly. He handed her the torch.

"I love you, Jake," she said, still looking at the circle of monstrosities before her. "I want you to know that. I've loved you since day one and I'll never stop. You're going to go on a little run with Officer Sawyer, okay?"

"I don't want to. I want to go home."

"Me too, sweetie. And maybe we will. But right now, Mommy has to take care of something. I wish things were different. I wish your dad was still around and I wish you didn't have to see all of this. And most of all, I wish Skeletor was still swimming around in his bowl. But wishes are complicated and so is life, so this will have to do."

Sawyer made to protest again but she pushed him back with his elbow. "Run!"

He followed her orders and before the Lords could close in on them, she removed the first coin from her pocket. Held the blowtorch high. "You want your coins? You can have them!" She flicked the switch and everything grew molten. She burned the coin in her hand, taking great joy in watching it turn a neon shade of orange that reminded her of the arcade on the pier, a place she'd gone with Jake and Donny to get away from the stress of everyday life. A place that was probably just rubble right about now.

The Lords screamed in unison.

The creatures of the sea wailed so loudly her ears rang.

And Tiamat, goddess of wherever the fuck she'd come from, was thrown from the largest snake, landing head first in the water.

Daphne hissed through her teeth as the gold singed her skin. She dropped the coin long enough to grab another. And another. And another.

Kneeling down with them in a row, she pressed the switch again. She did not stop as they liquified before her. Not when she felt the Lords struggling toward her, howling in pain. Not even when she felt so many dead hands touch her skin.

She did not stop until the coins ceased to be.

CHAPTER FORTY-FIVE

He'd watched Tiamat fall to her watery demise, disappear beneath the bay while screaming, howling as if the flames of Hell lapped at her flesh. Once submerged, she never resurfaced.

The other Lords grabbed at their faces, their liquefying skin. Their features bubbled like soup brought to boil. Sawyer saw the one known as Graysoul reach out with a hand melted down to the bone, more ghostlike than before, which didn't seem possible. The pirate grimaced. Sawyer didn't think ghosts could hurt, feel the agony that those left alive had felt, but at that moment he knew—Graysoul felt every flicker of pain, every torturous second. Green flames outlined his figure, licking toward the sky.

The rest of the Lords began to cry out. Together their pain-ridden outbursts sounded like a gale. They reached for Daphne, their fingers poking through the layers of green fog, but each one failing to touch their target. As she continued to melt every coin, Sawyer watched the Lords fall.

And then it clicked.

Each token represented one of their souls. Each time a token was destroyed, another Lord burst into flames. She moved on from the coins she'd stolen to the chest itself.

Sawyer covered Jake's eyes.

"Mom!"

"Sssh," he whispered into his ear, dragging the boy away from the docks. From the Lords. From the tokens. From his mother.

From damnation.

"Mom!" he shouted again, trying to break the bond of his protector.

Sawyer hugged him closer, picking him up off the pavement. Turning to run, he stole one last glance. She'd made him forget about his shitty childhood, his absent father, the local legends, and the fear he'd never become anything more—if he was lucky—than a high-ranking member of the Lea Bay Police Department. She'd given him hope that he could be something better.

Something better than his old man.

Deep in the shadows of the green mist, she was there. Somewhere. Fighting for her life.

Fighting for all their lives.

With Jake in his arms, he ran until he couldn't anymore.

2 YEARS LATER

HOLTON, KANSAS

If you stare from the back porch long enough, past the field of tall grass, you can almost make out the closest neighbor. The backyard consists of a barbecue pit, a small patio, a full furniture set, and, of course, a playground set fully equipped with monkey bars and a corkscrew slide. The sky is blue—almost always blue—and the clouds seem to stand still against it. There is wildlife nearby and depending on which way the cool summer breeze blows, you can pick up their musk. Sometimes you'll find their droppings in the backyard. A border collie runs free, zipping back and forth, chasing the bone the man keeps throwing to him. He barks with delight.

This is a happy place.

"Watch this!" a young boy says as he jumps up onto the monkey bars, starts doing pull-ups. He can do almost forty now without wear.

"That's great," the man says, ripping the bone free from the border collie's mouth. "One day you'll do a hundred."

"I can do that many right now." The boy smiles. It fills his heart with this indescribable cheer. Like someone lit the most expensive candle in the world in the center of his chest. It'll never burn out, he thinks.

Maybe, he wants to tell the kid but doesn't. Instead, he shoots the boy a warm smile. The boy grins back and continues his impromptu workout.

The border collie is at the man's feet again. Wagging its tail, presenting its prize. The man cocks his arms back, then heaves the bone back into the air. It sails farther this time.

"Go fetch, Skeletor," he says, watching the dog race across the grass.

As the boy lifts himself, the man ducks back into the kitchen, gently closing the patio doors behind him.

"Having fun?" a voice asks from the sink.

Without turning, the man watches the backyard. He's proud of what he's accomplished. He loves the life he's living.

He turns to the woman. She's cleaning dishes. Dinner's in the oven. The smell of turkey roasting under a thick gravy fills his nostrils, and he thinks perhaps he's died and gone to heaven. Maybe he has. Maybe he died two years ago. Maybe he's a ghost and he doesn't yet know it.

"Always having fun." He saunters over to the sink and kisses his wife. He grabs her arms gently, and squeezes. It's a little gesture to let her know it's all right. Everything is fine. He isn't going anywhere. He'll never leave her side again.

Then he rubs her stomach, swollen with life.

"He hasn't kicked much today," she says.

"A watched kettle never boils."

"We should talk about names."

"I'm still rooting for Elvis."

They share a laugh.

Then silence.

He looks out the kitchen window with her head under his chin.

"I keep thinking back to that day," he says. The official White House statement named terrorists the cause, some radical group from the Middle East that no one has ever heard of, but those who'd survived know what really happened. Will never be able to forget.

"I keep thinking of how I left you," he says, and tears run freely from the corners of his eyes.

"Hey." She pulls his attention to her eyes. "Don't do that. I'm here now, aren't I?"

They turn their heads, stare out the kitchen window and into the backyard.

The boy is still on the monkey bars, sweating and smiling. Skeletor is running around like he's being chased by a bear, back and forth, back and forth. A butterfly dances past the window. He sees past all of it. Into the fields. Farther still.

There's no bay there. No water. The ocean is fifteen-hundred miles away in either direction. Sometimes it feels like it's much closer. Like it's a part of him. Threatening to douse that candle in his chest.

Jake drops from the bars. "One hundred!"

THE LORDS OF THE DEEP

a poem by unknown

Welcome, welcome
The Lords of the Deep
Bring us new fortunes
and all ye seek

For there be no tomorrow
no light and no shine
the beasts of yesterday
hath eaten the hands of time

So welcome, welcome
The Lords of the Deep
Bring us new pleasures
from lands of foul sleep

Call on yer masters
minions and slaves
lay waste to the cities
seek all ye depraved

Have a drink of rum
rounds for ye all
empty all the bottles
before all ye fall

Protect one another
from enemies of the Deep
for we shall sneak and slither
cut their throat while they sleep

Let loose the monsters
hidden in the dark
turn them loose on the town
while the uncharted we embark

Welcome our god
to our house of sin
leave now our gold
to the rest of our kin

Welcome, welcome
The Lords of the Deep
No ocean too endless
No star too steep

Lead us to battle
our queen from the sky
may the world be ours
and for you we will die

Welcome, welcome
The Lords of the Deep
Bring us new fortunes
and all ye seek

Acknowledgements:

Patrick Lacey – Thanks to my heavenly fiancée Emily Diana, as well as the usual suspects: Ryan Beauchamp, Adam Cesare, Matt Serafini, Scott Cole, Aaron Dries, Matt Hayward, Max Linsky, and several million others. Also, a shoutout to some guy named Tim Meyer. Some folks call him the Lord of the Deep. Probably just a nickname.

Tim Meyer – Thanks to my wife, Ashley Meyer, for putting up with my nonsense. Also, Matt Hayward, Chuck Buda, Armand Rosamilia, Frank Edler, Chad Lutzke, Terry West, D.S. Ullery, J.C. Walsh, Todd Keisling, Wesley Southard, and Tim Feely. I'd also like to thank Patrick Lacey, but I've never heard of him.

Patrick Lacey spends his nights and weekends writing about things that make the general public uncomfortable. He resides in Massachusetts with his fiancée, his Pomeranian, his oversized cat, and his muse, who is probably trying to kill him. Stalk him in Facebook or follow him on Twitter (@patlacey).

Tim Meyer dwells in a dark cave near the Jersey Shore. He's an author, husband, father, podcast host, blogger, coffee connoisseur, beer enthusiast, and explorer of worlds. He writes horror, mysteries, science fiction, and thrillers, although he prefers to blur genres and let the stories fall where they may. Follow him on Twitter (@timmmeyer11) or on his blog, timmeyerwrites.com.

SEVEREDPRESS

 facebook.com/severedpress
 twitter.com/severedpress

CHECK OUT OTHER GREAT DEEP SEA THRILLERS

THE BREACH
by Edward J. McFadden III

A Category 4 hurricane punched a quarter mile hole in Fire Island, exposing the Great South Bay to the ferocity of the Atlantic Ocean, and the current pulled something terrible through the new breach. A monstrosity of the past mixed with the present has been disturbed and it's found its way into the sheltered waters of Long Island's southern sea.

Nate Tanner lives in Stones Throw, Long Island. A disgraced SCPD detective lieutenant put out to pasture in the marine division because of his Navy background and experience with aquatic crime scenes, Tanner is assigned to hunt the creeper in the bay. But he and his team soon discover they're the ones being hunted.

INFESTATION
by William Meikle

It was supposed to be a simple mission. A suspected Russian spy boat is in trouble in Canadian waters. Investigate and report are the orders.

But when Captain John Banks and his squad arrive, it is to find an empty vessel, and a scene of bloody mayhem.

Soon they are in a fight for their lives, for there are things in the icy seas off Baffin Island, scuttling, hungry things with a taste for human flesh.

They are swarming. And they are growing.

"Scotland's best Horror writer" - Ginger Nuts of Horror

"The premier storyteller of our time." - Famous Monsters of Filmland

SEVERED**PRESS**

 facebook.com/severedpress
 twitter.com/severedpress

CHECK OUT OTHER GREAT
DEEP SEA THRILLERS

THRESHER
by **Michael Cole**

In the aftermath of a hurricane, a series of strange events plague the coastal waters off Florida. People go into the water and never return. Corpses of killer whales drift ashore, ravaged from enormous bite marks. A fishing trawler is found adrift, with a mysterious gash in its hull.

Transferred to the coastal town of Merit, police officer Leonard Riker uncovers the horrible reality of an enormous Thresher shark lurking off the coast. Forty feet in length, it has taken a territorial claim to the waters near the town harbor. Armed with three-inch teeth, a scythe-like caudal fin, and unmatched aggression, the beast seeks to kill anything sharing the waters.

THE GUILLOTINE
by **Lucas Pederson**

1,000 feet under the surface, Prehistoric Anthropologist, Ash Barrington, and his team are in the midst of a great archeological dig at the bottom of Lake Superior where they find a treasure trove of bones. Bones of dinosaurs that aren't supposed to be in this particular region. In their underwater facility, Infinity Moon, Ash and his team soon discover a series of underground tunnels. Upon exploring, they accidentally open an ice pocket, thawing the prehistoric creature trapped inside. Soon they are being attacked, the facility falling apart around them, by what Ash knows is a dunkleosteus and all those bones were from its prey. Now...Ash and his team are the prey and the creature will stop at nothing to get to them.

SEVERED**PRESS**

 facebook.com/severedpress

 twitter.com/severedpress

CHECK OUT OTHER GREAT
DEEP SEA THRILLERS

SHARK: INFESTED WATERS
by P.K. Hawkins

For Simon, the trip was supposed to be a once in a lifetime gift: a journey to the Amazon River Basin, the land that he had dreamed about visiting since he was a child. His enthusiasm for the trip may be tempered by the poor conditions of the boat and their captain leading the tour, but most of the tourists think they can look the other way on it. Except things go wrong quickly. After a horrific accident, Simon and the other tourists find themselves trapped on a tiny island in the middle of the river. It's the rainy season, and the river is rising. The island is surrounded by hungry bull sharks that won't let them swim away. And worst of all, the sharks might not be the only blood-thirsty killers among them. It was supposed to be the trip of a lifetime. Instead, they'll be lucky if they make it out with their lives at all.

DARK WATERS
by Lucas Pederson

Jörmungandr is an ancient Norse sea monster. Thought to be purely a myth until a battleship is torn a part by one.

With his brother on that ship, former Navy Seal and deep-sea diver, Miles Raine, sets out on a personal vendetta against the creature and hopefully save his brother. Bringing with him his old Seal team, the Dagger Points, they embark on a mission that might very well be their last.

But what happens when the hunters become the hunted and the dark waters reveal more than a monster?

www.ingramcontent.com/pod-product-compliance
Lightning Source LLC
Chambersburg PA
CBHW031954170626
46807CB00006B/2473